By Claudia Dey

Fiction

HEARTBREAKER
STUNT

Plays

TROUT STANLEY
THE GWENDOLYN POEMS
BEAVER

HEARTBREAKER

RANDOM HOUSE

NEW YORK

HEARTBREAKER

A NOVEL

Claudia Dey

Heartbreaker is a work of fiction. Names, characters, places, and incidents are either the product of the author's imagination or are used fictitiously. Any resemblance to actual persons, living or dead, events, or locales, is entirely coincidental.

Copyright © 2018 by Claudia Dey

Published in the United States by Random House, an imprint and division of Penguin Random House LLC, New York.

RANDOM HOUSE and the HOUSE colophon are registered trademarks of Penguin Random House LLC.

Published simultaneously in Canada by HarperCollins Publishers Ltd., Toronto.

Hardback ISBN 978-0-525-51173-1
Ebook ISBN 978-1-524-79893-2

Printed in the United States of America on acid-free paper

randomhousebooks.com

2 4 6 8 9 7 5 3 1

FIRST U.S. EDITION

Title-page and part-title images: © iStockphoto.com

Book design by Dana Leigh Blanchette

In love there is no because.

ALICE NOTLEY,
IN THE PINES

Contents

Part One

—

GIRL

This is what I know: She left last night. My mother, Billie Jean Fontaine, stood in our front hallway with a stale cigarette in one hand and her truck keys in the other. The light in our hallway was broken or dying so it flickered above her head, throwing shadows across her face. I don't know how long she was standing there watching me.

I was only feet away on the couch in my nightpants trying to arrange my body like the woman in that Whitesnake video. It was not going well. The television was on, and I had our telephone receiver pressed hard against my left ear. My ear had gone numb listening to Lana on the other end breathing heavily, which made me picture, unfairly, Lana's dog, a dog, unlike our dog, of low intelligence. Together in silence, we watched *Teen Psychic*. The show was already at the love line, making it close to seven o'clock, and 1985, and late October. *Teen Stewardess* was on next, and for this, I felt deep excitement.

I had my outerwear smoothed flat on my lap. With a black permanent marker, I was filling in the cap letters I had written across the back. I would debut and copyright these later at the bonfire. Note there is no such thing as permanent. Especially in a marker you find in a snowdrift. I also found my camo outerwear in said snowdrift, the snowdrift that borders the north highway outside Neon Dean's pink bungalow, which on Free Day can be a bonanza. A few other things to keep in mind at this moment: I had almost a hundred dollars in small denominations hidden inside the album covers in my bedroom, twelve jerry cans of gasoline stashed in the woods behind our house, hair to my tailbone I had recently tried to self-feather, and my mother had not come downstairs for two months.

"I am going into town." My mother spoke this astonishing sentence not to me but to the cold air around me. She had not left our bungalow since the end of July, and it was now almost three months later. Winter had set in. Outside, the trees were skeletal, and the hunters were urinating on their hands to warm them. The men called this dicking the hands. I dicked my hands to turn my keys. Same. Dicked my hands right there on my front porch. Same. Had to dick my hands to cock my rifle. This was the kind of talk you might hear if you went into Drink-Mart for some homemade alcohol. There, under a half-busted chandelier, listening to Air Supply, the men of the territory gathered to clean their rifles with their wives' old tan pantyhose while being stared at by a wall covered with the beautiful heads of our animals.

Air Supply. A band name none of us wanted to read into.

I joined my mother in the hallway. I had not seen her upright for weeks and now looked down at her scalp, the hair broken in places. Beauty, what is beauty? Beauty is cheap.

Beauty is common. Beauty is luck. My father, The Heavy—known for many things but mostly his severe facial issues—loved to say when he first laid eyes on my mother, it was not like the stories you hear about beauty. A man struck down by a woman's beauty. Taken by a woman's beauty. No. Not at all. My father liked to say when he first laid eyes on my mother, he had never seen anyone quite so alive.

She was wearing her indoor tracksuit. It hung from her frame and was the color of dirty water. I knew not to touch her, and this was difficult, so I pushed my hands into the large pockets of my nightpants. I had done my bloodwork that morning and was still feeling a bit faint. Moving quickly from the couch to the doorway, I was seeing sparks, and the strobe-light effect of the dying bulb above us was not helping, so I tilted my head down slightly and leaned against the wall, looking but not feeling casual. Of late, I had become a fainter, and this was a most useful quality as it meant instant departure to a dark and neutral space. When my mother and I used to talk, we agreed that *HELP* was a flawless word. That even if you reordered the letters, people would still completely get your meaning. *PHLE*.

My mother wasn't wearing her sport socks or her house sandals, the usual combination for a territory woman who finds herself indoors at home at night, which is always. Her feet were bare and marbled. Her toenails had yellowed, and her shins looked sharp and blue, as if they could slice through wood. In my bedroom, I liked to listen to hot men sing about hot women while studying the images of disease. We had very few books in the territory, but we did have one thick volume that contained nothing except pictures and descriptions of diseases. It didn't even pretend to offer advice or remedies— just gory, vivid photos of people from the neck down with their various inflammations, and their identities protected. The book gave me solace, and some basic Latin.

Though she wasn't moving, my mother appeared to be in a rush. She gripped the truck keys, making her knuckles white as chalk. I wanted to write BIRTH across one set and DEATH across the other. She studied my collarbone. You made this collarbone, I wanted to remind her, though I knew not to speak to her. She was in the middle of something and could not be interrupted. Or so she'd told me. In our last conversation. If you could call it a conversation.

I slid down to the floor and closed my eyes to steady myself. I knew my mother was still there because she had taken on a new smell. It was a mineral smell.

This past summer, shortly before she stopped leaving our bungalow, when she still went into town for Delivery Day and her shifts at the Banquet Hall, but it was clear something had come over her, I watched my father dig another man's grave. Poor, dead Wishbone. The women of the territory had gone to pay their respects to Wishbone's widow. Get her mind off it. Fashion her hair. Bleach her freezer. Put on the Rod Stewart. My mother had not. She stayed in her bed. She didn't turn to face us when she asked my father and me to please leave her there. She wasn't up for it. Wasn't feeling herself. I had just turned fifteen and was finally at the age where I could go with my mother to these sorts of events. Instead, I ended up with the men at the graveyard. My father was incredible with a shovel, and the men had to tell him when to stop digging, he had gone down far enough, there was plenty of space for a casket. For ten caskets. Jesus, The Heavy, the men said to my father chest-deep in the grave, pulling the shovel from his hands. Take a load off, the men said. The high mound of fresh dirt beside us, and then under our boots as we made our way back to our truck, identically hunched and with our arms touching. My father and I sat in the front seat for a long time. I had been trying to tan my face though it was becoming clear I was allergic to the sun. So far, this is not the best day of my life, I wanted to say to The Heavy. What has come over her? I wanted to ask him. Do you even know?

All around us, the men in the graveyard wore mirrored sunglasses. Some were shirtless and looked barbecued in the July heat. They would alternate the positioning of their hands on their shovels so their musculature would be even. My father did none of these things. Sitting in the driver's seat, he was an uneven man blinded by the sun. I looked through the front windshield to the sky, which was such a bright blue, I felt embarrassed by it. Strategies for happiness. My mother had said it was important to try to come up with these. I pictured a supply plane dropping nets filled with useless, shiny things like mesh bathing suits and white leather furniture. I wanted a headlamp that worked. I wanted a Camaro. I wanted a *Le* in front of my name. Pony Darlene Fontaine. Le Pony Darlene Fontaine. Le Pony. That's what everyone will have to call me from this day forward, I said to no one.

Eventually, my father turned the key in the ignition, and Van Halen came on. It was the tape with the angel on it who even as a baby you could tell would be a future convict. I loved that tape. It was all my mother had been listening to for months. I would watch her in our unfinished driveway, staring into the middle distance in her winter coat while the truck shook with the music.

My father wrenched the tape from the player. He threw it into our backseat. I don't even know, his face seemed to say, I don't even know. I made a visor out of my hand and put it above his eyes. He drove home like it was an emergency.

THIS WAS THE SMELL my mother was giving off now in our front hallway—an unfinished space, an open body cavity, an open grave. Our dog came bounding down the stairs and wound herself between my mother's legs. I worried the force of her would knock my mother down. I watched my mother's heart lift the threadbare fabric of her tracksuit. I searched for the Latin translation of *cancer of the dreams*. I pulled myself to standing. Our dog sat at my mother's exposed feet, taking my place. Our dog had perfect posture. She did not want your companionship. She wanted your throat and your hot parts. She loved only my mother. She was too old to be alive. All around us, the men and women of the territory chased after and screamed for their dogs. Our dog had never run away. Our dog had never barked. Not once.

My mother went for our front door. She had to kick things out of the way to get to it, agitation like a shock. There was a blue tarp in our living room, hanging behind our television set, where *Teen Stewardess* had just begun, and through it I could see my father's shape. *LHEP*. A high whine. He was sawing through lumber. He would have his hearing protection and snowmobile goggles on. He was adding a room to our bungalow that would be a room just for my mother. Where nothing would be asked of her. Where she could return to her thinking, to what she called her native thinking.

My mother pulled the front door open with her sure grip, her athlete's grip, and the northwest wind came hurtling in at us. It was a wind that could carry tires and shatter glass. You had to walk with your back into the northwest wind. There was a partial moon, and you could see the snow was blowing sideways. Our dog paced at my mother's feet, lush and frantic. It had been months since she had truly felt the weather. She had braids all through her coat. My mother, looking ahead and then back, her mouth moving slowly, but sounding like herself for a moment, said with tenderness, "I had forgotten all about you." I told myself she was speaking to me. At last, she was speaking to me.

My mother came to this place as a stranger. Now I feared she was retracing her steps out. Returning to a world she had refused to describe to me. Billie Jean Fontaine. Billie Jean. Was that even my mother's real name?

WE LIVE ON a large tract of land called the territory. When the Leader and his followers first laid claim to it some fifty years ago, they called it Upper Big Territory. Now, it's just the territory. The descriptors were redundant. Aerial view: two thousand square miles of forest. Population: 391. We started as a single busload searching for the end of the world. Now, look at us.

We didn't spread out.

The north highway cuts a straight line through town, and this is where you will find most of our local businesses. The residential streets branch off from the north highway in a grid. They are not named. In the territory, we go by bungalow number. Lana's is 2. Neon Dean's is 17. Ours is 88. Guess how many bungalows are in the territory? Exactly. One of my favorite jokes is to pretend I'm lost. I will be riding my ten-speed in my mother's powder-blue workdress, her purse strapped across my body and her ATV helmet on, and I'll see someone at the edge of their property, and I'll flag them down and say, Yeah, so, hey, there I was on the north highway, made a couple of turns, and now I am just all spun around. Just totally lost. Cannot seem to find my way back home.

Bungalow after bungalow, built all at once when the territory began. Small cement porches. Snowmobiles and swing sets in the yards, and the girls with show hair long like their mothers', long like their dogs', and the men and boys shaved to near bald. Let me give you the lay of the land. The men love to start a lecture this way. Our dogs are white here, and there are no leashes. It is acceptable to make a leash-like mechanism for your children, but not for your dog. Your dog is an animal and to forget her nature is to forget your own. If you would like to see a dog on a leash, turn on your television. We will barbecue under a tarpaulin for our dogs in the dead of winter, but we will not give them names. You. Come. Here. Get. Names are for our people not our dogs. If you would like to see a dog with a name, watch *Lassie*. It's on at four. Duct tape in medicine cabinets. Radios with batteries carried from room to room. Always the sound of a truck in the distance. Knowing the trucks by sound. Who is approaching. Who is not going home. Deadbolts on garage doors. A bear on your property after the thaw. Motion-detector light. Gunshot. Beards a sign of mental damage. Gunshot. Tanning beds in our sunken dens, and many of our people the shade of anger. Smelling like coconut oil in line at Value Smoke and Grocer. None of the men going by their birth names. Wishbone, Sex-eteria, Hot Dollar, Fur Thumb, Visible Thinker, Traps. The Heavy. Let me give you the lay of the land: men, women, children, loaded rifles. Hearts stop. Dogs, trucks, winter, fucking. Hearts break.

See that lone white bungalow? Now, see the lone window looking out from beneath the roof on the south-facing wall, the one with the black sheet for a curtain that appears to have a single word spelled out in duct tape? That is my bedroom and the word is B E Y O N D. From below, you can only really make out Y O, message enough.

WE HAVE A travel agent though no one has ever left the territory. We call her One Hundred as she is either very close to or just past that in years. She has been here from the beginning. Her left pupil is wiped out and translucent with blindness, but otherwise, she is more fit than most and works nights in the back of Drink-Mart at a card table on a foldout chair. If you buy her a drink, she will pull out one of her four black gym bags, unzip it slowly, and show you her away pamphlets. The gym bags are called North, South, East, and West. Given the North is all we know, no one chooses North and it is clear that bag is empty. South, East, and West our broadest men can barely bench-press.

In the cold months, we can't bury our dead. Our people try to die in the summer. If you don't, your body is put on a cot and wheeled into the walk-in freezer of the Death Man's shed, a square of lumber, fiberglass, and Freon tubing twenty steps from the sliding back doors of his well-maintained trailer. He has gulls on his property though he is nowhere near water. While the Death Man is soundless, his gulls whine and screech and dirty themselves, and we tell them, Stop your commotion, we know what mourning is.

We all find it difficult to look at the Death Man when he walks by us in town. The dead have their secrets and he knows them. His bullet eyes, his bleach vapor, his unmarried, mannequin hands. If you die, the Death Man will be the last to touch your naked body with all its private codes. Not your mother, not your girlfriend, but the Death Man and his indoor gloves. The thinking is: Normal men volunteer to fuck women or fight fires, not store the dead.

When the thaw finally comes, we catch up on our funerals. We call this time final resting. For the first month of the thaw in April, sometimes May, we have a funeral every third day. If someone dies during this time, bad luck, their corpse must wait its turn. While it is stored in the Death Man's shed with the others, we are consoled it does not have to linger there through those long months of the sky in its deep freeze when our people are tanned but heartsick, immortal gulls cawing and bombing like psychotic confetti.

You won't see a gull anywhere else in town.

The entire territory comes out for a funeral. Even if you just sawed off your finger or lost an eye, you come out. In the beds of their matte black trucks, the men put their shovels. They try to keep their Man Store denim clean when it is time to fill the grave. The territory men wear sunglasses whatever the weather. Sunglasses never come off. The women don't wear sunglasses, and their black mascara runs down their faces. They don't bother to wipe it away. A beaten face is a grieving face. Last thaw, the trend was electric blue.

A special-order cassette stereo plays our final resting tape—instrumental—and Shona Lee, her bangs flipped back, her voice holy, solos:

GOOD TIMES, BAD TIMES—

Around the grave, we huddle in a mass until one of the men steps from the scrum to speak. A bottle of local alcohol is passed until it reaches the man in his tribute. He drinks while he speaks, but he does not smoke. Here, at final resting time, women smell like women and men smell like women. No one can light a cigarette for the heavy hairspray, aftershave, and perfume. We smoke the moment we are back in our trucks and speeding to the Banquet Hall with the windows down. Even the children will smoke after a funeral. They are expected to.

Every man in the territory has his portrait taken yearly from the age of thirteen onward. Sometimes the man will pose beside his truck or his dog or his girlfriend or, depending on his fitness, in a clean tank top holding up a barbell or the closest, heaviest thing. Bag of concrete, glass table, propane tank. Sometimes the portrait is just the young man's face, which can make you feel you never knew him. Never noticed that scar or that chipped tooth. When you walk into the Banquet Hall after the burial, our cots and IV poles pushed to the side, the buried man's portrait is propped up on the stage. A bouquet on either side of it. A lineup forms and everyone in the territory gets a moment before the portrait. You can touch it, kiss it, and make as much noise as you want, but once you walk away, you have to pull yourself together because you, then all those around you, could lose the point of the endeavor. As grief manhandles, it can be manhandled. This is what we tell each other, followed by, depending on who you are talking to, hard sex or light punching.

It is very rare the portrait is of a woman, and if it is, she poses with her children, and if she does not have any children, she poses with nothing at all.

THE FOUNDERS GOT OFF their bus here only because they discovered they could go no farther—no farther than our property, bungalow 88, also known as the Last House. You see, the north highway ends in the territory's only water source. It is directly behind our bungalow. We call it the reservoir, and now, in late October, it is mostly covered by a thin skim of ice. Where you can see it, the water is not blue but gray, branches floating on the surface, a few plastic bags. No one will go near it. Not even us, the teenagers, with our frayed cuffs and our open coats and our blue lips daring each other with money we have stolen. No way. Get real. Dream on. To our people, water is certain death. The reservoir is certain death. From my mother's bedroom window, you have a perfect view.

Our bungalow is the only one in the territory with a second story and a basement, features added by its former occupant. Our bungalow is fully carpeted, eleven hundred square feet, and split-level. Our bungalow is open concept, and the color scheme is gold-black-beige. You'd think everyone would want to live here. They don't. Our bungalow is the end of the world.

Yo.

"PONY DARLENE FONTAINE! Pony Darlene Fontaine!" I come to just in time to see the teen stewardess's plane break apart. She is over a flatland when the cabin of the plane suddenly bursts open on one side, and the passengers, still strapped into their seats, are sucked out and into space. Worst luck. Permanent winter. Pointless to call out. The teen stewardess throws herself on top of a baby passenger. She and the baby float down on a piece of airplane, and the teen stewardess tells the baby they will make their home under it. You can make a home out of anything, my mother said to me once. Home is in the soul. You will spend your life trying to get back to it.

"Pony!" It's Lana yelling at me through the receiver, which is dangling off our beige couch. "Did you see that? Did. You. See. That." Lana, at moments of great excitement, will speak with the cadence of a telegram. We arrange to meet in tight clothes outside of her much nicer bungalow at ten o'clock. To go to the bonfire. The pit party. A full hour. Later. Than. Anyone. Else.

I hang up and look through our front window. The truck is

not in the driveway. She did go into town. Did she go into town? I am briefly stopped by my own reflection. This happens when you can watch yourself grow. I am tall. Perhaps too much length in limb. I wouldn't have minded being a bit more covert, physically. Perhaps slightly less face. The face is a little more niche than I might have liked. The full lips, the thin canopy of a mustache. The failed haircut. The dark, shy eyes. I am not the star of the night soap; I am the visiting cousin. The one in the Pinto no one will kiss. I have a line of safety pins tapering my nightpants. I knot my DEVOTIONAL SECTION T-shirt just above my waistline in case there is a boy in the woods smoking the cold fog, and looking in at me. Wanting me. A boy I have never seen before. He wears a black suit and has a black dog and a few terrible habits that don't hurt anyone. I roll down the waistband of my nightpants and rotate my melancholia. Front on, profile, rear view. What is not to love? Some of it. Around my neck, I wear a large stopwatch. I took out the clock part and put in the back of Billy Joel's head from *Glass Houses*. We have many album covers here and very few albums. Most have been destroyed by overuse. I have no idea how Billy Joel's music sounds, but I like the look of him in his heeled leather boots and crime gloves about to seriously trash a house. I lift my arm and angle my body. All I need is a rock.

"Did she say why? Did she say for what? Why did you let her leave? Why didn't you come and get me?" The Heavy is covered in sawdust. It is trapped in his eyelashes, his shirt collar, his knuckles, the hard scars of his face. He has his snowmobile goggles around his neck. I do not have sufficient answers to his questions. I assure him she will be back any minute.

The Heavy runs out to the driveway to follow my mother in our new truck only to remember it gone; she took it. "Damn it." He pushes past me to the living room phone. He has sweat through his outerwear in three large circles. Two under his arms, and one, a bull's-eye, spreading across his back. We agree the dog got out behind her. I do not tell him my mother was wearing her indoor tracksuit, no socks and no shoes. That she walked into late October without shoes. Was she even wearing a coat? With only the dog. Her keys and the dog. The Heavy calls Traps, his oldest friend, on speed dial. "She said she was going into town." He pauses. "She took the truck."

Seventeen years ago, my mother showed up in the territory in a wreck. Three months ago, she drove our previous truck into a tree on an iceless day. A day without weather. Impossible to total your vehicle on that July day. The women of the territory gathered in Rita Star's kitchen to review the crash. Rita Star had one of the few businesses in town not located on the north highway. She ran it out of her small, wood-paneled bungalow.

Rita Star's Tanning Emporium, Fitness and Palmistry

The women of the territory tucked their ponytails into their waistbands and sat on Rita Star's leatherette chairs under her hazardous light fixture. Rita Star had a strange and flammable hobby. Light fixtures made out of old Delivery Day baskets. The women concluded my mother was a woman who made her own obstacles. Why, the women of the territory asked each other in Rita Star's dim kitchen, why in a world that is mostly obstacles would you make more for yourself? What sort of woman would do that? I mean, who would do that? And besides, who can leave her house at that hour, the dinner hour, when everyone needs everything?

WE HAVE ONLY the one truck. "We have only the one truck," The Heavy apologizes to Traps when he walks through our front door. "I know," says Traps, erect as a centaur, "I sold it to you."

Traps's face is eager. He smells like aftershave, cologne, and truck interior. Like a man at final resting. Snow melts and pools around his cowboy boots, leaving a ring of water on the ground, on my mother's winter coat. It was her coat she was kicking out of the way. Why didn't she take it? She loves her coat. When the territory had been warmer than any year on record, she had worn her coat all spring. I pick it up and hang it on her hook by the front door. We each have a hook. We used to be that kind of family.

The Heavy makes me swear I will stay in the house and, when she comes back, call Drink-Mart, and the men there will get the message to him. He will go with Traps in his truck. Everyone knows Traps's truck. Traps is the only man with fog lights in the territory, and while this is annoying, it makes flagging him down easy. Since Traps owns the truck lot, Fully Loaded, he has access to certain features for his vehicle, and our men have to accept it when they are told the features were limited edition and no longer available. It was a one-time thing only, man. Sorry, man, sorry. No one sells regret better than Traps.

Traps also controls the fuel supply in the territory. In a giant padlocked shed at the back of the Fully Loaded property, he stores jerry cans filled with gasoline. Above the entrance to the shed, there is a video camera. Traps watches the footage from his trailer, also on the lot, where he conducts his business, surrounded by collages. This is his true passion. Traps cuts images from magazines and combines them on large pieces of paper. He hangs them in his trailer and angles spotlights above them. When a man buys a truck, he will comment on the collages, and Traps will remind the man the collages are for sale. Traps rotates his padlocks and wears a necklace of small keys. His neck is thick as a python. He also has keys buried throughout the lot. Only Traps knows where the keys are and which ones will unlock the stack of padlocks on the fuel shed. If a man wants fuel, he places a request, and within a day, Traps provides it. I need time, Traps explains to the man who wants the fuel and then sweeps his eyes over the lot. The man has no choice but to wait for Traps's call. Sometimes, talking with the men, in his trailer, Traps will hold his lighter to his tongue and see how close he can get it. Once, when a man came in after the death of his wife, Traps pulled out the first aid kit and put a Band-Aid on the man's heart. He then put one on his own heart in solidarity. No man knows how full or empty the fuel shed is. Territory men have considered trying to break in but lost their nerve. They have considered setting fire to the whole thing but pictured the inferno, and themselves inevitably part of it. What it comes down to is this: If you want to move, you have to see Traps about it. Traps gives motion to our people. Traps is too important to kill.

"At least it's October," says Traps, studying our carpet, my mother's coat, the water stain made by his boots. "No one tries to die in October." His voice is rough. He clears it and then lifts his sharp, sad eyes to look at me. "Sorry."

I unknot and tuck my DEVOTIONAL SECTION T-shirt into my nightpants and watch from the open doorway as Traps has my father shake and brush the sawdust from his clothes, leaving a beige mound on our unfinished driveway and then folding his much larger body into the inferior seat. Traps moves around to the driver's side door slow as a man in the confident position of being needed. He throws me one last look. The truck peels off. It kicks up gravel and ice. The license plate says DEALR.

You would never know Traps had recently buried his youngest.

No Band-Aid big enough.

WHAT IF SHE comes back before The Heavy does? Will she walk through our front door and up to her bedroom without even seeing me? Will she pull me into her hard frame and whisper apologies and speak promises into my ear and swear she has returned? Will she hold my face to hers like a night-soap mother and say, I see you, Pony, I see you for all that you are? Will she work my hair into a design complex as engines? Will I ride my ten-speed to the bonfire and cause a stir with my new hair design? Will I stand near the flames, ignoring them yet well lit by them, and pull the pins out slowly and let the wind make shapes of my hair? Pony Darlene. Hot damn. Who knew? Even Supernatural will take notice. His ball cap under his hood. Showing just enough of his face. It's not like it's about sex with him. No. (Not that I would refuse sex with Supernatural.) It's more that he strikes me as the only boy in the territory I might have a decent conversation with. I heard Gregorian chants coming from his headphones. Maybe my pain has made me better looking. No. No boy wants the visiting cousin. Will I be able to tell my mother that she has been the only emotional weather in this bungalow for three months straight, and that I too have a lot of feelings? I have a lot of feelings.

I had forgotten all about you.

Yes. You had.

WHAT I KNOW about my mother's arrival in the territory my mother did not tell me. Lana did. We had gone by Neon Dean's bungalow. This was the end of July. Almost exactly three months ago. He and Peter Fox St. John were on Neon Dean's small cement porch sitting shirtless on lawn chairs, retrofitted with foam and old carpet, lifting bags of concrete over their heads. They were working out. Doing reps, they called it. And they were listening to Nazareth. "Love Hurts." We got off our bicycles. They looked us up and down. We had smudged charcoal around our eyes. Our bra straps were showing. They put down their bags of concrete.

"I know who shot J.R.," Peter Fox St. John said.

"Shut up, Fuck Pants," Neon Dean said.

Neon Dean was nineteen, four years older than us. He lived alone. Both of his parents were dead. He showered with his dirty dishes. He had a pet rat called Radical Feminist. Rad for short. He had a girlfriend named Pallas, who was tanned and cruel. She looked like an out-of-work wrestler. She had recently tried to self-pierce her tongue, and now she sounded like Sean Connery. How'sh tricksh? she would say when I biked by her in town. Lana and I were relieved she was not there. The boys were alone. They were checking us out. It was the first time, we agreed, we had been truly checked out, and it made us feel dangerous. We had very little money, but we did have our sex appeal. Neon Dean reached for his toolbox. He had $UPERIOR EXI$TENCE written across the top of it. He flipped open the lid. We bought two white pills and two yellow ones and then went into the woods to the metal husk of the founders' bus to get very, very high and try to make each other levitate, which is a lot harder than it looks on *Teen Spirit*.

True story, Lana said. To the max. She said everyone else had been born and raised in the territory. Everyone else could tell stories about each other's grandparents. Everyone else knew how the others liked their meat cooked. What color thread they had used to sew up their gashes. Your mother just showed up one day in a Mercedes sedan. What kind of vehicle is built that low to the ground? The territory demanded clearance. What kind of world does not? A place to be glided through. The people of the territory had seen Mercedes sedans on their night soaps. Green grass, high heels, tuxedos, endless unmarried fucking. A world without facial issues. Mercedes sedans. An impossible world. Was the woman in the low car an apparition?

Covered in dents and scratches, missing a front fender, muffler scraping the north highway. The woman fell from the driver's seat of the Mercedes sedan, the car still running, skinning her thigh badly and showing her underwear. It was underwear from elsewhere. Her upper portion smelled like gasoline. Her lower portion urine. She had sucked gas into her mouth. The people of the territory knew about siphoning.

The car radio was playing a song our people had never heard. A kind of music they could not get their heads to move to. A 5/4 beat. Think about that later. For now, one of the men reached in and turned off the ignition of the Mercedes. Our people did not let their vehicles run in May. Winter, sure. Winter, hell yes. But, May? Snowmobiles, generators, chainsaws—what would we do without fuel? When one of the broader men bent down for the woman, she flinched, and then put her arms around his neck. The movement, when it came, was swift and rabid. Feeling a rush, another one of the meeker men joined the effort, though the woman was so thin and without muscles that, not useful, he backed away.

Our people were frightened of the woman. We'd never had a complete stranger here. Never had someone just show up. Was she a descendant of the Leader? She looked like she could come from that stock. Fine bone structure. Luxury vehicle. Do we shoot her or do we feed her? The broad man who had picked her up carried her into Home of the Beef Candy, conscious her dress was up around her waist and her black underwear could not be bought in town. The Heavy was standing in line at the lunch counter taking the place of two territory men. The woman saw him, crawled out of the broad man's arms, stopped crying immediately, and placed her body against The Heavy's body. Body on body. Like that, her focus shifted. The Heavy bought her a meal. The woman ate like a predator. The Heavy bought her a second meal. Our people gathered around her, filling the restaurant, spilling out onto the north highway, looking through the window. The men knew to stand beside their wives. They all waited for the woman to speak.

Our people would say later, about your mother, Who knows, maybe women from elsewhere like men with facial issues. Your father had pulled off and burned the last of his bandages just that morning. The morning he saw your mother for the first time. FYI. No joke. Totally perf.

After that, Lana and I played a game we called Wanting. She went first: I want Sexeteria to push up the back of my skirt with his face. And then make me a very mixed tape. I want braces. I want a chain-link fence with red roses threaded through it. Real ones. I want a lace bodysuit with a mock turtleneck. I want to call my first son Everlasting. I want to spend a week in a hotel. I want the pill. And I want the territory to be rich again. Or at least how it was five years ago. And I want 9-1-1. I could have really used 9-1-1. And I want Def Leppard to know my name. Lana Barbara Smith. Lana Barbara. I am like that town in California, but minus California.

Lana and I were fifteen, which was only three years away from getting pregnant and married and pulling our hair back into ponytails of duty and service and wearing pastel dresses and taking the blood of the teenagers at the Banquet Hall and then sitting on the leatherette chairs in our kitchens to look out over the snowfields, our children in them, standing tall on piles of aluminum with rabbit feet around their necks and blowtorches in their hands. We have a very small window, I wanted to say to Lana. Urgent. Very. Small. Window. Urgent.

Some of the fathers had already started warming up to The Heavy. I was the only girl in the territory who did not have a Gold Lady Gold name necklace (because I was a virgin). I was the only girl in the territory who did not have a Walkman (because I was an untouched virgin). The fathers knew what this meant, and they were taking note of me for their sons, who, at this age, were just starting to get their nicknames. So while we got jewelry that was quick to tarnish or a Walkman that was sure to break, the boys got nicknames of infamy like Fang and T-Bone. The Heavy wanted nothing to do with the fathers. I wanted nothing to do with their sons.

OUTSIDE OUR BUNGALOW, the northwest wind has died down, and it has started to rain. I hear ice slide off the roof. It hits the hard ground and smashes apart, making my body jump. My mother left just over two hours ago. Her eyes flat, her skin the color of nicotine. Her parting words—"I had forgotten all about you"—echo in my head. If my mother has forgotten all about me, what's to stop her from leaving the territory for good? A space has opened between us. It feels uncrossable. A war, an entire sea. Me on one side. And my mother on the other, disappearing from view. My pulse pounds in my ears. My throat tightens. Don't cry now. Cry later. Cry in your sleep.

I turn on all the lights and climb the stairs. I consider calling Lana, asking her to come over, but she has no idea. The Heavy and I have kept my mother's illness a secret, even from each other. It's not like we agreed to this. We're the same. Do not enter. Private property. About the sudden change that came over my mother three months ago, we haven't spoken a word.

Her bedroom is directly across the hall from mine. She thought to close her door before she left.

On my wall, I have a black-and-white picture of Muhammad Ali that I tore from a magazine that's a decade old. Ali is holding up a piece of paper that says, THE SECRET OF MUHAMMAD ALI. When I have my portrait done, this is how I'll do it. Beside him is my blood schedule for the month. The days I have completed are x-ed out, and above it is a postcard Lana put in our mailbox that just says, *SIGH!!!* I have Ric Ocasek's face inside Samuel Beckett's hair in a frame beside my bed. He is wearing dark sunglasses and under him I have written DREAM MACHINE.

PONY BECKETT OCASEK.

Le Pony Beckett Ocasek.

The Secret of Le Pony Dream Machine Beckett Ocasek Ali.

I GLUE RHINESTONES around my eyes. I put on my mother's camouflage tracksuit and her gold hoop earrings. I have two books on my bed: my disease book, which from the Latin loosely translates into *Brutal Errors of the Human Body*, and a romance novel, *Chance Encounter*, that I stole out of a turquoise mother purse at the Banquet Hall. My album cover collection takes up half a wall. It is in milk crates. I have it organized by emotion. To be free is to have achieved your life. Someone said this once. I'll count my money later when I've got more to add to it.

I am going to the bonfire. Whether The Heavy comes back or not, I am going. I sat at my mother's door with my knees folded to my chest for the last two months. You can see the imprint in the carpet, where it has worn out and the vinyl floor is shining through. I pushed notes under her door. Notes I don't know that she ever read, or even saw.

I am not waiting anymore. I have plans.

Wantings.

I press play on my tape recorder, and the Gregorian chants come on. I borrowed them from the Lending Library after I heard them coming from the tormented headphones of Supernatural. I wanted to ask him if I could listen to them, but I had forgotten how to speak. We were lying side by side on the cots at the Banquet Hall having just had our blood taken. I was trying to subtly Whitesnake my body while he lay perfectly still, staring up, black paint on his jeans and smelling like woodstove, which was more than I could handle. His boots hung over the end of his cot. I pretended we were in bed together, that our cots were joined and the bed was a waterbed, and we were in a field where we wouldn't get shot or mauled. Sometimes I get lonesome for a storm. A full blown storm where everything changes. Someone said this once. Here, you have a rest. Here, you have some citrus. This one's a fainter. Oh, look at her go. Have mercy. The women in their puffed-sleeved pink dresses, talking about me, moving busily around me, gripping my shoulders, getting me to put my head between my knees and make it settle, then lift it up slowly, slower now, Pony Darlene. That's a girl. God, you look like your mother. Doesn't she now?

SUPES IS THE SON of Traps, the truck dealer, and his wife, Debra Marie, and he is by far the best-looking boy in the territory. He was also the youngest boy in the history of our people to be given his nickname. Let me give you the lay of the land. It is between the ages of fourteen and nineteen that a territory boy gets his nickname. He will be called by this nickname until he is buried at final resting. It is his nickname, burned into a piece of shellacked plywood, that will be placed under his portrait when the territory mourners line up before it to hammer out their grief.

Supes got his nickname when he turned thirteen. Supes was not like the other boys. Their running shoes worn through and thick with mud, sticks of dynamite between their teeth. Wade Jr., Ivo Jr., Gary Jr., Constantine Jr. Their voices took forever to break. Supes's voice went from boy to man in a night. He never lit things on fire. He never chased. Never barked. Was never breathless. The boy practically had light coming off his body. Where did he come from? Visible Thinker would think. The boy's clean tank top under his parka. The shape of his arms. At Drink-Mart, The Silentest Man spoke the only name he could think to give the boy. Matches striking. Glass against glass. The younger men tossed the name between them.

"Supernatural."

"Supernatural."

"Supes for short."

"Yeah, Supes."

"Supes."

The men of the territory laughed, and when the boy did not, they stopped laughing.

All of the girls wanted him. They loved their dogs, but they loved Supernatural more. In the graveyard, by the bonfire, Thursday night after Thursday night, they trained their eyes on the incline, the one he might walk over any moment. Sometimes his hood would show. Oh God, oh my God. The girls would elbow each other, throw fits under their outerwear. Quiet one, he is. The girls would flick their eyes toward him and then away, let their hair fall in front of their faces. I can do things to you simultaneously, the girls would communicate with their minds. This is serious. I have skills I can coordinate, combos I can execute. Make me your wife. But by the time the girls cleared their faces of their hair, Supes would be gone.

I wanted his soundtrack.

And possibly, him.

I fold the hem under and pin my mother's camo track jacket so it shows off my midsection. Better. Baby one night somebody going to strike a match on a tombstone and read your name. Someone said this once. SETTLE YOUR HEAD. This is what I have written on a flag above my bed. Settle your head.

I twist the knob and creak the door open to my mother's bedroom. I turn on the overhead light. It still works. The curtains are drawn. A knot of black bedcovers, and her pillow curved where her head lay against it. I look through her dresser drawers, her closet. I get down on my knees and run my hands over her carpet. I look under her bed. Lift the black bedcovers.

Nothing.

The room is empty.

THE DAY AFTER my mother crashed our previous truck into a tree on an iceless day was the day our people call Free Day. When I left our bungalow, my mother was in her bed with a white bandage across her forehead, raking her fingers through our dog's fur. Save for our totaled truck, our yard was empty. I held and kissed her hand three times and cranked her window open. You could hear the reservoir lap the shoreline. It was summer. Summer is a beautiful time here. Don't you see that, I wanted to say to my mother. See that.

Free Day is the day we put our unwanted objects at the edges of our properties, and you can just ride by and take whatever you want. Most of the items are in need of some repair, and these are clearly marked AS IS. I always started at Neon Dean's on Free Day because sometimes he left money or pills in the pockets of his old clothes. I had done my tour through town and had a Betamax, headlamp, and crimping iron balanced on my handlebars and had roped a shovel and a ceiling fan to the back of my bike. Deal with it. Hell yes. Focus Thine Anarchy. Pony Ali. Things were looking up.

When I got home, my mother's bedroom was in a pile on our front yard. Neon Dean's girlfriend, Pallas, a few years older than me, was rifling through it. She had human bite marks on her skin and my mother's belts fastened around her neck. Her friend was with her. I had seen her friend around. She was Rita Star's daughter, and Rita Star had called her Grace, and Grace wanted nothing to do with her mother. The women of the territory would sit at Rita Star's kitchen table in their ski jackets and white underwear after tanning in Rita Star's tanning bed and talk about their falling-out, and how unnatural it was for a mother to be separated from her daughter even though Grace lived right across the street in bungalow 21 on a mattress in Pallas's closet. Pallas had rigged a string of lights and nailed a final resting bouquet above Grace's head. All I need is tuberculosis. Grace laughed and changed her name to Future.

Future was stabbing her cigarette into the ground. She stood up. She had my mother's lotions, perfumes, waterproof makeup, and underwear stuffed into the large pockets of her daypants. She pulled on my mother's silver party dress and smoothed it over her body.

"When he sees me in this, he's going to name his dick after me."

"He is."

She found my mother's red ski jacket and put it on over the silver party dress.

"When he sees me in this, he's going to make me pregnant with his supernatural baby."

"He is."

"Futurenatural."

And then seeing me, Pallas said, "Seriously?"

And Future said, "Seriously."

I was wearing hunting glasses and Neon Dean's discarded camo outerwear, which had a white pill in the right pocket and five dollars in the left. I came to a stop in front of them. It was warm enough to kick up some dirt.

"Nice show the other day," Pallas said.

"Yeah, nice show at the final resting for Debra Marie's *baby*," Future said.

"Real nice."

"Real classy."

"We know all about your mother, Pony Darlene."

"She's a cheater."

"Yeah, we know all about her rampant cheating."

"Yeah."

"Yeah?"

"Yeah."

"So jealous of Debra Marie—"

"She had to kill her baby."

"Then crashing her truck—"

"So she could go to Fully Loaded and get a new one."

"Any excuse to go to Fully Loaded."

"Any excuse to see Traps."

"We know all about your mother."

"Poaching Traps."

"We know all about her cheating."

"But do you?"

"No, she doesn't."

"Why?"

"Because she's such a deep geek."

"Geek nation."

"Welcome," I said.

"Freak nation."

"Bienvenue."

"Mental like her mother."

"Demented like her father."

"As is," I said. And I dropped the white pill onto my tongue. And I ripped the five-dollar bill in half. And I threw my bicycle a shockingly far way.

And when Pallas and Future started at me and I didn't flinch, they turned to each other.

"I might just want to go home and get into my nightpants."

"Yeah, I'm tired too."

"Seriously, I did my bloodwork this morning and need some citrus."

And they left in their matching WANT IT MORE sweatshirts. Their sweatshirts hung down to their knees. Future's had a laminated pin on it that said, FAINTER. I had the same pin.

WHEN MY MOTHER first led me through the woods and down to the reservoir, I was shaking with terror. I thought I might throw up, and I told her so, and she said, "It makes our life so much better to have this other separate life. Just to know it is here," and she held me by the wrist. I was eight, nearly nine. When we reached the shoreline, she unlaced her boots, unclasped her workdress, pulled it over her head, and hung it from a tree branch. The water was still and gray, and the moon was in it white as a bone, and my mother stepped into the water. I gasped. She turned back and put her hand over my mouth. "Don't wreck it, Pony." And then I watched my mother from the banks of the black mud as she walked into the reservoir and then did a shallow dive. Would she be sucked down? Would her skin dissolve? Was this where all life began? Since when did my mother wear nothing under her work-dress? Where was her white underwear? Her beige bra? A starless sky. To it, my mother let out a cry. It was happiness. She cut through the water. I agreed with my father. I had never seen anyone quite so alive.

I begged her to teach me how to swim.

IT IS TRAPS'S TRUCK, not ours, that backs sharply into the unfinished driveway and fills my body with dread. A reversal meant to awe me. Traps knows I am watching from my bedroom window, the curtain drawn to one side. B E Y O N D. He shuts down his fog lights and pulls in all the darkness around us. My father gets out of the truck. His bowed head, his slow steps. This tells me everything I need to know.

In the territory, the boys are dragging tires, cabinets, wood pallets, whatever they can find to burn, to the graveyard. They have cans of lighter fluid in their back jean pockets and cigarettes in their mouths. They are wearing fingerless gloves, Yamaha vests, and scarves around their heads, tied into bandannas. It is ten below. They grip their handlebars and hold their bodies high off their dirt bikes and pedal hard. They cannot believe muscle has to rip in order to grow. They have playing cards in their wheels that go *tic-tic-tic-tic-tic-tic-tic*. They want the territory to show up on a satellite. They want the bonfire to be photographed from space. The boys think about space the way some boys think about girlfriends. They get stomach cramps thinking about space.

In their headphones, the boys listen to asteroids blazing through the atmosphere toward them. Later tonight, they will trade their cassettes by the bonfire while the leather of their running shoes melts.

"Which one are you listening to?"

"Maxell!"

"Oh, that one is killer!"

"You?"

"Memorex."

I don't want to tell the boys the asteroid's approach is the sound of the tape running, and the sound of its impact the tape coming to its end and then clicking off. I don't want to tell them their tapes are blank tapes, and Deep Space Tapes is a fraudulent business run by the older, smarter brother of Peter Fox St. John, and they should just hit up the Lending Library and check out the Gregorian chants. They're in the devotional section.

SEVEN THINGS shortly before 10:00 P.M.:

1. The boys of the territory have the same shaved hairstyle as monks. Monks are their own deep space tape. Correlation.
2. There are a million asteroids on a crash course with the earth. This is not the kind of thing you tell a boy whose running shoes are on fire.
3. I put on my mother's perfume, and I do this exactly

the way she would have. I spray my wrists and then
I run my wrists up under my hair, and, in that instant,
I become a woman.

4. At night, I reliably think about death. I have no aunts,
no uncles, no siblings, no grandparents, and when my
mother and father are gone, I will be the last Fontaine
living in the Last House. Urgent.

5. The reservoir is the result of an asteroidal event, which
the astrophysicists also call an impact event. A person
could organize her timeline into impact events. This is
one approach to understanding a life.

6. While asteroids are, in their own catastrophic way,
totally romantic, what the boys of the territory want
most is a girl rolling off them saying, That was fucking
amazing.

7. Tonight, that girl will be Lana. Lana Barbara
California as she will come to call herself.

"You need me," Traps tells The Heavy when they come
through our front door, bringing with them the bitter air. On
our small cement porch, we have a partial telephone, a broken
fridge, and a large piece of chipboard with an *88* painted on
it. My mother used to trim my nails on our front porch. I
would lie on the cement and she would hold my feet in her lap,
and she was radiant. The men kick the ice from their boots
and push the door closed. Traps refuses to go home to his wife,
Debra Marie, should something come up. He makes a "no
way" sign with his hands and calls her on speed dial.

Debra Marie has just suffered what the territory calls its

worst tragedy in nearly twenty years. The women of the territory talk about it and how she has not cried once. Not broken down once. Not mentioned her dead child once. The women can't even tan. They can't drink their coffee. It's hideous. It's cruel. The women feel a weight in their chests, heavy as bronze. Debra Marie, oh, Debra Marie. Poor Debra Marie. It wasn't her fault. Was it?

After the final resting, when we were leaving the Banquet Hall, even through the commotion, I overheard the men of the territory talking to Debra Marie. They hulked before the black square, which stood in place of the portrait, a bouquet on either side of it, under three floor lamps, and they kept their sunglasses on and did not know what to do with their large arms, like bouncers with nothing left to guard.

"Noble Debra Marie."

"Noble."

"If you were a man, that's what we'd call you, Debra Marie."

"Noble."

"Your nickname would be Noble."

"Yeah, Noble."

"Noble."

"HE NEEDS ME." Traps tells this to Debra Marie over the telephone. Quickly, not wanting to tie up the line. I can see Debra Marie on the other end. Her plain hair arrangements, her purposeful body. She would iron her indoor tracksuit but never put it on. "He has only the one truck. Unlike us. The single vehicle." Traps adjusts himself and looks for cigarettes.

"You have your own truck. Unlike the Fontaine mother, you have your own truck. And it's fully loaded." Then he pauses to listen and says, "Okay, okay, almost fully loaded," and he lights a cigarette, one of my mother's cigarettes. "She'll be back. Nowhere to go." And he glances for The Heavy, to share this small encouragement, but The Heavy has left the room. "Pony was the last to see her."

And then Traps turns his eyes on me, and lets them go soft and pleading on my mouth. My supple, athletic mouth. I can see him working out the timeline in his head. Two nights until Saturday night. Two nights until I walk the side of the north highway in my button-down and pencil skirt with my perfect waistline-to-ass ratio. A 0.8.

THE SECRET OF PONY DARLENE FONTAINE

THREE MONTHS AGO. Nighttime. When the men of the territory were going to and then leaving Drink-Mart, clusters of them smelling medicinal and exhaling turbines of smoke, clapping each other hard on the shoulder, on the back, a half hug here and there, then dispersing into their trucks to one-eye it home and fall asleep on their wives in their nightdresses, I walked the shoulder of the highway in my white button-down and black pencil skirt. I had a plan. This was step one. I carried a clipboard and waved down the trucks, knowing only one of them would come to a full stop. All of the passing territory men called out, "Pony." They rolled down their windows. "Pony Darlene Fontaine." Reaching out with a lotioned hand, I introduced myself as The Complaint Department and asked the men the question I was desperate to be asked, "What is troubling you?" Then I gave them my card with my toll-free number, 1-800-OH-MY-GOD, should they wish to discuss their troubles further.

The men laughed. No one complains here. That is not the territory's way. Complaint is a form of self-degradation. Hardship is a matter of perception. The men quoted the Leader. The men were missing teeth. They were missing fingers. They were missing testicles. They had slipped disks. They ate the tendons of animals. The organs of animals. They carved them up and gave thanks. Thank you for your meat. They delivered their babies. Their babies became teenagers. Men hunting women. Women hunting men. Men hunting animals. That is how it goes here, Pony Darlene, the men called out, and tearing up the gravel, sped home.

"My only complaint," Traps said to me, too loud, bit of a slur, throwing on his emergency brake and unlocking his doors, "is that you won't blow me in the back of my truck." And, step two, I blew him while he said my name over and over, and when he was done I directed him to his fuel shed, where, step three, he took off his heavy necklace of keys, while looking at me under his security camera. The look was exaltation and the Saturday night sky was dark. However grainy, Traps would watch the video of me waiting for my payment, step four, one full jerry can of his gasoline—one hundred miles of transport—again and again, pausing it at certain moments, when he could really see my face.

———

I HEAR TRAPS opening and closing our kitchen cupboards. He is looking for the alcohol and concluding his call home to Debra Marie. "We did a tour through the territory. The Heavy doesn't want to do a door-to-door. Not just yet. Says it's a family matter. A private matter."

Tonight, Traps will drink himself to sleep on our beige couch. Too much, too little. He still finds this hard to gauge. He will be standing, talking, drinking, taking, killing, talking, drinking, standing. And then unconscious. Debra Marie loves crime shows. Murder shows. Shows where the plot rests on violence. I wonder when she will stop dragging Traps's faithless body to comfort. When there will be a trail of blood in his wake. An antler plunged through his heart. "Besides, it's Delivery Day tomorrow, and no territory woman in her right mind would miss Delivery Day." He agrees with himself: "No territory woman would miss Delivery Day."

My father is lying in the half-built room on a hooded chair, and because of the tarp, and the work light he has set up in there, we are both a bright blue. Is she missing? I want to ask him. You can tell me. I can handle it. I can't handle it. "You need to get some rest," I say instead to my father, and I unlace and pull off his boots, tug at the cuffs of his jeans. I was with him when he bought the jeans. "Not too tight?" The Heavy said to the salesmen, who nodded with their arms crossed, which was a confusing set of messages. "Denim is a tight and captivating weave," the salesmen said. The Heavy bought them in a moment of hope. Hope makes you buy clothes that don't fit you. A brawl to pull off, the jeans hold my father's shape and appear to be standing, a former fighter turning soft.

"I love that perfume," he says.

Three things he does not say: Where are you going? When will you be back? Won't you be cold?

My father, who never raises his voice. Never goes to Drink-Mart. Does not listen to music. Does not watch television. He fears he will miss something real, he explains. Life is about paying attention, Pony.

Traps watches me closely as I lace up my boots and throw on my camouflage outerwear. Camo on camo. I open the front door. On the back of my outerwear are the words I was coloring in earlier with Neon Dean's impermanent marker, when my mother came down the stairs in her indoor tracksuit, a stale cigarette in one hand and her truck keys in the other. Fifteen years of blank tape running out and clicking off. The asteroidal event. The impact event.

CAN'T TOUCH THIS

THE NORTH HIGHWAY is silver with ice, and Lana is riding behind me. This is our usual formation. Tonight, we're just trying to stay upright. The road is slick. The shoulder better. At least there's some traction. In the distance, we can see the bonfire, sparks shooting up into the low black sky. Of note: This is exactly what I see before I faint. Same panorama. I listen to protest rallies and sporting events (also in the devotional section). I love the sound of a crowd. I put the tapes into my cassette recorder, and I feel surrounded. I pump my fist in the air and nearly wipe out. Lana lets out a howl behind me.

When I arrived at Lana's bungalow, she was at her bedroom window. She had teased her hair and was holding a crowbar in her hands, vigorously working the bottom of her window frame. I knew she would be sweating. She was a sweater in the first degree. Nerves or yearning.

Two years ago, Lana's mother died. Caution. Steep drop. Lifeguard off duty. The women of the territory decided the cause was inconsolability. Soon after her mother's death, Lana's father married a girl just a few years older than Lana. This is how it goes in the territory. In the rare instance a woman dies, it is expected her husband will remarry. Children need a mother. If a man dies, his widow remains a widow. Children need a mother, and they still have one. Lana's mother's portrait is wrapped in a black bedsheet and stored in their toolshed. Lana's stepmother's name is Denise. Her portrait hangs above their mantel. In it, she wears a very tight sweater and Vaseline on her eyelashes, and a smile that seems to say, I am pretty sure I am being paid for sex with food, shelter, and beauty products. Her name necklace, given to her by an exboyfriend, says DENIS.

Lana's mother's color scheme was violet. Now, Lana's bungalow is red, and her stepmother sits sidesaddle on the shag carpet in their living room, watching television and eating from a large bowl. She is pregnant, and most nights, Lana's father stands in their driveway with his truck running, staring into his high beams until his eyes sting. When Lana screamed at her father, "Admit it, there's a stranger in the house, and she's evil! Admit it, Denis is pregnant with another man's baby!" Lana's father put a lock on her bedroom door and painted her window shut.

I watch Lana fall to the ground and walk unevenly to her ten-speed. Her father has rigged their front yard with motion-detector lights. Lana's father reminds me how completely I have slipped from The Heavy's view. Maybe it's the camo on camo, I joke to myself. A joke is a disguise. Don't you think there is always something unspoken between two people? Someone said this once. Paint my window shut. Worry about me. I want my father, The Heavy Fontaine, to paint my window shut. I want my father to worry about me. I want my mother to come home.

"You are totally talking to yourself," Lana says and looks back at her bungalow, bungalow 2. "Teen prison break. Seriously. I might have just broken my wrist. Is everything all right? You look like Cherie Currie. Only after a fight. And before a hunt. With longer hair. And more height. And less fame."

"Thank you."

"And maybe poorer and more isolated."

"Let's roll."

"Psyched."

Lana has tied a strip of leather around her neck. She is wearing a snowmobile suit and her steel-toe, steel-shank boots. She has belted the snowmobile suit and cut off the arms. She has her wool socks pulled up above her knees. "It's the closest I can get to lingerie," she says. On the back of her armless suit she has written HIGH HOPES. She digs her heels into the ground.

It's frozen. Even The Heavy couldn't muscle through it. Winter in the Death Man's shed. "Damn-o that camo. I can barely see you. Don't get shot!" Lana says. Then a tremble to her lower lip. "Seriously. Killing you would kill me." She laughs. "1-800-OH-MY-GOD."

I DID NOT NAME the complainant (as much as she tried to get it out of me), but I did tell Lana about The Complaint Department. One July night, in the founders' bus. Two pink pills, three blue ones. This was soon after I secured my first jerry can of gasoline. Nineteen more to go.

"It's not like kissing on television," I said.

"Duh," Lana said.

"Not even close."

"Okay."

"You have to really relax your mouth. See? More. That's better. That's good. Your mouth goes a lot farther back than you think it does. Remember when we took our emotional measurements? We thought I would have the broader shoulders, but you did? The actual measurement of your mouth will astound you. Blowing will free you from the emotional measurement of your mouth."

"Exciting."

"And could have a domino effect on your other body parts."

"Bonus."

"Despite the name, there's no blowing."

"Okay."

"Don't blow on it."

"I won't."

"Don't blow on the dick."

"I won't. I mean, when the dick shows, I won't blow on it."

"By the end, it will not be unlike the headbang."

"All right."

"You'll feel it in your neck in the morning."

"Okay."

"If you need a break, you just tuck the dick under your hair and up behind your ear. Rub it against your jawline. You are in charge. This is an exchange and you are in charge of the exchange."

"I am in charge."

"Regardless of depth, pacing, and tongue placement, this is the most important part. You are in charge."

"I am in charge."

"Don't worry."

"You know that's hard for me," Lana said.

And then stoned, so stoned, Pony Ali, Le Pony Ali of the Superior Existence, I said, "This might be my one natural talent."

"You are so lucky, Pony."

The small voice. The large darkness. It opened up between us. And I was suddenly no longer stoned. I was so unstoned. So unlucky. Pony of the Inferior Existence.

Of course that July night I had been thinking about the scene I left at home. It was Free Day. The day after my mother totaled the truck. My mother, a fresh cut above her left eyebrow where she hit the windshield, almost invisible under her black bedcovers, our dog the only one allowed in there with her, and one floor below, my father building a room, which, let's admit, is not for my mother but for him. His alternate jeans and his outerwear folded in a neat stack on the ground. While other territory men drag razors across their scalps and weep into black towels, my father wets his hair and combs it off his face with his fingers. He leans over our kitchen garbage and trims his beard. He is the only man in the territory with hair, and this is because of his scars, because before Debra Marie and Traps, my father's tragedy was what the territory called its worst tragedy. And right now, my father is sleeping on a hooded chair. A chair he built for my mother after she said—and we could see she had been crying—"If only this chair had a hood." A chair to keep her coming downstairs. To keep her sitting with us. Our people are a sitting people. When the women of the territory aren't drawing blood at the Banquet Hall, they are sitting across from each other and starting with "You good?"

My father called it the Easiest Chair. Not the easier chair. Not the less difficult chair. But the Easiest Chair. My father, The Heavy. My father, the heaviest.

The sun was rising, and with it, I could read the graffiti on the ceiling of the founders' bus, and it was all about love, which seems to be all about addition, about surplus.

person + person
person + person
person + person

Where were the minus signs?

———

THE PIT PARTY. The boys have set what they can on fire, and the girls are sitting in a loose circle, leaning on headstones, leaning on each other, flames as high as their bungalows. Perfect circles are for other people, people who don't have the dead in their way. Lana and I add our bicycles to the pile. I hand Lana her three pills. "Ready?"

"Amped."

I put mine on my tongue. Yellow, pink, blue. We swallow them together.

"Sit on my face, Pony Darlene!" one boy yells. He pronounces *face* like *fay-uhssss*. He has small bleeds on his jaw from shaving. He jogs around the bonfire holding a can of butane in the air. He has drawings up and down his bare arms. Fangs, knives and tires, guitars, bikinis and telephones, the Death Man, an IV drip, and words cap-lettered—BLOOD, JUSTICE, LADIESMAN. He pounds his chest and says, "What do we have left to burn?" He pronounces *burn* like *bee-yurnnnn*. The pills kick in.

Neon Pony.

Welcome.

Bienvenue.

"I'm the Secret Service!" yells another boy. He is looking at the girls and needing the girls to look back at him. They won't. The girls, who have all had sex encounters, have their names on their necklaces. They glint by the fire. Their hair falls far down their backs and is picked up by the black wind. It takes on a new form with every gust. Touch it. Touch me. I am the softest thing going. "Nature wants girls and kills boys," one girl says. She is wearing an eye patch, and I know it's because she needs it. "I tried to make alcohol from potatoes," one skinny boy says, "and my father duct-taped me to a chair for two days." The other boys hold themselves and laugh, "Two days!" And the skinny boy laughs though I can see he is sore, and was after love.

The girls pass a bottle, drinking through a straw to quicken the effect. The ones who did their bloodwork this morning are seeing spots. They fall back and take in the sky. "This sky is so dull! Do something, sky! Do a meteor shower or something! Feel me up! Make it summer!" The girls grin until they show their gums. They untuck their shirts and knot them under their breasts. They fold the waistbands of their pants down so the edges of their hipbones come up. My hipbones. You like them? They're new. Softness bracketed by hardness. Copyrighting this look, the girls think, copyrighting this whole look, my best look, and when the girls sit up, "Head rush," they stare down at the ground to settle it. Their blood multiplies itself, racing to occupy the spaces that need occupying. They train their eyes on the incline, the one Supes might walk over any minute. Love and a cough cannot be concealed. Even a small cough. Even a small love. Someone said this once.

One night, almost two years ago, Lana and I snuck into her father's truck. We wanted to steal his cigarettes, his small change. Whatever we could find. He had just married Denis. "She brought a belt to the marriage," Lana said. "Seriously. She showed up with a belt. That was it. A belt." We wanted to steal her father's truck.

"I can drive," I said.

"Not well enough," Lana said.

Like every matte black truck in the territory, Lana's father's had a CB. We dialed through the frequencies, getting mostly static. "Come in, come in," I said. We were both in our night-dresses, had badly crimped hair and whatever press-on nails we could press on. "Come in, come in." And then a girl's voice came through, "I read you." Lana grabbed the microphone. "Go ahead," the girl said. "I'm pregnant," Lana said, lying. My mouth dropped open. "I need help," Lana said, not lying. The girl began her instruction. It was Pallas. Before she got together with Neon Dean. Before she got tanned and cruel, and tried to pierce her tongue. After her fourteenth birthday. When she got pregnant with the Delivery Man's baby.

"Okay, girl. Listen close. You have to starve yourself, but make it look like you are suddenly eating like that woman on that show. The one who can't leave her house except by a crane. Then, hard as this is, you have to wear baggier clothes. Like a widow. Never let anyone see you naked. You can use duct tape and girdles to pretty convincing effect. Ask Rochelle. Or Lorraine. Or even Tristan. Tina had skills with the whole weight-lifter belt, shrink-wrap thing, and Tiffany with those junior-size pants. You can only stop a pregnancy from hap-pening on night soaps. Or, and this is a last fucking resort, you do the Mother Trick. You break down and tell your mom, and when she is done hitting your pretty face, she gets her owl feathers and her foam and hides them under her bed, and starts stuffing herself to the appropriate measurements. Inches versus time. Watch your inches. Watch your time. Parallel baby. And she suffers with it. The nausea lays her right out. No one can touch her. No one can see her. And when you start to feel the hellishness coming on, you wait as long as you can, and then your mom drives you out to the forest with some cough syrup or whatever you can get your hands on at Drugs and More Drugs. We all know the forest is for the babies. It grows for the babies. To have them, to hide them if you have to. And you get that thing out of your body and against hers. Make sure your father doesn't figure it out. Make sure he doesn't catch on. Seriously. That's on your mom. And you. Fathers hate to be tricked. Remember Stephanie. But seriously, if you can pull this off, you will make both your parents so happy. Your mom will seem young to your dad, and your dad will seem young to our men. You handed your youth over to them. They should be giving thanks inside. But seriously, you have to be ready. Something can happen between you and the baby. You just have to commit to the motions. Make a list of the motions. You can't get lost. You have to know what to do next. Have the baby. Hand over the baby."

AROUND THE BONFIRE, the territory boys approach the girls. They have new shoulders, new jawlines, and are looking for kicks. A boy comes up to Lana. He wears a tire chain for a necklace, has a pine twig behind his ear. Across one set of knuckles, he has written PAIN, and across the other set, PAIN.

"Seriously, let's reproduce. I'll give you my chips."

"I can buy my own chips."

"You can have my headphones."

"So?"

"You're pretty."

"Ew."

"What?"

"Stop trying so hard."

"Okay."

"Effort is repulsive."

"Okay."

"Your effortful smile. Your kingdom of effort."

"Okay!"

"You have the voice of a beggar."

"Sorry?"

"Don't punctuate your questions. A territory man presents his questions with flatness."

"Will you do me."

"It's just don't be keen. Seriously. It's gross."

"Okay."

"Besides, what are headphones without a Walkman?"

"Okay. Here, take my Walkman."

And Lana and the boy leave the loose circle for the dark space behind Shona Lee's husband's headstone. Lana knows that if she becomes a mother, she will never listen to her Walkman again. But still, Lana +.

I NEED TO GET some air. Lately, I have been hyperventilating in my sleep. This can be accompanied by a wet face. Love. Brutal error of my human body. Underneath my pillow, I keep a picture of a coach. A glossy image I tore from a magazine. He is wearing a collared shirt and a headset. He has his arms out and he is yelling. This is bullshit! Take a deep fucking breath and wipe your face on your black bedsheet and get back to it, Pony!

My mother has been missing for five hours.

I leave the bonfire and head for the woods that border the edge of the graveyard. The boy with the can of butane follows, and when I say, "Get the fuck away from me," he says, "Do you need CPR?" And when I give him the finger, he returns to the bonfire, throws his can of butane into it, and yells, "Heads up!" (*Heeyed-zyup!*), then looks to outer space. "Did you get that?"

Pallas, performer of the Mother Trick, has a little sister now. She's four. Every night, the girl begs Future to let her sleep with her in her closet bed. Future says sure and blocks the image of her own mother, Rita Star, from her mind. The sound of the girl's silvery breath. She sleeps on the mattress with her arms above her head like she's just landed on it.

It's a new kind of darkness with my mother maybe roaming it. Don't you scare yourself! Don't you crack on me now, 88! You've got a plan to execute! Pony Supreme! Chin up! Chin the fuck up! I can see the Death Man's trailer from here. He's done some landscaping. I cannot picture him touching anything living. His furniture is plastic. His gray, featherless birds are on the roof of his shed. They don't seem to eat or migrate. They just dive-bomb us, wailing. We're so annoyed by the birds, but maybe they are trying to tell us something, issue some type of warning?

I wish I had a cigarette. I wish I smoked.

MY MOTHER WOULD never talk about her life before she arrived in the territory. She didn't like to remember it, she told me. This was her life now. Her only life.

When Shona Lee's husband, Wishbone, shot himself in the chest last winter, Shona Lee called my mother and asked her to come over. Said she wanted me to come too. Had a soft spot for me. We stood in Shona Lee's driveway. Shona Lee lit a Virginia Slim and talked about walking a brave line. She wore a leopard dress, blue eyeshadow, and her dead husband's plaid outerwear. A week before, the men of the territory had knocked on her door. It was early November. The middle of the night. The men stood on her small cement porch, all of them looking in different directions. Shona Lee was confused by the men and so called for her husband. When he didn't answer, she checked their bungalow. Surely he was in it and this was her worst dream. "What is love if not a space for horrors to grow?" she said to my mother, and my mother agreed. An accident. He had been fully loaded, the men tried to explain to Shona Lee, something close to a joke. A woman's despair can be so hard to take. When Shona Lee was told the next morning the ground was frozen and her husband would spend the winter in the Death Man's shed, Shona Lee begged to see his body. She was told no. Once a corpse is handed over to the Death Man, it is never seen again, but Shona Lee was already walking away when the men told her that. She knew the rules.

The weeping went from bed to sink, floor to shower, vacant room to vacant room, and so much time balled on the bed. Shona Lee could not stand her widowed self. "Enough," she said, and with her widow money bought twenty jerry cans of gasoline from Traps and an animal print dress from The Woman Store. She was set to drive the two thousand miles south to the next nearest town. "You're the only one who knows what's beyond the territory." Shona Lee lifted the tarp and showed my mother her truck bed. It was filled with fuel. I had the crazed heart rate of prey, but was trying to appear cold and bored like the teen wives on *Teen Wives*. Like Denis. Arms crossed, eyes half rolled back. As much as I pressed my mother, this was the one line of questioning she would never submit to. What is beyond.

"You will be a stranger among strangers," my mother said, and I could feel a charge run through her. "Why can't a woman be more than one person in a lifetime?" she continued. "Why can't she be two or three?"

"I will be a stranger among strangers," Shona Lee motivated herself.

And that summer, while I sunburned nearby on an emergency blanket, The Heavy dug Shona Lee's husband's grave, and then Shona Lee stood over it singing Led Zeppelin with the voice of God. She sang over the drone of the horseflies. Her husband was in the ground. He had a place. She had a place. This savage place, her only place. She didn't want to be a stranger. She wanted to be known. Shona Lee remained in the territory. No one has ever left it. And only she came that close.

SHORTLY AFTER my mother's arrival here, Rita Star swore she saw a picture of her on television. The name on the screen was different than the one my mother had used to introduce herself, but the face was the same. She'd cut and dyed her hair, but any novice knew that was the first thing you did to bury your past. Wanted or Missing, Rita Star could not recall. She searched and searched, flicking through her channels, but the picture of my mother did not come back into focus.

Hearing about the picture, the other territory women searched and searched. The Heavy's thin fox of a stranger is going to murder me, steal my husband, and make a nice den for herself out of my den things. "You are glued to that damn television," their husbands would rant. The women didn't know how to make sense of it. Rita Star was a gossip. She was lonely. She would come over and sit at your kitchen table, and tell story after story, and not know when it was time to stop talking and leave. This was long before she invested in her tanning bed and opened her palmistry business. Her young daughter basically lived across the street with Pallas Jones. Who the Grace girl's father was, none of the women could say with any certainty. She had no husband, and in practical terms, Rita Star had no child. What do you even call that? The women had no name for a woman without dependents. Nothing feeding from her body. Nothing feeding from her hands. One knife, one fork, one spoon, one bowl. The emptiness of her bungalow. Should the women really believe this lone woman of mediocre fitness or was she just looking for attention? The women decided against believing Rita Star.

They all came to my parents' wedding, and the men and women of the territory marveled at my mother, this woman who had appeared at their lunch counter with her short hair and her short dress now with her long hair and her long dress. How quickly she looked like one of them.

But sometimes, they felt unsettled by her. She seemed to

clock the way they held their bottles of alcohol, their Delivery Day baskets, how they spoke, where to accentuate, when to laugh, and our people looked at her and thought: Lassie. "The thing about Lassie," the women would say to each other when my mother was not at the table, "is that you watch the show and you think it's just this one single dog doing all these things, but it's actually many dogs that look exactly alike, and they all have different talents. This one is good at wagging its tail. This one is good at jumping over logs. This one is good at sitting. This one is good at fetching. This one is good at heeling. This one is good at playing dead." And when my mother crashed our truck on that July evening, and it was towed through town to be salvaged at Fully Loaded, Rita Star's story returned to the minds of the women.

The hood bent into a tree shape, the glass cracked where my mother's head hit the windshield. Once the bleeding was under control, my mother needed only one small bandage. But still. Parts of her had come loose in the crash, the women said to each other. A life has its rigging.

I was up to my mother's collarbone when she taught me how to swim. I didn't want to learn. I only wanted her—anything that told me what she felt, loved, protected, lied about, thought of, had been.

I GUESS THE TEENAGERS of the territory don't see me, Camo Pony, when I make my way back to the fire. One girl is talking about being courted by a widower. I sit behind a headstone to listen. I fold my knees to my chest. In Latin, *cancer of the dreams* starts with *somnia*.

"What widower?"

"The Heavy?" And this makes the teenagers howl with laughter.

"The Fontaine mother isn't dead!"

"She's just missing!"

"In the territory, missing *is* dead."

"The Heavy—"

"Sick."

"Plus, the facial issues."

"Double sick. Seriously. Sick galore."

"My mom told me he used to be hot. Superhot. Before . . . you know."

The girl being courted says she likes the widower's bigger truck and cleaner stuff, and how he doesn't just walk around all the time in a black towel, eating off his barbecue with his dog, you know, the update to basic sonic and video technology, the light fixture advantages, but the graying body hair takes getting used to. Big-time. Revulsion can come pretty quickly and has to be integrated for a dimensional sex encounter, when it is time for body on body, for *65 and *69, which, the girl explains, "comes down to the difference between facing my hot rocking body north and facing my hot rocking body south."

"Show us," the girls say, "show us how you do the widower."

"Better than the dick channel," one boy rasps when the girl is done.

"Okay. Losing your mind. Hard or easy?"

"Hard."

"Killing yourself, hard or easy?"

"So easy," says Lana.

"How would you know?" Then the skinny boy remembers Lana's circumstances. Her dead mother, and her new mother, the ex-girlfriend of Peter Fox St. John, who misspelled her name on her name necklace, but she still wears it even though Lana's father bought her one with her name in full and made of a purer gold, and Denise is pregnant with the Delivery Man's baby, and she painted their whole bungalow red, even the toilet seats, and Lana's father might be the one who's inconsolable now. "Sorry, Lana," the skinny boy says. And hating his voice more than ever, "I'm really sorry."

And everyone falls quiet, waiting for Lana to break down. Then Lana says, still very, very high, "Lana Barbara California!" and a cheer goes up.

"High hopes!" she says.

Another cheer.

"Leaving the territory, hard or easy?"

"Impossible."

"Don't even."

Some of the older girls who are invited to sit at Rita Star's kitchen table tell the others my mother left our bungalow in her indoor tracksuit and no shoes shortly after 7:00 P.M. How could they know that? How could they possibly know that? And she has not been seen since. No sign of the truck.

"Where is the Fontaine mother pacing without her shoes?"

"She could be right there."

"Don't!"

"Watching us."

"She could be crouching to the ground like an animal."

"Behind that headstone."

"She was that small."

"Small as their dog."

"Their dog is massive."

"She was filled with a disease," Lana says. "Mental damage."

"It took her hair, her muscles."

"And now she is out here."

"Getting closer, getting closer, getting closer."

The snap of a twig. A stirring all around.

"Wait."

"Did you hear that?"

Their hearts leaping all through them. Their fingertips going numb.

"Did you hear something?"

"Seriously."

And then I'm standing there, and the boys and girls of the territory are shrieking, "You can't just sneak up on people like that!"

"I didn't mean to," I say dumbly.

"You fucking scared us!"

"Sorry."

"You scared us so bad."

"Sorry."

I want to tell them they're wrong. My mother soaped my body and sang me to sleep. She taped my drawings to the walls. She got down on her knees and brushed the knots from my hair. How you're growing, she would say, I can't keep up with your growing, and she would laugh and kiss my neck. Tell me a story, she would say when I got older. Tell me about your day. Thrill me, she would say. You thrill me.

And the boy who had the can of butane comes to stand beside me and says with perfect pronunciation, tracing lines across the air with his hands, as if he is reading the words off a headstone, my headstone, "Pony Darlene Fontaine. Even her mother couldn't love her. 1970 to—"

Gunshot.

And the boy falls to the ground, taking me with him, and some of the teenagers scream and cover their ears.

"Don't be mean." Coming down the decline toward us, his rifle aimed at the sky, and then his rifle aimed at the boy. "Don't be mean," Supernatural repeats himself. His ball cap under his hood. Giving just enough of his face.

In the territory, when a woman has a baby, she's attended to by another woman. This is the territory's way. Let me give you the lay of the land. While birth is beautiful, it's primarily a fight.

Fifteen years ago, when The Heavy in his shoulder-length gloves followed my naked mother, in a state of manic concentration, out of our bungalow and into the front yard and then back inside to our living room floor, he suggested Debra Marie come over. She could place a damp cloth on my mother's back and say the thing territory women say to each other: "A woman's body knows just what to do."

"Ha!" My mother, four feet around, turned to my father

and said, "I am a phenomenon. I am multiplying. I am one becoming two, and then I am two becoming one, and as I do this, let's admit Debra Marie's help will be a small act. She will not be feeling. I am feeling. I am feeling everything there is to feel." Then my mother hissed, "Debra Marie," and begged for an apple. When The Heavy gave her the closest thing—they were two days before Delivery Day with only frozen goods in the house—my mother broke the frozen side of caribou in half with her bare hands, and I was born.

A tiny girl in his arms. The Heavy didn't know why he was choking. There was a problem with his body. "You're sobbing," my mother told him. Was the baby sweating? No, he was soaking the girl with his tears.

MY HEAD IS in the lap of Supernatural. Repeat. Situation critical. My head is in the lap of Supernatural.

S.O.S.

Supernatural. O. Supernatural.

He gets up and helps me to my feet. He looks down at me. He is extremely tall. Could there be a taller man? Yes, but not here. Maybe The Heavy. Yes, The Heavy. "You passed out." I look around. We are alone in the graveyard. I am having trouble summoning language. The bonfire is mostly embers. Everyone has gone home. "Fainted."

I had pictured this so differently. Now is the moment when I name-drop the lights in the sky, and Supernatural falls in love with me, but instead I say, "I listened to the chants." And then what I don't say: I slow danced to the chants. Embarrassed,

I lift my hands to my face. No sense of mystery. Visiting cousin. Pinto. Kissless. The rhinestones are still there. Good.

"Are you about to faint again?"

"No."

"Phew."

He is moving strangely. "My legs fell asleep," he mumbles, and then he stands very still.

I see the charred can of butane.

"Did you kill him?"

He shakes his head. "I am so not a murderer."

The tall boy in the black jeans with the rifle at his side. He has a scar that runs through his top lip. I don't think I have ever noticed it before. I don't think I have ever stood this close to Supernatural before. Seen so much of the face under the ball cap under the hood. When did he get the scar? It looks new.

WHEN WE WERE CHILDREN, our mothers dragged us here while they tidied the plots.

"You good?"

"You good?"

"You good?"

The women never answered the question; they just traded it between them. When my mother and I walked over the incline and joined the circle, they always commented on her hair design. She had the most elaborate hair designs in the territory. I would sit on the edge of her bathtub and watch her twist and pin her hair. Her gold hoop earrings, her gold eyeshadow. The pale pink workdress, the red ski jacket. All around us, the boys of the territory ran between and climbed the headstones, rolled tires, lit cardboard on fire, chanted, "Fight, fight, fight."

"Graveyard getting big," the women said.

"Graveyard getting bigger than the town."

And the widows would break off in their rubber aprons and dish gloves, their cleaning supplies in their pails, their shorter ponytails like pets at their coat collars, to clear their husbands' headstones of dirt and snow.

"When did the headstones start getting uneven?"

"Who's to say this one gets a bigger headstone than that one?"

"This one's headstone's bigger than my chest freezer."

"This one's bigger than my bungalow."

And the children pinned their arms to their bodies and rolled down the small decline. Clay, rock, and scrub. The girls played at having their blood drawn. Faking dizzy, "I did my bloodwork today. Get me some citrus." And the boys, with their fathers' old tools, built makeshift ladders, hunting platforms. Every stick was a rifle. They had knives in pouches and sharpened wood into spears.

"Oh come on, you two," my mother would say.

"Join the others!" Debra Marie would look from me to Supernatural. And we would leave the mothers and walk toward the children. We wouldn't look at each other. We wouldn't talk to each other. We would stand there with our hands in our pockets and search for the next moment.

———

SUPERNATURAL BRUSHES OFF my outerwear. He straightens it.
He touches me the way my mother would. What is this feeling? I put my head in my hands. There's a pressure against my
skull. A metallic taste in my mouth. Drugs? Fear? Love? I want
to ask him if there is any word on my mother. An alarm
sounds. A rapid, high beeping. It's his watch. He has a digital.
Black, plastic. He presses a button to turn it off and a blue
light comes up: 6:45 A.M. She has been gone close to twelve
hours. "No word on your mother," Supernatural says, and he
puts his hand on my shoulder. It startles me. "Sorry," he says.
Did he just read my mind? I need to go. I get on my bicycle
and try to ride away from him as fast as possible. "Are you all
right to get home?" he calls after me. I don't answer him.
"Hey, Pony!" The sun is breaking up the horizon. "What did
you think of the chants?" he asks. I pump my fist in the air. I
do not even come close to wiping out.

Next life. Waterbed, field, be there.

THE MORNING AFTER the bonfire. The Delivery Man pulls
into the loading dock of Value Smoke and Grocer. He always
arrives right at dawn. Two young girls in ski masks and nightdresses come to a stop beside me and get off their dirt bikes.
They are shivering with the cold. Slender and breathless.
They are wearing rings made of duct tape. I can see the paint
under their fingernails. They hold their arms on a diagonal
against their bodies. I recognize the injury. They launched
themselves from their bedroom windows, their nightdresses
looking like parachutes, but not performing like them. The

girls roll up their ski masks. They are sure not to cry when the Delivery Man steps down from his rig. This man is in love with me, the girls tell themselves, and he is going to take me to a place where they never run out of eggs, bullets, or Vaseline.

The Delivery Man has two gold teeth. He wears a hat a horse could drink water from. He moves like there is nothing in his way. Because of the length and barrenness of his trip, he hauls extra gasoline in jerry cans. I can see he is careful to keep these separate from the fresh goods. He unloads crate after crate. He unzips his gray leather jacket. A T-shirt that says LIBRA. A bandanna tied at his neck. Workboots. He has cuts on his knuckles from fighting. His hair is short in the front and long in the back. Neon Dean leans his head into the loading dock. The Delivery Man brings his hands down hard on a keyboard made of air. They exchange envelopes and call each other Brother.

Once the delivery truck is emptied of supplies and filled with bags of teenage blood, the Delivery Man drives back to the perimeter of the territory, one mile outside of town. He eases off the gas pedal, making pauses with his foot. "Oh, oh, oh, oh, oh, oh, oh, looks like I have run out of gasoline." The young girls on their dirt bikes catch up to him. They walk through the trailer part after the sex part and hold up the red bags. "Our blood! It's so pretty! Look at it in the light! Did you know your blood has particles in it?" the girls say to the man, his rough throat, his smooth body. They sing purely,

TEEN BLOOD,

ALL THE WAY—

Then the coughs of new smokers.

I wait my turn in the passenger seat. I stare out through the Delivery Man's tinted windshield. Sky, forest, and the north highway cutting a sure line through both. My future. Just behind me, there is a partition that snaps on and off. It is partly open. This is the Delivery Man's bunk. Single mattress, walls of burgundy tufted leather, picture of Heather Locklear, a carton of menthol cigarettes and a stack of instant soups, a jar of pickles, tasseled vest, jeans in a ball. The Delivery Man's dashboard and steering wheel are fake mahogany. His steering wheel is worn down in two places. Where his hands spend the most time. On the knob of his gearshift, he has written KEEP ON.

The Delivery Man tells the girls he is making poems out of them. He is a stray and the road is his home. He asks the girls what their favorite television show is. He tells them he is going to be on it. He doesn't know when. When he says "guest star," the girls hear "death star." With a switchblade, he carves whatever he can. Here, a wolf. Here, a woman. Here, a flower. And he gives them gifts of mangled wood. The girls lift their nightdresses. Across their stomachs, they have written their phone numbers in permanent marker. "Memorize it," they say to the Delivery Man. "I got photographic recall," he says to the girls. And he closes his eyes, drags his tongue across his teeth. "Life is about making something new," he purrs. "When you make something new, that's when you know you're truly living," and the territory girls picture babies. In the territory, babies are the only new things. "What do you see in those two thousand miles?" the girls ask him, but by then, the Delivery Man has grown tired of them. He deadpans, "Trees." Then, he has to persuade the girls to get off the truck. "You'll miss your mother," he says, looking past them.

The Delivery Man gets into the driver's seat.

"So?"

"So."

I give him my Complaint Department face. He takes off his leather jacket. He has a tattoo on his right bicep. It's a triangle. Along each side, it has a word.

"You can't have it three ways," the Delivery Man says to me. "But you can have it two."

I open up my camo outerwear. "I want it fast," I say, showing him Supes's rifle, "and I want it easy. Now, give me all your money or I'll dump your gasoline."

"TIME TO DO a door-to-door," Traps says to The Heavy when The Heavy raises the blue tarp and joins Traps in our living room. It's morning, early, Friday. The Heavy's arms at his sides, hands making fists. Supes stands there too, his long straight body in the same position. Traps lifts himself off our beige couch. The surge of alcohol and the private fantasies of men hang all around him. "Hello, Son." Traps glances at Supes, who barely lifts his chin toward his father. His eyes are fixed elsewhere. He does not pull back his hood, take off his ball cap, but I can see what he is looking at. The portrait that holds him.

"Son." The Heavy nods his acknowledgment to Supes and makes his way to the kitchen sink. He puts his head under the faucet, running it beneath the cold water. Then he stands and combs his fingers through his wet hair, pulling it back off his face. "Sir," Supes says to my father. And then, one quick look in my direction, and he is gone. Not the kind to say goodbye.

And where the hell have you been? The Heavy does not ask me as I take off my camo outerwear and put it on my hook. My mother's coat is still in a heap in the front hallway. All of us taking care to step over it.

Sometimes, at final resting, we don't have a portrait, and so we stand before a black square, a bouquet on either side of it, under three floor lamps. We need something to touch, to kiss, to talk to. When we came home from the final resting for Debra Marie's youngest, The Heavy confronted my mother. "Why did you have to go and make a scene like that in front of the portrait? Why did you have to go and make a scene when Debra Marie didn't even make a scene? There wasn't even a portrait and you had to go and make a scene? Making a scene in front of a black square, what is that? Why did I have to pull you from the black square when the child's own mother held it together?" My mother would not answer my father. She got in our truck and drove into a tree.

Climbing the stairs to my bedroom, I can hear Traps call Debra Marie on speed dial. "We need you here at the Last House. It could use a mother's touch." And, a man bad at whispering, he whispers, "And so could Pony Darlene. Have mercy. She just got home from God knows where looking like"—bad whisper—"I don't even want to say"—(but you know he can't help himself), and from the top of the stairs, I watch him touch his FULLY LOADED belt buckle, then run his fingers over his stained teeth, his sharp cheekbones, his stubbled jaw, and order his features into glory, authority, former handsomeness, cunning, sympathy—"her mother."

I pull back my bedroom curtain. The town is just waking up. The men swing their screen doors open and let their white dogs out. The women load their smallest children into the backseats of their trucks and head toward Value Smoke and Grocer. They will wait in line with their Delivery Day baskets trading details. She was last seen around 7:00 P.M. Indoor tracksuit, no shoes. No word yet. No word. The Heavy told Traps he'd left some outerwear, a spare rifle, and some fuel in the cab. That could be the difference between. I don't want to say it. Life or death. Sure could. It was Rita Star. Rita Star who said Billie Jean left the house in the first place. With the dog. Just the dog. Did Rita Star see Billie Jean? She said she was walking by. How did Rita Star just happen to be walking by bungalow 88 at that hour? Going for her constitutional. As only she could. 7:00 P.M. Thursday. Not seen since. Thirteen hours. Billie Jean Fontaine. No shoes, no coat? Was she wearing a coat? And like a brain sickness, the women will bat these same few facts between them; they won't make any progress. At this point, there is no progress to make.

"HUNTING IS WAITING." Traps was on our front porch with my father. I could hear them from my bedroom, which is directly above it. He wanted my father to come hunting with him. This was when we had chairs on our small cement porch rather than broken things. About five months ago. Around the time Traps's and Debra Marie's baby was born. A warm night. My window was open. The horseflies hadn't come out yet.

"The hunter must be able to distinguish sound." Traps loved to lecture my father. "Let me give you the lay of the land. Wind can confuse and other animals can confuse. He must be able to slow his heart rate, keep his pupil size intact, hold his water, hold his functions so he can separate out the sounds of nature. When he sees his target, he cannot think of where it is coming from and where it is going. He cannot think of what might be following it. He just has to commit to the motions. He can't get lost. He has to know what to do next. The Heavy. Are you even listening to me?" asked Traps.

"No." Then there was a silence, and my father said, "Nothing to tell me, eh, friend?"

THE TEENAGERS WHO don't have to do their bloodwork today are still asleep. I can see their flags in their windows: TAKE MY CHANCES. REMEMBER LAST NIGHT. LOSING STREAK. CALL OF THE DEEP. WAIT FOR ME. Words written with duct tape or scissors. Neon Dean has two small holes for his eyes to look through. The ones who do have to do their bloodwork are climbing wearily onto their bicycles and heading toward the Banquet Hall. The boys with blue circles under their eyes, headbands made from old black bedsheets, duct-tape cuffs at their wrists, the thick chains they used to pull the cabinets, tires, and wood pallets to the bonfire now looped into necklaces. And two girls, arms linked, walking slow and conspiratorial. They have braided their hair together. You can't get lost. You have to know what to do next. Have the baby. Hand over the baby. Lana flashes through my mind. Her belted, armless snowmobile suit. Her teased hair. I know she will call me later. She will breathe heavily and then say, eventually, I want Pony Darlene Fontaine to forgive me. Impossible. Right? No. Possible. She will leave a postcard for me. Sorry. No. *SORRY!!!*

There is Sexeteria in his hairnet on his DIY skateboard, riding past Hot Dollar's Hi-Fi Discount Karaoke and Sporting Lounge on his way to open Home of the Beef Candy. The skinny boy unlocking the front door of Gold Lady Gold, the shop that employs him part-time. And Supes. I can see Supes running along the shoulder of the north highway. The long stride. Dressed like a thief. The insulated black hoodie, the black jeans. He has the same boots as the Delivery Man. Beige, size twelve. He is just south of our bungalow, and just north of the activity of the town. He will have to go through it to get home. Bungalow 1. He turns back toward our house, the Last House. I know he can make out my shape in the window, the last Fontaine.

Yo.

He runs a little farther, and then he cuts into the woods. The part of the woods opposite the woods where you'll find the founders' bus. The part of the woods none of us will go near because of the sinkholes that started forming in there five years ago. Beware. Keep back. Unstable ground. Has he lost his mind? I lift my window, lean out, and scream, "Danger!" No one even turns around.

I LIE NAKED on my bed counting money.

I snap the elastic off and peel each bill from the roll. Higher denominations than I ever found in Neon Dean's old jackets. Twenties, fifties, a couple of hundreds. I put on my hunting glasses; I need a tinted lens. I have pine gum in my hair. I smell like fire, cold air, and the end of my mother's perfume. Between my fingers, the money feels like velvet. I'll store these big bills in my disease book. I have been saving for three months. It has been three months since my mother crashed the truck. Three months since my mother lost her rigging. Three months since I made my plan to get it back. "You have to have a plan, Pony," my mother always said. "You have to have a plan." *THE SECRET OF PONY DARLENE FONTAINE.*

"YOU HAVE GOT to be kidding me," the Delivery Man said. "You have got to be fucking kidding me." "No," I said, "I am not kidding you. I am not fucking kidding you," and I leaned against the passenger-side door with plenty of room to point a rifle. One spacious rig.

The Delivery Man gets paid by the mile, he told me. His name is Gerald. Named after his father, who he never met but his mother loved to talk about. Everyone calls him Ger for short. His girlfriends call him Leger, which in French means gentle. "Fuck," he says again, slapping a plush roll of money into my nonrifle hand. I tell him I have always wanted a *Le* in front of my name.

"What's your name?" he asks.

"Ha," I say. "Good try."

He flirts, "Le ha. I like you, Leha."

"You like everyone, Leger," I say, and I tuck the roll of money under my camo outerwear and into my sports bra.

He is not actually a Libra. He stole the shirt from a girl-friend's trailer one night when he had to make a quick exit. He knows he can be bad, he says. That he has a hundred sons and daughters. But he does believe people are good. He is good. When it gets right down to it. Good and bad. "I am more than one thing," he says. "Most of us are more than one thing," I agree, and then I ask him with my teen-wife face, cold and bored, nothing to lose, "On your way here, did you see a black truck, a matte black truck? A woman driving and a white dog in the passenger seat?"

He reaches behind him. Finds the sample-size bottles of Old Spice, Drakkar Noir, lights a cigarette, blows smoke rings, and then looks at me. "Wouldn't you like to know."

DEBRA MARIE PARKS her truck beside Traps's truck, which means she parks on our front yard. I watch her open the driver's side door and step down from it. She is wearing my mother's low blue heels. She does not walk so much as shuffle. She glances up to my bedroom window. I pull the curtain closed.

I remember my mother giving the shoes to Debra Marie at our party. This was five years ago. I was ten, and when I was falling asleep that night, I asked my mother why she gave away her second pair of good shoes to Debra Marie Linklater. They didn't even really fit her. My mother had such narrow feet, and Debra Marie's were a different shape altogether. "I could tell she liked them," my mother said. When she spoke, my mother smelled like alcohol and cigarette smoke. She put her fingertips on my back and she drew things. She leaned over me and brushed my hair away from my ear, moved it to one side and whispered, "I don't think she has been given very much. Without people expecting something in return." I wanted my mother to stay. And she did. In her party dress, her white heels. She lay down beside me and pulled me close. The hallway light was on, and I could hear the music downstairs. The adults' laughter came up in waves. It sounded like they were putting on a play. They all knew what would happen next, how it would end. All of them were together in the same world for a night. All of them except my mother.

Debra Marie steps over my mother's coat and into our living room. Traps moves to kiss Debra Marie's cheek. It lands on her chin. She keeps her shoes and coat on and holds a hand to her mouth as I come down the stairs.

I still have the hunting glasses on. I wear my mother's DAY OFF sweatshirt and her tan pantyhose. My hair is parted deeply to the right, and on the left I have a single braid. It hangs down to my hipbone, and only ten steps away, just upstairs in my bedroom—seventy square feet, color scheme is black and white—I have over one thousand dollars stored in my disease book between (loose translations) "Sad Lower Quarter De-

rangement" and "Lust of the Neck Skin." Someone get me a
Camaro. Sign me to the teen channel. Get me my own show.
Teen Hustler. Teen Fainter. Someone get me a dark room with a
mattress in it and a deadbolt on the door. I am so tired. Faint-
ing does not equal sleep. I can't go on, I'll go on. Someone
said this once.

"Hey, Debra Marie." I lift a hand, a weak, starved wave.
"Hi."

"Hello, Pony."

"How's tricks?"

"Have mercy."

"I will. I will totally have mercy."

It is then that I see, for the first time, what has become of
the bungalow. With Debra Marie Linklater in it. Her straight
spine, her powdered face. Her angry, gray eyes. Knives, bowls,
and plates are piled high on the counters. Cupboards strain
from their hinges. Some of the cupboard doors have fallen to
the floor. Spilled dog food. Black bedcovers. Black towels. To
walk from room to room is to kick things out of the way.
"Debra Marie," my father greets her as he hurries past her to
the front door. It is then that I see what has become of The
Heavy. His bloodshot eyes, his chapped lips, his densely haired
neck. Agony, with its high pitch, having set into and lined his
skin. "Oh Heav," she says, looking after him as he exits our
house and gets into Traps's truck. "Heav," she says to herself
when he is gone, her eyes now drained of anger. I have never
heard anyone else shorten my father's name. Only my mother.
"Heav, short for Heaven," she loves to say. "Heaven."

———

AFTER SHE CRASHED our truck, my father confronted my mother a second time.

"Were you trying to kill yourself?"

"No, Heav."

"Were you trying to kill yourself?"

"I said no."

"Because it looks to the people of the territory like you were trying to kill yourself."

"I wasn't."

"First the scene at final resting. Now, this. Maybe you were trying to kill yourself."

"I just, I needed a break."

"So you drove into a tree."

"Yes, but not hard enough to kill myself."

"We'll need to get a new truck. Is that what you wanted, a new truck?"

"No."

"You wanted to go to Fully Loaded?"

"No."

"Is there something happening between you and Traps?"

"*Traps?*" My mother's voice was spiked with hate. I had never heard it like that. "If you track my movements, if you climb your ladder and stand on your platform, and you stalk me, you will see I have not been to the truck lot for some time."

"You know I hate to hunt, Billie Jean."

I listened from the hallway. There was a long silence, and I could tell my father had another question, but felt he couldn't ask it. I moved to stand in the half-open doorway. My father was looking from my mother to the dog, like he expected the dog to speak. He pushed the dog off their bed, and he cleaned my mother's bandage. I watched my father stanch the bleeding and dress the wound. The dog sat with her attentions on my mother. She would have none of The Heavy when my mother was in the room. Even though my father credits the dog with saving his life. I had only minutes left, The Heavy told me, and she stayed by my side and she spoke to me. The dog wouldn't let me go, Pony. She made me hang on. She's a nurse. She's a killer.

Two MONTHS BEFORE she crashed our truck, I could see my mother was compensating for some new fragility. Surely, this was temporary, I told myself. Nothing of my mother's nature. My mother with her hard grip, her athlete's grip that had broken in two a frozen side of caribou. But, even though she still dressed and moved with purpose around me and toward me, I could feel her withdrawing.

I watched her as she went through her days, putting on her gold hoop earrings, taking blood at the Banquet Hall, climbing into our truck, stepping down from it, carrying the stew from the stove to the table, carrying the pot from the table to the sink, but it was as if she was filled with small hurts. And, she was preoccupied. Dishes would crash to the floor. She developed a problem with time. She would iron a pair of The Heavy's jeans for an entire afternoon. Braid my hair for an entire morning. Once, she stood in the middle of our kitchen holding a dish towel that was on fire. I took out the disease book from the Lending Library but could find nothing. My mother's ailment was internal. Undocumented. I would have to track it.

I started to lie under my mother's bed. I had at least three inches above me, and as she thinned, and I thinned, four. She had no idea I was there. Swimming with her in the reservoir had taught me to control my breath. The dog knew I was there, but she allowed it. Did not nose around. Did not make a sound. She had watched my birth, watched my childhood. I guess this made for some kind of loyalty.

"If I had to choose between a man and a bear, being in a confined space with one of them, I would choose a bear." Who was my mother talking to? Shona Lee? I would *69 the number later. "I fear if a man walked onto the property, he would murder me. Murdered women are found in wooded areas"—she laughed a contained laugh, not the laugh I knew—"I am living in nothing but a wooded area." She was still in her pale blue workdress. I could see it falling over the side of the mattress.

I missed the sound of my mother's voice. Her low voice. Her pronunciation was just slightly off mine. Especially when she was tired.

My mother told me when I was a baby, she used to pace the upstairs hallway with me in her arms for hours. Then she would pace the whole house. Up and down the stairs, into the living room, my bedroom, her bedroom, the bathroom, and back along the hallway. She could not get me to sleep. I didn't cry and fuss; that was not it. I was a passionate baby, my mother said. Social. I just wanted her company. Didn't want to miss a moment. And this made it so difficult for me to fall asleep. Finally, one night—she was almost hallucinating, she said, she thought she was going to die, just die if I didn't close my eyes—my mother put the telephone receiver to my ear. She said the dial tone calmed me immediately. It put me right to sleep. She described the dial tone as eternity. Nothing happens there, Pony. You won't miss anything. For the first few years of my life, my mother said she, The Heavy, and I slept on top of their black bedcovers with the telephone receiver between us.

"What is going to get me? Exactly." My mother spoke quickly, and then she fell quiet. "What is going to get me." I waited for her to hang up. And then I remembered the bedroom telephone was broken. The Heavy had torn it from the wall and ripped it apart with his bare hands.

FOUR THINGS shortly before 11:00 A.M.:

1. It was Traps's number that was the last to call when The Heavy tore the phone from the wall.
2. Now it is in pieces on our front porch beside the broken refrigerator and the hand-painted *88* sign on chipboard.
3. My mother was speaking to the dog.
4. And it was the dog my mother heard speaking to her.

DEBRA MARIE OPENS our living room window, then clears an area for herself on our couch, and sits with her outerwear folded on her lap. Her name, DEBRA, at her neck, in rust. She is in her pale yellow workdress, a black leather fanny pack at her waist. I know it is full of tape and gauze. She must be due later at the Banquet Hall. She puts her outerwear back on. I find my mother's red ski jacket and sit beside her.

"Traps thought it would be best if I stay here with you."

"Not necessary."

"Necessary," she says, and she looks ahead, not to me, her breath cutting through the frost.

I know Debra Marie thinks disorder is a weakness in character. A mess is weakness. Even a stain on a dress. A run in a stocking. I know she parts the world into the weak and the strong. I know she is trying to place me. To place us, the Fontaines. "You cannot imagine how much cleaning I have already done today, Pony Darlene," she says, "and how much I still have left to do." Her hands are raw. They rest on her knees. I can see the edge of her face powder, at her hairline, where she left off this morning. DEBRA. Twenty years of Traps Linklater. Two mysteriously beautiful children. And now only one. A minus sign for Debra Marie. The most unbearable minus sign.

After her youngest died, I would see Debra Marie in town. Parking in front of the Banquet Hall, getting takeout at Home of the Beef Candy. You good? You good? I know a human heartbeat has an irregular rhythm, and a sick heartbeat a regular one. Debra Marie's sick heart. Her dull, regular heart. In our living room with the sun between us, I consider touching Debra Marie.

"I'm sorry," I say to Debra Marie. "I'm so sorry."

My eyes glass over. And then I start to hyperventilate like I do in my sleep. And Coach tells me to calm down. Wipe your face on your sleeve. Chin the fuck up. Okay, okay. Love does hurt. Debra Marie does not stroke my back. Does not pull me close. Does not do any of the stuff my mother would.

Instead, she springs from the couch. She walks over our things like she has conquered them. Her hands to the walls to steady herself. When she finds the living room phone, she wipes it down with the cuff of her outerwear and starts dialing. "Mercy." I hear her use this word over and over, call after call, her mouth against the receiver, and then thinking better of it, mouth pulled away, "We have to help. Something has gone very wrong here." As if I am not animate on the couch, and cannot hear her. "The house reveals the woman," Debra Marie goes on, cupping the receiver. Then in a sharp whisper, "She must have been very disturbed when she left it."

Debra Marie hangs up the phone and turns her wild attentions on me. She has a plan. She is executing her plan. She is plan oriented, fiercely so, and I will comply.

"Settle yourself there in front of the television."

"I already totally am."

And Debra Marie flicks it on, and I see sex clearly, graphically and professionally lit for the first time. "What can I say, I am hot for dick." My mother and I had watched The Heavy angle the antenna on our roof, like all the territory men, move it this way and that, while we kept an eye on the television through our living room window and would shout when he got it right and run back in to our night soaps, and let The Heavy get down from the roof on his own.

I did not know we got the dick channel. I did not know bungalow 88 had that kind of reception. Then I remember

Traps slept on the couch last night. "All I can think about is dick. Dick gives me a fever." The woman in the intense outfit goes on about dick to the man, shined with oil, standing over it. "Have mercy. Where's your mercy?" And Debra Marie searches the room as if God too dwells here, then she shuffles in front of the dick, waving her hands, fanning her outerwear, dropping a blanket over the television, finding the socket and unplugging it, but not before I feel I am really starting to understand something about men and women and dogs and myself.

"BLACK TRUCK, white dog, woman driver." The Delivery Man reviewed my question, draped his bar-fight hands over his jean zipper. "Hmm. Let me think on that one." And then his hand and its environs stiffened, and he looked at me with eyes that said, I'm dying, and I said, "Ew." No. No way. I was not going to lose my virginity to the Delivery Man. That would close my very small window once and for all. Pregnant, married, pastel dress. Oh wait. I could do the Mother Trick. Oh wait. No mother to do it with.

"YOU HAVE NEVER seen anything like it." Debra Marie makes her last call. "Not even on that show, you know the one. The hoarder one. Where they found the old sister and the old brother. The house was so crowded with things they couldn't even fall to their deaths. They had pianos and boats in the house, shoes of every size. To get from room to room, they had made tunnels. The sister was found sitting in a chair. The brother was stranded in one of the tunnels. The tunnel had collapsed on top of him. Beside him there was a tray of food. The sister was waiting for her dinner, and the brother was bringing it to her. It took a full month to find the body of the brother in the tunnel. A full month even though the brother and sister, when they died, were only a few feet apart."

I want a brother who brings me dinner.

I want a brother I can die with.

The last Fontaines.

RUSHED—WAS SHE IN a panic?—my mother had worn her waterproof makeup to the burial of Debra Marie's baby. In the graveyard, no mascara spilled down her face. All around us, the territory women fell to the ground. The men got them to their feet and stood behind them, held them up. Riding shotgun to the Banquet Hall, they called my mother heartless. A woman with no heart, the women sobbed, and they smoked with their windows rolled down, wind thrashing their trucks. Then at the Banquet Hall, my mother broke the territory rules; she made a scene in front of the portrait, and she continued to make the scene when her turn with the black square ended and the next territory mourner stood before it. Debra Marie. Noble Debra Marie, still as a headstone. The Heavy had to drag my mother away from the black square, her large dark dress folded in his arm muscles. She had animals coming from her throat. "Let's go, Pony," he said to me. "Now." The women of the territory watched us leave. They watched my mother's unbeaten face with their electric blue ones.

"What are you staring at?" I yelled at them. "She's sad! You're sad! What's your fucking problem?"

"Enough," The Heavy said, not raising his voice, and he urged me then pushed me out of the Banquet Hall and into our truck, and we drove home in silence, and that was the moment my mother slipped away from us, from me.

Soon after, my mother stopped sleeping at night and slept only during the day.

"You're all turned around," The Heavy said to her.

"Daylight is obscene," my mother said back.

And I tried to see how daylight had become that for her. She used to attack a mess, but she had stopped being able to do things in the daylight. She would do her circuit, scanning the rooms, but not do anything about what she saw. If a room needed straightening or a meal needed to be made, she couldn't do it. When The Heavy asked, "Why?" she said searchingly, "I don't know." Then she put her hand on the hot stove top and said, "See, nothing." She pulled a knife from the drawer and put it through the skin between her thumb and first finger. "See, nothing." She pulled at her hair. "See, nothing." And hit herself in the face.

"My wife has a disease." The Heavy bent his large body forward and spoke quietly into the living room telephone.

"You had better tell her that," One Hundred said gently. And The Heavy hung up, stared into our empty fridge, his face held by the rectangle of light, and then he ripped the door off it.

"She is lost," he tried again with One Hundred. The next day One Hundred painted a large *88* on chipboard and dropped it off on our front porch, beside the broken fridge and the partial telephone. She left a casserole, and with it, a note that read, *To help your Billie Jean find home.*

Night became my mother's time. She could wander. Night didn't ask anything of her. It did not shame her. I was under my black bedcovers, and The Heavy was under his. The house was dark. There was nothing to be done to it. I would hear her bedroom door open, her quick footsteps on the carpet, and then she would do her circuit: down the stairs, around the kitchen, into the living room, into the basement, and back up the stairs. The sound of her walking helped me fall back asleep. With every circuit, her footsteps slowed. And then I would wake up scared because she would be standing above me, her hands on my chest, checking my breathing. Or sometimes, just her face so close to mine.

She stopped coming downstairs. She stopped washing her body. Her bedroom had two windows. One looked out at the yard, the other onto the reservoir. She stood before the windows. The Death Man's gulls in a gray knot on our yard, and only three hundred steps away, the water. Why did these birds of water not return to their natural place?

When she moved, my mother did not make use of her joints. Her legs remained straight. When she lay on her bed, she placed a stiff arm across her body. Beneath it, her organs pained her. Her skin hurt. Her teeth were sore. Just under her collarbone, she was being rushed at, drilled. The Heavy tried calling some of the territory women.

"She is not herself," Shona Lee explained.

"Exactly!" he shot back. Exactly. But Shona Lee left him alone with that. He was deserted with questions. For The Heavy, it was the most upsetting thing. Where does a *herself* go? And how can a man bring a *herself* back home?

"WHEN YOU LOOK OUTSIDE, you see the woods. You see the town, the people of the territory. I don't see the woods, the town, the people. I see a set."

"I don't understand," I said.

My mother tried to further explain her state. "It's like a film set. All of it. Nothing is real."

"Still don't understand."

"When you look at me, you see your mother."

"Yes. I see my mother. I am looking at my mother. I am looking at my mother!"

"When I look at you, I don't see my child. I am not looking at my child."

And my mother was like the other women of the territory, gasping and shuddering, when she said that. Like we were at final resting. My final resting.

After that, my mother stopped speaking to me for days on end, and the change that had come over her accelerated. The muscles of her body, that of a runner, withered until her indoor tracksuit hung from her frame. When she moved, I could see her elbows and her ribs, her nipples. The Heavy tried to bring her things on a tray. The things mounted. Her bedroom took on a stench. The stench of the discarded. Just a couple of months before, my mother had emptied her bedroom, emptied her drawers, her closet. Her party dress, white heels, gold eyeshadow, pale pink workdress, gold hoop earrings, hairpins, perfume, tan pantyhose. Anything that had come close to her body she lifted into her arms and left in a heap at the edge of our property for Pallas and Future to rifle through. Free Day. A day for the broken and unwanted, as is.

Her head was teeming with sentences. I stood at the end of her bed and tried to read the ticker tape of her mind: Who is this girl asking me to identify her haircut? Telling me she has feathered her hair? Do I like it? Wanting to swim. Wanting to light my cigarette. Wanting to tell me a story, tell me about her day, thrill me. What is this about a plan? You have to have a plan. Loading our truck bed with jerry cans of gasoline. Twenty jerry cans. She is about halfway there. She is saving money. She has saved up so much money. Heading south. Taking me and The Heavy away from here, beyond the territory. Getting me back to where I started. Getting my rigging back. *Myself* back. She is practicing her driving. Lana lets her. On her father's truck. At first, she didn't, but now she does. Lana's paranoid, but telepathic. Friendship is telepathy. Love is telepathy. We used to be telepathic. Why is this girl so angry? Holding the receiver to my ear, talking about eternity?

"I am in the middle of something," my mother spoke at last. "You have to stop interrupting me."

And my mother's hair collected into hard strands. Her skin turned sheer as paper. She was bloodless. She was heatless. She was gone. The Heavy did not have to tell me. The way she moved, the sounds she made. From Lana, in the large darkness of the founders' bus, I had heard the stories. All skin, all bone, all animal. By the time my mother left, she looked just the way she had when she arrived.

In their rubber aprons and dish gloves, their cleaning supplies in their pails, the women of the territory set down their mops and tie their scarves over their mouths.

"Have mercy."

"Yeah, I already covered that with Debra Marie."

It was clear that, at first, we had tried to stack the magazines in the corners of the living room, but the towers grew too tall even for The Heavy to add to, so we laid them out on the floor, which could have been read as a strategy against the mice. I had constructed a second bedroom for myself, moving a spare mattress beside the couch, and around it, piling coolers and unusable electronics, a crimping iron, a ceiling fan, a Betamax, so that if I chose to sleep there, nothing could sprint across my face. I did not admit it was my night mother who frightened me. Her ghost touch, her eyes that never closed.

The television, and behind it, the tarped-off section of the house being built for my mother. The blue room. For my mother to return to her thinking, her native thinking. "To return to *herself*," The Heavy said to me one August night, guiding lumber through his Skilsaw. But as quickly as The Heavy could build it, termites started in on the wood. The beams framing the room had begun to slope and thin. "A difficult room," The Heavy said, pulling down the hood of the Easiest Chair.

In small armies, the termites were making it to the furniture so the edges of our tables were pocked, legs of chairs uneven. The women tested the furniture, and if it was weak, they cracked it over their thighs and fed it to the bonfire they had going on our front yard.

A red squirrel had made its way into the house, so The Heavy and I had set up a trap in the cooler at the end of my makeshift bed, a string from the open lid to his hand, peanut butter on a slice of bread inside it. When the squirrel went for the bait, The Heavy slammed the lid shut. Carrying the cooler outside, The Heavy set it down and then lost his nerve. He could not flip the lid open. What if the squirrel was hurt? How could we send it back to the wild?

Earlier that spring, we had seen a deer frozen in midair. It had been running, we supposed, from a bear, and following its mother, had reached a gully, and when it tried to jump, its hooves got stuck in the overhanging brush, and the more it struggled to free itself, the more ensnared it became. The mother deer could not get at it and the bear could not get at it, and the deer was frozen like that in midair. "Nature is unsentimental," my mother said when we told her the story. Looking at the cooler, The Heavy shook his head. "I can't do it. I can't free the squirrel." And he glared at the woods. "Not to that."

Now, the squirrel's tail is in one of the women's rubber gloves, its spine flexing back and forth. "Was chewing through the electricals," she tells the others. The squirrel's open mouth nearly reaches her hand. "Now that's a sure way to lose a family to fire."

"Reservoir frozen over can do nothing for an inferno."

"Not frozen over yet."

"Soon enough."

"Losing a family to fire."

"Let's not talk about that now."

And the woman hurls the squirrel like a discus from our bungalow and into the flames. Her necklace says PAMELA.

WHEN A PART of the night sky split away from itself, The Heavy and I watched as it flew at me and then grazed my face. The Heavy, concerned the bat might get tangled in my hair, and his hair, picked up his badminton racquet and, sweat dripping into his eyes, swiped at it until we heard contact. We flicked on the lights, all of which worked back then, and searched for the body of the bat, eventually finding it, small as a coin and soft in my hand. The Heavy and I agreed, in its stark workings, only death could tell you a thing's true size.

"Will you look at this?" The women have made it up to my bedroom. They stand in my doorway. Mops and pails. Hair the color of gunmetal. I am lying on my bed, on top of my disease book, looking up at my SETTLE YOUR HEAD flag. Is it getting dark out? It is. Despair.

"God. Oh God."

"Will you look at these walls?"

"What do you even call that?"

"What, all the handwriting there? The charts?"

"You call that—"

"The walls of the insane."

"That's what you call that."

" 'Questions Answered versus Questions Unanswered.' "

" 'Daytime versus Nighttime.' "

" 'My Mother versus The Heavy.' "

" 'My Mother versus Herself.' "

" 'My Mother versus Me,' " one of the women reads. "Will you look at that? Covers a whole wall."

FIVE THINGS shortly before 6:00 P.M.:

1. When the women return with cans of white paint, they don't know whether to put the cans down on the hallway carpet and then lift their hands above their heads.
2. Or just lift the cans in surrender.
3. It has become no problem for me to kick a door closed while pointing a rifle.
4. Even when empty, a rifle will always be perceived as loaded.
5. I told myself that to study my mother was to know her still.

Lying under her bed, I recorded my mother on my Deep Space Tapes. If she said something I could not understand or did not want to hear, I taped over it with something I did. I turn on my cassette recorder now and listen to her low voice, the low voice I love. "Nostradamus. Now that is a name. The time to die is during a storm. We have the trees all wrong. When we picture their tops, we look up to the branches. But it is the root systems, these are the faces of the trees, and they are underground. A man should have a packet of salt in his pocket should there be occasion to salt something. A child is the only true astonishment."

Men do not bring mothers back. Women do not bring mothers back. Children bring mothers back.

IT WAS FIVE years ago, the night of our party, when The Heavy was zipping my mother up and she started to talk about not feeling old but looking old. "Big difference," she said. The guests would arrive in an hour. I could tell my mother was nervous. The Heavy got her to swing her hair around to the front of her party dress so he could really get at the zipper, the zipper was giving him a hard time. Her hair was to her tailbone, and he said her hair—while he loved it, wanted to make a cave out of it and live there and have a hundred more daughters— was slowing things down. I watched her fine-boned feet lift off the floor as The Heavy worked the zipper. "Everyone thinks it's a gradual decline, but the truth is aging is catastrophic. One night you have a certain face, and the next day, upon seeing people, you have to tell them who you are. All at once. And it's not just time. Everyone thinks, Oh, it's just time. Blame time. But time is content. Time is nothing without content. Time is the speeding vehicle. Content the fiery crash." And my mother turned to me. "Can I borrow that?" She climbed our stairs unsteadily, half-zipped, with my roll of duct tape. I had been making a belt with it.

When my mother came back down the stairs and walked the length of our living room, an extravagant, radiant thing, The Heavy thought to take her portrait. "It's time, Billie Jean," he said. I was too stunned to sit at my mother's feet and gaze up at her, as was our people's way, and The Heavy was too stunned to order me into his frame, so there was my mother, alone, in her zipped-up party dress, the silver one, with rhinestones glued around her eyes, and The Heavy deciding on a close crop. "What a portrait, what a portrait." My mother remained perfectly still. I had never seen her so still. She was always in motion. Always between things. Talking to herself. The list in her head, and then her laugh, uncontained. But, she sat, looking into the camera, searching the camera, not knowing how to smile on command. I remember how The Heavy moved the emphasis between the words. "What. A. Portrait." Her narrow feet in her low white heels, just slightly crossed at the ankles. She had seams that ran up the backs of her stockings. The Heavy put his camera away, and my mother had me sit on the floor in front of her, and she worked my hair into a design that matched her own.

It was my mother's portrait that held Supernatural's attention this morning when he stood in our living room. In his large beige boots. His thief clothes. Standing on my spare mattress, keeping his balance. His arms at his sides, hands clenched into fists.

My mother's portrait hangs above our mantel, felted with dust. I watch Debra Marie reach for it and wipe it down until it gleams.

"What is that noise?" The women press their ears to the wall.

"It's here too."

"And here."

"Oh I know that noise," says one of the broader women—tight ponytail, chipped tooth, CHERYL—and she finds the ax. "Get that Pony Darlene Fontaine outside."

It's dark now. A million stars. An October night. Nearly twenty-four hours since my mother walked out this same door. I stand on our front porch. Broken phone, broken fridge, *88*. That about sums it up. I look in our mailbox. A postcard.

SORRY!!!

LOVE, LANA

Telepathy, after all.

I STAND BESIDE the bonfire with Supernatural's rifle in my hands. We have never had a bonfire on our property before. The Heavy would not allow it. The small bodies of bats, squirrels, and mice. Animals. Generations of animals. Broken electronics, empty coolers, black towels. Black bedcovers, dirty dishes, broken furniture. Spare mattress, crimping iron, ceiling fan, Betamax. Out the front door and into the bonfire. The broad woman, Cheryl, still holding the ax, stands in our front doorway and watches the snakes that have been living inside our walls throw themselves in mounds across the hems of her nightpants and her sport socks inside her house sandals, all of which she will later soak in a bleach solution. Pamela diverts the snakes into the fire.

Vacuums, dustbusters, power drills. Fixing the tanning bed in the basement. "I have just the thing." The blue room completed. Wall built. Tarpaulin pulled down and into the bonfire.

I watch the women mob the house. They move between the windows. Mothers in my house. Mothers circulating the rooms. Mothers standing in the window frames. Not my mother. "Step back there, Pony Darlene, you're starting to smoke." A bucket of dirt is thrown onto the flames and quickly refilled.

I reach for the ignition of the nearest truck. The keys are in it, but looking behind me, I see there is no way I will be able to back it out, not with the way the group has parked their vehicles. Just when I go to investigate the last vehicle to arrive—Shona Lee with a Delivery Day basket full of fresh goods for us—I hear a voice over the CB. Static. Static. It's Traps's voice, searching. "Traps here." Static. "Do you read me?" I take on the voice of one of the mothers. "10-4. Over. Come in. Come in, Traps."

"We did our door-to-door and another tour through town, checked everywhere. Nothing." Traps says he and The Heavy will start back. Ground is frozen. Gives them some hope. Winter is on its way. No one tries to die in the winter.

"How's"—he pauses—"Pony Darlene holding up?"

"She's"—I pause—"emotional."

"Yeah, she sure is. Hard to understand how a mother could leave her own daughter behind."

"Sure is," I say to Traps. "Sure is."

Has she left? Has she left me behind?

I LEAVE THE TRUCK and run around to the back of the house. The last time my mother took me down to the reservoir, I refused to go in. It was the middle of the night, late September.

One month ago. Perfect for freezing to death. No way. Get real. Dream on. She would hardly speak to me, and suddenly her face was hovering above my face and then she was holding me by the wrist and dragging me to the water.

I watched her from the shore as she did her circuit. From one end to the other, from one end to the other. There was always a circuit to be completed. There was no moon, and I could barely make out her body. She stopped in the middle of the black water and called out, "Time me!"

"But it's so cold!" I shouted back, raging in my nightdress and my nightpants.

"Time how long I can hold my breath!"

"It's almost October!"

And my mother took a succession of quick, shallow breaths, then arched her back, and dropped beneath the surface.

I am standing three hundred steps from the reservoir and haven't even thought to check it. But, I would have heard her go in. I would have heard her dive in. I would have heard the entrance. No. This is not true. Why didn't The Heavy think to check it? Surely, he did, and the water is not a concern. Right? Impossible. Right? The Heavy knew about her swims. He never wanted to learn and once, in a fury—"Why did you have to go and make a scene like that in front of the portrait?"—threw his outerwear into the water. My mother dove in and brought it back to him. She stood naked on the shoreline, and she slung the wet jacket onto her shoulder. She swayed her hips. She always found a way to be forgiven.

My mother had never asked me to time her before. She had never held her breath like that. I shifted from foot to foot, trying to stay warm. I counted as she had asked. Devotional section. She was impossible to say no to. And it was in the water that she most resembled herself. The *herself* The Heavy and I so desperately missed and were trying to bring home. I blew on my hands and put them in the large pockets of my nightpants. Thick beds of fallen leaves on the water. Branches bare and black against the sky. Birds hanging in the air. Not the Death Man's. Were they the Death Man's birds? When it had been one minute, one minute and a half, nearly two minutes, I panicked. She had been under for too long. Do I run and get The Heavy? Then, what could The Heavy do? What could The Heavy possibly do? He didn't know how to swim. How could he help?

When my mother resurfaced with a long gasp, she paused for a moment before making her sure, fast way toward the shore. She pulled herself to standing, her ravaged body, all planes now, all arguments. She did not notice I was naked. I had just waded in. I was taller than she was. I was stronger. I was going to save her. With her blue lips, looking up at me, convulsing with the cold, all my mother said was "How long?"

"Too long."

I turn to run up to her bedroom. Only from her window do I have a clear view of the water. Before I can reach the back door, a shape comes at me from the woods. It's our dog. Ice in her fur has shrunk her by half. I lower myself to the ground to meet her. She is shivering. I pull her to me. I stroke her back. I hold her snout to my face. It is soaked with blood. She leaps at me. She knocks me down. And then she sits with her perfect posture, and for the first time, she barks.

Part Two

DOG

You asked me for it. My opinion. Many times. You were desperate for it. You would stand in front of the mirror. I would lick my fur.

At the beginning of the affair, it was about eyeshadow, gold or blue, belt or no belt, hair up or hair down, but by the end, it was about your name, about your body, what to do about your body. Where to place your body.

I am not sure you heard me. Just before you sprinted to the truck and slammed the door so I could not get in and over your lap to the passenger seat, forcing me to follow your tail-lights through the ice (love is the highest humiliation), I am not sure you heard me. So here it is: gold, belt, down, Billie Jean Fontaine, rest it, bungalow 88.

You have been gone for a full night and day now. Missing. No signs, not one. It is the first time, since we met, that I don't know where you are.

Come home.

My opinion.

———

How DID IT START, Billie Jean?

Where did it go wrong, Billie Jean?

Two years before the affair began, you came home to me empty. "Nothing of substance," you said when I inquired after your time with the wives and the widows. What a shock, I said, and you laughed. I would go anywhere with you, but after so many pointless encounters, I refused to go to the graveyard. Headstone Saturdays. I had my limits. I could not stand the anxiety of the other dogs, their minor confusions. And worse, the women's narrow conversation. Standing there in those heavily treaded boots that could kick through oak, yet never would. Those sexless dresses. Puff-sleeved with foam at the shoulders, the high necks, the high waists. Under ski jackets. The light coating of hair on the women's faces. And their mouths moving, issuing words, but furthering nothing. Speaking only about the weather, about time. As if life is only weather and time. You are standing on top of death, and all you can ask is "You good?"

You good? You good? You good? Are these women full of batteries?

We agreed the better question was You bad?

How bad are you?

How bad can a person be?

FOR SO LONG it was just the two of us up in the bedroom. Was it two months we shut ourselves in there, Billie Jean? Or was it three? Pony Darlene would know. She tracked everything. On her walls in permanent marker. In that disease book she was writing. Always open on her bed, her body hunched over it, legs crossed, the Latin dictionary beside her. She did drawings of what she saw, the hidden ailments of every person in the territory, and she gave the maladies names. In her large clothes, her nearly hipbone-length hair. What an exquisite child. The only child I could stand. Children are manipulators, hysterics, vaudevillians. Not Pony Darlene. She is a tactician.

In the bedroom, time did not matter to us. Weather did not matter. Spring, summer, fall. How could the weather matter? Time? Tell us how time could possibly matter. Birth. Love. Murder. *These* were the forces we were contending with. The tragic impulses of the heart.

There was a wooden light fixture above the bed. Whenever we referenced God, we would instinctively look up and see that light fixture. It was a light fixture that imitated a candelabra. I hate any form of imitation, especially when I am looking for God. I know, I know. You told me countless times. The light fixture came with the bungalow, and you and The Heavy, after Pony was born, never got around to updating it. A child will do that, you told me. A new child will prevent a woman from properly appointing a room. A new child will occupy a woman's every thought.

The bed was a double bed with a dark wooden frame. Mahogany, I think. Casket wood, I would say. Ha, you would say back, sounding just like Pony Darlene, and you would lie like a corpse, your hands clasped on your chest, a pretend bouquet held over your vital organs. There were two side tables with reading lamps. You had a stack of books on your side, your name necklace, wedding ring, and whatever pins you pulled from your hair, and on his side, The Heavy had whatever he dug from his pockets at the end of the day. Bolts, small change, keys, stray thread, a black ink pen. You loved to watch him empty his pockets onto the side table and then drop his jeans. His clothes held his smell. Sweat, dirt, industry. His belt buckle would make a thud on the floor. You loved the consistency of his motions. You could not read the mind of the man, but from his body, you knew what would come next.

The bedding was black. Traps Linklater—one gold incisor tooth, one dark blue thumbnail, one prominent U-shaped scar on his forearm—and his wife, Debra Marie—impassive, long-suffering, ironing her husband's money at night, working the expression *house arrest* through her mind—had given you a fur throw for a wedding gift. It was intended for the bed, but you and The Heavy found the throw repulsive. You did not want to sleep underneath a murdered animal. You pictured Debra Marie feeding the fur through her sewing machine, affixing the satin backing under a fluorescent light, moving silver pins between her teeth. You knew Traps would trade her in for a younger face, a tropical vacation. You pictured Traps stumbling onto the north highway with an ax through his skull, Debra Marie following him out of habit. You thanked Debra Marie profusely for the throw, folded it, and stuffed it into your closet, which was, until you crashed the truck on that July evening, filled with your belongings.

Due to Pony Darlene's display of fury, the throw was the only thing those young women took from you on Free Day. They were a few years older than Pony, loose, spiteful, and overtanned. A casual hygiene. Matted hair, coral lipstick. I thought they looked exhumed. Pony was not intimidated by the young women. I watched as Pony rejected her peaceable nature and put forward a different one. Like The Heavy, Pony hated all forms of conflict. She would do anything to avoid it. But on this day, Pony crisscrossed the yard with her arms spread, her bombastic stride, and she was vicious. She was defending her territory. She was defending you.

You were asleep, and I did not want to nose you awake, return you to logic, tell you that in giving everything away, a person does not get everything back. I spent my first year of life watching The Heavy make wishes. He would walk from room to room trading in comforts. I will do this if only that. He gave up his hot coffee, his wool socks inside his boots, the pillow under his head. For his sister, for his mother, for his father.

The girl with the deeper tan rode away with your fur throw across her shoulders like a demented queen. Her friend, gauze and tape up and down her shapeless arms, the face of a trance, followed. You lay on your back in the corpse posture we joked about. You had the complexion of pavement. The Heavy came into the room and dressed your wound. His motions were tender and efficient. He was a natural nurse. Your eyelids were moving. I knew you were dreaming. I believed you could confront and repair a life in your dreams. I did not want The Heavy to wake you. You were concussed from the crash. I would wake you in an hour. I knew about concussions and how they could change a person.

Despite my objections, The Heavy roused you. He started to shoot questions at you. You deflected him expertly by giving him just enough of the truth. His pupils dilated as he listened to you. He swatted me off the bed. This, I can handle. I am a fucking animal. I will always be the most punk in the room. Pony Darlene watched us from the half-open doorway. She had cleared the yard of your belongings and run everything into her bedroom, taking the steps two at a time.

I'll do this if only that.

IN THE BEDROOM, there were two medium-size windows. One looked south onto the town. The low, squat bungalows all built from the same beige bricks, and fronting them, gray porches of crumbling cement. A mess of television antennae. The black driveways. The identical trucks.

I found it amusing the founders of the territory had fled suburbia only to re-create it here. They got off their stolen silver bus in their tennis shoes. A city transit bus. What city, they had deliberately forgotten. The city name had been wiped out, scratched at by a key or a knife blade, and then shot at several times. OR BUUST, it said in large cap letters in the oblong slot above the bus's windshield.

The founders had a Leader. He spoke about systems, creating new systems, and an end to hierarchies, both real and self-imposed. He argued a dome was the highest architectural form. He had the body of a fencer, a luxuriant head of hair. His face was average, but with a large mustache that divided top from bottom and eyes the green of the sky just before a squall. His teeth indicated wealth, a history of orthodontists, his diction too. He was a learned man. But his education did not matter. The Leader's talent was persuasion and this was talent enough to begin a new civilization. Who is with me? I am. All the way. This was a common rallying cry among the founders. All the way. Under his suit jacket, the Leader wore a white smock that came down to his knees. No one spoke of it as a hospital gown. He called himself John.

Young women fell in love with him. John stared at them until they could not take it, then ignored them so long they doubted they were actually there. On the bus, John erected a curtain around his seat, and behind it, held consultations. He studied the area just above the women's breasts and read their futures off it. He told the women they were born disrupters. This was exactly what they wanted to hear, and they offered to thank John with their bodies. Give him children. A legacy. "I am a monk," John told them, "but the kind who will fuck you." He was fluent in seven languages and used them all when he said the coarse word. The women described him as touched. Sometimes, John would sleep in the overhead compartments. Sometimes, he would ask one of the men to lock him in the luggage hold beneath the bus. Once, on the way north, he saw a field, a gray horse in it, and climbed onto the animal's back while his followers watched awestruck as he tore across the open. His head would fill with numbers. Distances, fuel amounts, outside temperature, inside temperature. The date, the hour, the second. The bus picked up every hitchhiker. Some wore tube tops and gas masks. One woman wore a housedress. Her hair neatly combed back, a furtive look, and a sign in her hands that read, AS FAR AWAY AS POSSIBLE. John eyed her like he was hypnotizing her. She left her bag in the ditch. No possessions needed when you have your freedom. In the territory, she would become known as One Hundred.

The founders' bus sat forty-eight passengers comfortably. By the time it arrived in the territory, there were ninety-seven of them. John was the last to disembark. In each hand, he held a rope, and at the end of each rope was a large dog straining against him. The animals came up to his waistline. From the cargo area, he unloaded a bullwhip, spare fuel, paintings of sparrows he was unable to sell at rest stops, and in a leather trunk, his vast inheritance. He had been on many canoe trips and had spent eight summers working in remote logging camps before he had his breakdown. He could drive a truck through a mud slick, start a cooking fire in a blizzard, swim an icy lake with a hammer in his hand should he need to bash the surface, and when it came down to it, not die in the wild. John had a satellite phone. He needed five large trailers, a mess tent, and a food drop. He knew the snow would come in three months. They had three months to build.

Dense woods to the east.

Dense woods to the west.

Behind us, perfectly framed by the north-facing window, the water.

You were obsessed by the water.

You spoke to me long after you stopped speaking to The Heavy. To Pony Darlene. We could hear The Heavy just below us, building a room for you. Working from a drawing he did when he sat at the end of the bed and asked you several times in a row, What do you need? Seeing your wet face, your devastations piling up. What do you need? What do you need? What do you need? Sizable question. Beautiful voice. The kind that could be on the radio in the middle of the night listing off plant varieties, cloud formations. Eventually, to your husband, you said, "Privacy." You needed to be left alone. Beneath the black bedcovers, you held your secret. Your soft body, your secret body.

The Heavy ran the word *privacy* through the circuits of his mind and arrived at the idea of the room. Black ink drawing on white paper. He showed you the plan. You moved your head and The Heavy took this to be approval. He had an elegant hand. I remember when Pony Darlene was born, she fit inside his hand. He held her there. It was the only time I saw The Heavy cry, when there were already, in his short life, too many occasions. In his daughter's face, he could see his sister's. His shaking body lulled his new daughter into sleep. He cried for the miracle of her. First you, and then her. "Tell me," he said to you, "tell me nothing will ever separate us."

You did not lift the blue tarp to see what The Heavy was building for you—not once—and this added to his devastations, also piling up, of which you, remote, defeated, changed, had become the only source. He made a sloping roof that was translucent, and the walls of the room were entirely composed of glass. Beams of wood at the corners, holding the whole thing up. I would bring progress reports to you. I would say, Do you know how difficult it is to build with glass in a climate like this one? If not angled and treated correctly, the whole thing could crack and shatter in an instant. And for a man to do this alone. With no crew. To hold up plates of glass and to position them properly. I would watch The Heavy, his arms outstretched, and think: Love is dumb. Dumb as muscle. Love will lead a brilliant man to build a glass room in a wild north-west wind that wants only for him to fail. That wants to pull out his teeth. Make his eyes burn. Scar him over and over and over again.

And Pony Darlene. She would sit in the hallway with her back to the other side of our bedroom door, a hot slice of des-peration. We could hear her long body slide down the wood, to the carpet, and then she would fold her knees against her chest. Arms wrapped around herself, head down. She would have a warm red mark on her forehead from staying in place, unmoving. Signs of endurance, of great stubbornness. I won-der where she got that from, Billie Jean. She spent hundreds of hours like that. A whole portion of her youth. Waiting. Waiting for you.

A dog understands waiting.

Come home.

I could hear Pony Darlene's pulse on the other side of the door. I could smell her worry. It was frantic, livid; it circled and consumed her. She stopped eating. Some nights, she would pull herself up and bang on the door. By then we had a lock on it. You had told The Heavy you needed a lock, and he was so yielding. Wanting only to please you, to make you bet-ter.

Pony Darlene started to pass notes under the door. I would see the ends of her fingers, her nails painted red, the skin around them bitten raw, and I would pick up the notes with my teeth and bring them to you. I felt for the child. The notes had a thin coating of sweat on them. She palmed them before sliding them into the room. They were quotes. *To be free is to have achieved your life.* That kind of thing. My favorite was *I can't go on, I'll go on.* Samuel Beckett. A sadist, but Pony's deepest crush. She would go to her Lending Library and find what she thought was beautiful, and transcribe it for you. She would spend her days there. She had a stack of loose-leaf paper, white, and she would tear it into strips, and on the strips, write down the quotes she thought might coax you out of the bedroom. She used other people's words. She worried her own might take you somewhere darker.

Her closest friend, that enthusiast Lana Barbara, had lost her mother two winters before. A bottle of homemade alcohol, a handful of pills. House sandals, sport socks, the toolshed. A straight arrow to death. The mother's determination haunted Pony Darlene. For Pony, you were a storm, Billie Jean. A dangerous and unpredictable storm.

"The people in this place don't name their dogs, and I think that's barbaric," you said to me in our first conversation. The Heavy had carried you to the Last House. In his arms, you were frail, shorn, but your eyes were vivid and alert. I could see you would miss nothing. My admiration was immediate. I was one year old. "To name an animal is a form of love," you went on. "I know you saved The Heavy's life. And I know, if it came down to it, you would save mine." You ran your fingertips along the backs of my ears, and then dug them in, moved them back and forth. You could climb a cliff face with those fingers. I let my eyes close. "What will I call you?" you said.

I opened my eyes. Gena Rowlands, I said. Call me Gena Rowlands.

"Gena Rowlands." Your voice had so much breath in it. "Pleasure."

There was a period when you were really into your body. You were more content naked than dressed. You would close the door to the bedroom, and you would lie down beside me on the gold carpet, and I would think, Is she imitating me? Is she trying to be funny? But no, you were testing yourself: Can I do what I want to do? I want to lie on the carpet like a dog. Can I do that?

"Can I lie on the carpet like a dog?"

You already are, I would say.

You would do these exercises in the shower: touching your toes, touching your knees, your hips, your shoulders, your head, and then you would turn the faucets and make the water freezing, and you would rub and slap your skin, lift your arms and push your face into it, and I would tell you that you were a lunatic, and you would say, "I am getting my blood going. I am getting my blood going." And then we would run along the empty highway—the abandoned part that continues west from the bungalow, navigable only on foot—and if any hunters happened to see us and ask you why you were running, what was chasing you, was there a black bear, a moose, a wild bison, you told them, "I am getting my blood going." Soon, we would be running in the woods, where no one could ask you about it.

The en suite bathroom was the most notable feature of the master bedroom. Ten months apart, both you and The Heavy were brought back to life in the bathtub while I sat on the tiles beside you, not panting.

When the bedroom became too stifling, and you could not catch your breath, I would lead you to that other tropic. I would pull myself over the lip and into the tub, and you would unfurl your exhausted body on the cold floor. The porcelain against my fur. The square black tiles against your skin. They gave cool order to your being, you told me.

As much as you had repressed it, the story of your childhood came back to you. I was the only one you shared it with.

When you were a girl, the things you stole from your mother were the things that came from farthest away. Little brooches, rings, hair clips. Precious things. Sentimental things. Gifts from your father, who traveled all the time. You watched your mother as she overturned her bedroom looking for the thing you had stolen, and you helped her look for it, and when her distress reached such a level, you tucked the thing into her thick carpet and then lifted it proudly in your hands, and she said, still on her hands and knees, "You are such a good finder!" You didn't want the thing. You wanted the praise.

Think of what I buried for you, Billie Jean. My small captures. The careful arrangement of bones under your pillow. Kneading your bedcovers back into place. You called my paws artful.

You lived on a cul-de-sac in a wealthy neighborhood outside a major city. The houses on your street were box-shaped, and the lots they sat on, sprawling. There was plenty of space between you and your neighbors. Easy to commit murder here and get away with it, your mother said to you once, and smiled broadly. Or be murdered, you thought to yourself. Your mother was a homemaker. She wore her hair in a large bun. She had a plastic dish that she held to the back of her head, and she wound her hair around it to give it volume. You pictured the dish transmitting secret messages to her. She always seemed to be listening for something you could not see. She was an obsessive reader. She would sit straight-spined on the couch and move only to empty her ashtray or to get a new book. The conversation she wanted was the one in her brain. You learned early to keep your thoughts to yourself. You knew your mother's talents had been wasted. Like a private joke, she dressed every morning as if it were night. Furs, velvets, silks. When she walked through your house, her gold bracelets knocked together. She wore high heels all day even if your father was traveling.

Your father was a surgeon. He operated on the hearing impaired and, when you were a girl, pioneered a procedure in which he extracted the smallest bone from the human body and replaced it with a prosthesis, returning sound to his patients. Soon after, your father flew all over the world to teach other surgeons. Though he hardly knew you, you were the one he told everything to.

When your father came home in his long, cream-colored car, he put his arms around your mother, shortened her name, and promised to take her to Europe. You watched them from your bedroom window. Standing in the driveway beside their expensive car. Your mother's heels sunk into the soft gravel. Your father's hands cupped your mother's jaw, tilted her face up to the sky. Why wasn't she happier?

One night, after one of his longer trips, your father entered your bedroom and, pacing, lay his thoughts at your feet. He ensured your mother was not within earshot. "Love is a force," your father said to you. "You understand me?" your father asked. You were thirteen years old. You were at your desk in your flannel nightgown. You had new braces on your teeth that made your mouth bleed. Your body was in riot. Your brain was too. You had skipped a grade, and this had isolated you. You had no friends. You had never kissed anyone, let alone loved anyone. "Yes," you lied. You were grateful for your father's attentions, and wanted to make them last. "Love is a force," you delivered his words back to him, buying time as you strained for insight. "Like electricity," you added, surprising yourself. "Yes!" your father exclaimed too loudly and then, collecting himself, sat at the edge of your bed and put his hands on his knees. His fingers were positioned in such a way you felt he was about to begin playing the piano. You heard the minor chords in your head, the complex music. Just above it, your father spoke. He was desperate. Beside himself. You found this expression disturbing. His eyes took on a faraway look—you pictured smoke rising from them—and he told you he was in love with these other women. "I am just so in love," he confessed. And his love became your problem.

"I get it," you said, feigning weariness.

"I am just so in love," your father said again.

"It happens."

Your mother must have taken off her heels, her gold bracelets. Neither of you noticed your bedroom door open just a
fraction as you outlined what you saw to be your father's options, and then at last, exposing your age, begged for vivid
descriptions of these other women, imagined yourself sleeping in a new bed under a less cavernous roof. You too were so
in love. Suddenly your father looked at you like he had no idea
what you were talking about. It was so confusing. He was in
love and then he wasn't. It spooked you. When you reached
for your father, you expected your hands to pass through him.

Soundless in the hallway, with the hearing of a panther,
your mother would never fully forgive your betrayal. It lodged
itself, hard and dark, inside of her.

How I LOVED to eat your underwear. Better than steak.

YOU STARTED TO take your time before you left the bungalow.
Though I hardly needed to be tipped off, this was what did it:
the consistent placement of your body in front of the bathroom mirror. Pony Darlene would sit on the edge of the bathtub, wearing ripped black pantyhose and some kind of shirt
that she had cut to show off her waistline, her biceps, her
sternum—sex had started its sure course, a lightning forking
through her body—and she would cross and uncross her long
legs and, looking up, watch you watch yourself. You were mes-
merizing. You would ask Pony for her opinion, though the one

you wanted most was mine. Something was taking hold of you. Something of substance.

You were preparing to be seen. To be touched. But, by whom?

Remember when you and The Heavy brought home a second dog?

That night, on the front yard, while I sat at your feet, you said, "I don't think I have ever seen anything killed that quickly."

Hosing down the other dog's blood, The Heavy asked, "Have you ever seen anything killed?"

"I guess I haven't, but our dog is not the attacking kind."

"When pushed, we are all the attacking kind." The Heavy turned off the hose. "Billie Jean."

"Yes, Heav." And then you stroked my head. "Lucky us."

Have you ever seen anything killed? *I guess I haven't.* That was one of your first lies to The Heavy. Those were the early days. When you were still growing your hair. It was about shoulder-length when you made him promise: "I will marry you if you ask me nothing about my past." The Heavy put his hand to his chest and he vowed to it. He was not a liar. The Heavy never could lie.

The morning of your arrival here in the territory, as he was unwrapping and then burning the last of the bandages that had kept his blood inside his body, he kept repeating the phrase *new start.* When he ran his rough fingers across his wrists, he could feel the scars forming. He knew they would harden over time, grow over the bright blue thread Traps had used to sew him up. The body was reliable after all. My reliable body. My new start. The Heavy said it over and over again. He believed in its possibility.

Gently, I argued against the concept. New start. It was beneath him. It was a motto for men capable only of short sentences, to convince people of thin truths. It was for inferior men. Men who lived above suffering, who turned their eyes from it, forced their minds blank.

We are what we have lost, I countered. Here was a way of thinking we could tear apart together. Thinking that reminded us we were alive, and what an inconsistent experience that was proving to be. We are what we have lost, I offered again. But, while The Heavy searched my eyes and seemed to find comfort in them, he was in his own world.

This man, when he was nineteen, when he was still known as Jay Jr., returning from the woods one August night with his best friend, Traps. Traps already had his nickname. Traps already had his wife. His son. Traps had a coyote slung across his back, her paws tucked under his armpits. Jay Jr. had nothing but his rifle at his side. They stepped onto the shoulder of the highway and were stopped by the sight of men and women running, and sparks in the air. The men and women were running toward the sparks. They sometimes built bonfires. They cleared their yards, and whatever they could find was burned. Cabinets, tires, wood pallets. They called them pit parties. The sound of cries and screams, and still Jay Jr. and Traps thought the cries and screams were a pit party. As they got closer, they could see the women were in their nightdresses. They were running with buckets of dirt. They had to push their bodies into the northwest wind. Reservoir is too far away, the men were shouting to each other. Some of them were naked. We'll never get to it in time. The men were pacing in front of the Fontaine family bungalow. They were unable to do anything. They had never seen a house on fire before. Who knew a fire could spread so fast? Taking a bungalow faster than a cabinet, faster than tires, faster than wood pallets. It was a matter of minutes, the stunned men would say to each other the next morning. It was a matter of minutes, The Heavy would hear this in his head for years to come. No amount of dirt, no amount of water could undo it. No one could get to them. Jay Jr.'s mother, father, and sister. No one could get through the flames. Jay Jr. tried, though. The people would say, A fine boy, a good boy, a courageous boy, a boy who tried to put out a fire with his face.

Don't know why a week after the fire, when The Heavy took a jagged hunting knife to his wrists, knowing to cut up rather than across, Traps had to use the conspicuous blue thread to sew him up. He pulled The Heavy from the bathtub, the pink water, his clothed body, his face washed of color, his eyes fixed on the wall, hard to tell whether he was still alive, and he laid him out on the bedroom floor. "You will never know how I love you," The Heavy said when consciousness flashed through him. He was not speaking to Traps, not speaking to me. He was speaking to the subjects of his heart. He never raised his voice. Never cried. Like me, he never barked. Not once. He had taught me that to announce your wants was to leave yourself open to betrayal.

Traps had an entire sewing kit with him. I watched him

unzip it. The small spools in two rows. I watched Traps deliberate. There were a few other colors that would have matched The Heavy's skin and, in so doing, distanced him from his injury rather than reminded him of it. Traps took notice of me looking at him, and he lied, "The blue thread is the strongest thread. What's your fucking issue? You're in my fucking way. Go kill something. I am sorry about your mother, all right? That was an accident. All right? Can you please stop fucking staring at me? Please?"

Traps has a deep red scar on his right forearm. I bit him there so he would not be able to sew himself closed. He would have to go for help. Drive with his left hand, the right barely attached to his body. The scar is oval-shaped, the shape of my jaw, and you can see it both on the top and on the underside of his forearm. My mother had taught me to unlock my jaw only once I felt my molars meet. This way, I would not sever the arm, but I would damage the nerves permanently. Whenever Traps turned his key, pulled down his zipper, lifted his mug, touched himself, shook a hand, made a deal, counted money, shot his rifle, steered his truck, his forearm would flare with pain. Something like an electrocution. With it, he would be compelled to think about me. About my mother.

I waited until he was finished sewing The Heavy's wounds before I bit him. I was a week old.

You and The Heavy had that party. This was five years ago, and the whole territory came out for the party. I was never a dog's dog. The dogs were in the yard chasing each other in circles, climbing each other's backs, and barking into each other's mouths. And then running for no reason at all. What is play-chasing? Something I will never understand. I was much more interested in your stocking legs. You had stockings with a shimmer in them, black seams up the back. You took them out of the package just for that night. I watched you roll them up your legs. It took almost ten minutes. You spent an hour with toilet paper wound between your fingers and toes, red nails held up in the air, drying. You spent the day behind a clay mask so your skin would be moist when people came in and put their faces against your face.

"It's aspiration that keeps you young," you said to me, gluing rhinestones around your eyes. "Wanting. Wanting to be something, wanting to go somewhere. Even wanting a different nose, different legs is a kind of aspiration. Even vanity is aspiration. But when you see those things you want are not going to happen for you, you enter the state past aspiration. The striving stops. Everyone thinks it's freedom to be past aspiration, past striving, but it's not. It's defeat. It's when your face starts to fall. Striving is antigravity." Then you took a roll of duct tape and plied a silver band to your hairline, holding back a quarter inch of your face.

You studied yourself in the mirror. In a vast and prolonged way, you stood there and took in your image, the long hair, your perfume smudged beneath it, the lean neck, the lustrous mouth, slightly parted, the fight of your jaw, all that you've dreamed and had to conceal, the dark, shy eyes, love flickering through them, and your daughter one floor below, how your only wish was that her life would supersede your own, then you said, "Youth. Tell me. Why would I ever go back there?"

Efficiently, you pulled the duct tape from your face and, to it, returned time.

When you were finally dressed, you came down the stairs, and surveying you, The Heavy took your portrait, then kissed you hard on the lips and rubbed his hand over your ass and then the small of your back and then over your ass again just before the doorbell first chimed. He would take you later. Twice. "Heav short for Heaven," you would say. "Heaven." Every table was covered in food and bowls full of cigarettes. Platters everywhere. Even the top of the television had a platter on it. Glasses and bottles were lined up on the bar. There was a punch bowl with cherries floating in it. Pony had covered the basement floor in old mattresses, and all of the children were jumping and doing somersaults. One boy lost a tooth. One girl collided with another girl and briefly knocked her out. When they were hurt, no one told their parents. One girl peed in her dress, and two boys were having so much fun, they started to cry uncontrollably and then fell asleep in a corner. The girl who peed in her dress went upstairs, and without anyone noticing, took a dress of Pony's and then hid her own dress in Pony's drawer. When you found the wet dress a few days later, the overwhelming smell of urine, you stroked Pony's head and told her never to feel ashamed. It felt so good, she didn't even tell you Lana's wet dress was identical to her dress, but not her dress. I knew how good it felt; you stroked my head all the time.

Who needs to bark?

Nothing like this had ever happened before in the territory. The people gathered to mourn the departed or to burn things, but never for a house party. It was the month of March. At last winter was loosening its death grip. The days were getting longer. The people could aim their faces at the sun. The ground underfoot was softening. Soon the dead would go into it and the dark heads of new flowers would rise. The people felt a heat build in their bodies. They needed pleasure. A natural rule breaker, a woman from elsewhere, you were the only one who could have set off this kind of release.

Five couples had sex in the toolshed, and a few people had their way with themselves on our bathroom floor, peanuts scattered everywhere. And there was one group thing. Later in the night. Under the badminton net. Four women. Three men. And from that group, a single woman with a painful-looking ponytail and a chipped front tooth went on with two men in a truck bed.

Now you tell me, who are the dogs?

When Traps and Debra Marie arrived with their boy, Will Jr. (finally, a child as private as Pony, my kind of child), Debra Marie handed you a small cake wrapped in tinfoil. When she saw the platters and the bowls, she saw her cake was not the right size of cake for the party. She had mistaken the scale, and this had a diminishing effect. A woman is the cake she brings to the party. Her cake was small; she was small. She had mistaken the scale of you, mistaken the scale of the party. It was a different kind of party. "What a party!" That is what everyone was saying. "What a party!" There was a stereo set up and there were speakers in every room of the house. You had twelve songs and they kept playing over and over. The songs had an order. They were slow and then fast and then slow again. You called it the rotation, and the rotation was exactly what everyone wanted. Even if they did not mean to, people were moving. They were moving on their way to saying hello to someone, on their way to the bar. They put their hands on their own bodies when they moved, and then on each other's bodies. Pretty soon, people were dancing.

Debra Marie handed you her cake and then her coat, and then she took off her shoes.

"Don't do that!"

"Beg pardon?"

"Don't take off your shoes!"

"But, I wouldn't want to track dirt!"

"I don't care about dirt!"

"Sorry! I can't hear you over this music!"

"It's a party!"

"What?"

"I don't care about dirt! It's a party!"

And when she refused to put her shoes back on, you took her hand and pushed your way through the crowd while everyone watched you, thinking, Where are those two going? and you brought Debra Marie in her stocking feet up to the bedroom. I could tell it was erotic for everyone to watch you lead Debra Marie up the stairs. I could tell it was erotic for Debra Marie to be standing with you in our bedroom. Debra Marie had no name for that feeling.

"Does your dog always stare like that?"

"Yes, she does."

"She doesn't blink."

"No, she doesn't. She's a good, loyal bitch."

"Beg pardon?"

"I said she is a good, loyal bitch!"

I really do come across that way.

And you laughed while Debra Marie, upon your insistence, squeezed her very different feet into your second-best pair of shoes, low blue heels, but not before taking a good look around.

"You should have seen this place when we moved The Heavy in."

"Oh, I know all about it," you said, even though you didn't. Such a smooth liar. Such a long and beautiful neck. You have the neck of a movie star.

The Heavy had held you to the same promise. You would ask him nothing about his past. You did not need to. His face and his wrists told you everything you needed to know.

"You arrived fairly soon after that. Let's see. The Heavy moved in here in August, and you arrived the following May." Debra Marie concluded her story about you, to you. I could hear her heart pounding. Below you, the women of the territory were pulling down their hair. It fell to their knees, their ankles. Under it, they swayed their bodies. For once, they were imitating you. The next morning, your living room floor would be gold with pins. Whatever lasting, subconscious hesitations the women had about you disappeared that night. They threw off their guards. They too wanted to put their hands in yours. Be led somewhere by you. But, the women were used to Debra Marie having all the luck. Her rich husband, her mysteriously beautiful son. "Will Jr. was one when you arrived in the territory." Like you, Debra Marie measured time in her child.

Then Debra Marie turned her face to the north window. Her strong nose, her small mouth, her eyes wide and gray. The clear view of the reservoir: pump at one end, hoses running from the water to the pump. "Don't know how you can look out at that thing day and night. I sure couldn't. And I don't know how Heav does it." She blushed when she said that. "Looking out at the thing that might have saved his family, and didn't. Oh poor Heav." You joined Debra Marie by the window. You could feel she had become hot. Her feet were damp inside your shoes. If I put my jaw around her ankle, she would taste of salt. You had never heard anyone else shorten The Heavy's nickname; in doing so, she was telling you something. Something about The Heavy's past. Something of her possession.

You had underestimated her. You felt power leave your body and enter hers. You were not one to lose. "I love the view," you said to the reservoir. "And I love Heav," you said to Debra Marie, pointedly.

Then seeing over Debra Marie's shoulder in the half-open doorway her large, gorgeous boy, who, at the age of thirteen, had just received his nickname, you said, "You know what? I am going to get changed."

"What?"

"I am going to change my dress."

"Now?"

"Yes! I'm bored of this dress and feel like wearing another one."

And Debra Marie watched you move your sensational body out of one long dress and into another one, not noticing her boy, transfixed. "Zip me up?" Debra Marie, thinking you were speaking to her, did as she was told.

THE HEAVY. It was the only nickname The Silentest Man, proprietor of Drink-Mart and husband to One Hundred, could give to the nineteen-year-old when Traps dragged him from the cinders and steered him into the bar. While One Hundred (the only rider of the founders' bus still alive, and the only one to have known John the Leader, thereby appointed the territory nurse) tended to Jay Jr.'s wounds, The Silentest Man lined up bottles of alcohol for him. The young man went about drinking the amber liquid until his anguished world gave way to another one. A black square. Jay Jr. looked into the black square. The Silentest Man looked into Jay Jr. Fire can jump a river. Pain can fell a man. "Heavy," The Silentest Man said to the boy.

The Silentest Man had watched Jay Jr. for years—since the day he turned thirteen—coming close to but never settling on his nickname. All of the other young men in the territory had their names. Traps, Fur Thumb, Wishbone, Sexeteria, Hot Dollar. They had declared themselves so flamboyantly. Naming them had been easy. Although Jay Jr. had a seriousness about him, he also had an inner liberty The Silentest Man admired and felt ready to name him for. If Jay Jr. had not gone hunting with Traps that night, his nickname would have been Liberty. The fire might not have happened. He might still have a family. If Jay Jr. had not gone hunting with Traps that night, he might not be the last Fontaine. Looking at the boy, his boots still smoking, his face raw from the burns: "*The*

Heavy." The Silentest Man thus reinforced the name. It was the right name. The Heavy was the only young man in the territory with secrets, secrets he knew how to keep.

Jay Jr. had slept with a woman. He thought of her now. The smell of fire filled Drink-Mart. His lungs were tight with smoke. An iron taste in his mouth. Sex was a revelation, but he was careful with it, never promiscuous. He was not greedy. Had never been drunk. He did not love this woman. He was enthralled by her body, but he could not see the future in her. Was not one to fake it. He knew what love was. About love, he had no doubt. His love had belonged to his family, and his family was dead. In a matter of minutes. The Heavy threw up on the floor of the bar. The Silentest Man covered it with sawdust. Traps stood nearby, feeling useless, stung and unsure why. The Heavy passed out with the hands of One Hundred stroking his hair and trying to mend his face.

In the territory, the announcement of a nickname is met with celebration. Not The Heavy's nickname. It produced an awkwardness among the men. Evoking only the tragic fire, The Heavy's desperate attempts to rescue his family, nearly getting to his sister.

When he ran at the blazing house, The Heavy had to throw off the men. They hung from his arms. Held him by the boots. Tried to tackle him and pin him down. The Heavy pointed his rifle at the men and shot the air just above their heads.

At the front of the Fontaine house, there were two metal supports that held a roof above the small cement porch. His sister's bedroom window looked out onto the roof. She used the roof to sneak out at night. The Heavy climbed the supports. He said, "Pony." This was his nickname for his sister. "Pony." He said it again. She followed him everywhere. Pony. The Heavy got his hands on her burning window frame and was working it open when the window exploded and the roof he was standing on caved in.

The Heavy's father had started the fire. His wife was having an affair with his best friend. The Heavy's father was smoking and then, upon his wife's admission of guilt, held his cigarette to their bedroom curtain. His wife found the gesture elegant, a gesture that did not fit in with his usual ways, which reminded her of a bear. She had no time for the next thought. The Heavy's father could not believe how fast the fire was. How beautiful. How it climbed. The Heavy's father was a romantic. He pictured his son. Soon, he would kill an animal. Soon, he would find love. Smoke obscured the room. He could no longer see his wife. He could hear her making sounds. He did not know her necklace was on fire. He put his fist through their window and ruined his hand. He understood he had punched the wall, and the window was nowhere to be found. Neither was his wife. Everything was on fire. The bed. His shoes. His hands. Fire was loud as bones snapping. He had no one to make this comment to. He was a social man. Unlike his son, who only faced inward. God, he could be hard to reach. He pictured his daughter. All he could see was the night, and her slicing through it. She was trouble. He did not know she was only feet away. The fire jumped across the hall to her bedroom and consumed it. Around her bed, her father had hung a white lace curtain. On her wall, she had a poster of a shirtless man. Under it, she had written YOU ROCK MY WORLD. In a room of smoke and flame, his daughter had fallen asleep with her headphones on. She was waiting for the asteroid to make impact.

The men of the territory accepted The Heavy's name, but uttered it with a distancing tone. They could not punctuate it with a clap to his back. They could not shorten it. Make a nickname of his nickname, as they liked to do. There were no jokes to be made with the name so the men tried to avoid using it altogether. The man who was never greeted, never joked with. Already an isolated man, The Heavy rarely heard his name called. What was meant to create closeness had the opposite effect. The Heavy preferred this. Besides, there was only one voice he wanted on his name, and it was yours.

Heav. Short for Heaven.

My mother was the sole survivor of the fire. She refused to leave the bungalow, but was within reach. By her fur, The Heavy pulled her through the blown-out living room window after the roof to his sister had collapsed. He handed her off to one of the men. When my mother went to run back in and was stopped, she bit through the arms of the men, went for their chests and necks, until they locked her in a nearby truck, and she chewed through the interior. That is where I was born. A week later, my mother was run over by Traps speeding toward the Last House with his sewing kit.

When a dog is born, her mother tells her everything she thinks her pup will need to know. We do not, the way humans do, assume the future.

But have you left the fire? I would ask The Heavy. You can leave the fire. You don't have to stay loyal to the fire. The fire does not have to be all that you see. I would say the things my mother had before me.

THE DAY AFTER your party, the men and women of the territory woke up in their truck beds, under the badminton net, on the bathroom floor. Had they looked through your medicine cabinets? Yes. While you crawled on your hands and knees, picking up hairpins, tumbler glasses, and half-smoked cigarettes, adults snuck from the bungalow into daylight. Pony was still asleep on a bare mattress in the basement, her friend Lana's leg thrown over her, and The Heavy was upstairs on your bed. The rhinestones had fallen from your face. You tried not to leap to conclusions.

A quarter mile away, the men gathered at Drink-Mart. Their eyes were bloodshot. They needed fixing. What had you done to them? They could not even joke about poison. *I'm all out of love, I'm so lost without you.* The Silentest Man did not have to be asked to turn off the Air Supply. "What is the softest drink?" The men shook when they asked One Hundred, who had grown weary of healing them and had, just that morning, nailed a piece of chipboard over the INFIRMARY part of the Drink-Mart sign. "The gentlest, kindest drink?" The men flirted with the old woman. She poured it for them, then left the bar and walked across the highway and northwest to a small clearing in the forest where she had her lawn chair set up. She loved to sun herself. She would arrange her clothing into a sort of bathing suit, oil what she could, and close her eyes.

Upper Big Territory was a gold mining town. The fathers

of Wishbone, the Death Man, Hot Dollar, Fur Thumb, Traps, and The Heavy had discovered gold a year after they stepped off the founders' bus. Shortly after, their Leader, John, went for a swim in the reservoir and never returned. John had lived in the bungalow they called the Last House. Wanted to be at the northernmost point of the territory. When he vanished, his followers left the Last House unoccupied as if he might come back to it. They were used to him disappearing for a day, two days, but this time, the days stretched into weeks. Every morning, his followers checked the shoreline to see if his body had washed up on the black mud. One morning, the black mud had a glimmer to it. The people of the territory had struck gold.

On her lawn chair, under the blazing sun, One Hundred grew thirsty, and she returned to the bar. The Silentest Man handed her a drink. She always drank her drink while The Silentest Man fixed her a second, identical drink. He did this now, and she thanked him. There was love when his skin grazed hers. A life together. Barefoot, One Hundred walked back to her clearing, but where her lawn chair had been set up there was now a gaping hole.

Crowding around the crater, the teenagers of the territory could not believe it. They thought they had missed an asteroid. "Classic," they commented to each other. "Finally, something happens here and we miss it." One girl, Pallas Jones, said she had actually heard the approach and was the first to get here on her dirt bike, but by then, it had already hit. Others agreed the sound was furious. Still others thought only of the night before, and having sex for the first time under a large coat on a pile of mattresses on the cement floor of the Fontaine bungalow basement. The crater was deepening. The teenagers stepped back and watched the earth open.

The men looked from the sinkhole, the result of an abandoned mineshaft, to the frontier, and saw it for what it had become. Yes, there may still be some gold deposits in the territory, but they had become too difficult to extract. The fog downed planes. The cold broke metal. So much of the time, the men worked their instruments in darkness. It was cheaper to do this type of thing elsewhere. That is what they were being told, and had been told for years.

But this was the only place the men and women knew, and they didn't want to leave it. They didn't think they could. They had to come up with a different way. Supplies were no longer flown in. They were driven in. Once a month. A single truckload. Milk became expensive. You can make a lot out of very little, the people told themselves, and they competed for austerity. The men counted out their cigarettes and smoked them to the filter. They cut their hair. Their hair, which had been long and full like the women's hair, went into the bonfires. When their gums grew weak, the men pulled their teeth. "Complaint is a form of self-degradation," the men said to each other. "Beauty is a state of mind." The words of John the Leader became more resonant than ever. "Hardship is a matter of perception." The women pulled down the hems of their children's clothing. Paperbacks were ripped into chapters and parceled between the bungalows. With duct tape, everything could be used more than once. Babies smelled like mothballs. A woman could no longer change her dress midway through a party. There was no second dress to wear. There were no parties. There were no joyrides. Trucks were driven with purpose. All materials had purpose. The men thought about starting in on the forest, and did briefly, but faced the same obstacles. The fog, the cold, the dark. They needed a new export. Something lasting. Something endless. Something that could renew itself. Look within.

Blood. The world always needed fresh blood. And blood became the new export of the territory.

You told me your surroundings were blurry when you fell from the Mercedes sedan, the rush of transport from the highway to the lunch counter. The arms that held you were the wrong arms. The man's smell was wrong. His skin against yours made you bristle. The body never lies. And then, through the door to Home of the Beef Candy, a chime of bells, and there he was standing at the lunch counter. The Heavy. He turned to you. You didn't even see the ravaged face. What you saw was the body of a fighter. The sheer solidity of him. And then the eyes. Green, bottomless.

While you recovered in the Last House, and your name— Billie Jean—was spread throughout the territory, the women circled the dark blue Mercedes sedan (painted that color by you in the big and empty parking lot of a mall). It was a car that did not understand clearance. The territory demanded clearance. Opening the glove box, the women found a pair of underwear. One of the women held the pink underwear up with a finger and let the sun shine through them. "I could do that to my underwear with a pair of scissors," she said, then reconsidered. "Our men can never see this underwear," she warned and went to light them on fire before being stopped— "Fuck!" clutching her ankle—by me. They scoured the car floor but collected only a few old wrappings for foods they already knew. Hands on the upholstery, between the seats, under the visors, inside the armrests: nothing worthy of their time or contemplation. They went to the trunk, and when they found it sealed shut, key not working, grew excited. *Crack,* the supplicant whine of the hinges, and one woman, crowbar in hand, lifted out a white plastic bag containing something small. "Is it a baby?" The women emptied the bag. A white button-down. A black pencil skirt. SERVER stitched on the right breast pocket of the button-down. A change of clothes. Clothes for a different climate.

They scrapped the sedan. They would circle you, instead.

The women left the plastic bag by the front door of the Last House alongside a second plastic bag. Clothes for this climate. An indoor tracksuit, an outdoor tracksuit, beige bras, white underwear, wool socks, heavily treaded boots, a winter coat. They left a note explaining the clothes' designations as they had been declared by John.

A woman's white indoor tracksuit is meant for domestic operations inside the home. It should not be seen by anyone but immediate family. It is most appropriately worn first thing in the morning and just before bedtime. It should not be worn for longer than thirty-minute intervals, and is considered strictly a bridge outfit between nightwear and daywear. A woman's camouflage outdoor tracksuit is solely for work on her property. It can be seen by neighbors though this is not optimal. To protect herself, limited use of a woman's outdoor tracksuit is best.

THE WOMEN HUNG AROUND on the porch, but were not invited in.

I watched The Heavy lower you into the bathtub. He soaped your body, and then placed your body between clean sheets, and then, joining me, stood by the door, waited for you to wake. The startled look you had when you did. Then recognizing the bedroom, recognizing him, and lifting your arms. Love. For the first time, you felt love. Love was uneasy. Who knew?

When you were strong enough, you would hand-wash your underwear and hang them to dry from the shower rod in The Heavy's bathroom. There was always a pair of underwear hanging there, pink then black then pink then black, and I felt so sharply how your underwear was underwear from elsewhere. The Heavy had had only one lover by the time you came to us, and she had very different underwear. White. Territory-issue. Futureless.

The Heavy talked about how you were the only woman I took a liking to. "Are you going to eat my throat while I'm sleeping so you can have her to yourself?" he would ask while running his meaty hand through my fur.

ONE NIGHT (we had buried Lana Barbara Sr. that day), you whispered to me, "I am done with young men." You and Pony had gone swimming in the reservoir. No wind, and your black final resting dresses hung from a tree branch, not moving. Later, when Pony was in her bedroom, in front of her mirror, repeating chants from her cassette recorder, practicing the splits so she could one day do them across the hood of a speeding car in a glam metal music video, we were in the bedroom, and you looked at me in the way that says, Hold me to this, Gena Rowlands. "I am done. I am done with young men." And then you paused. "Make me swear to it."

No way, I said.

My mother had taught me that, like us, human beings are composed of instinct above all else.

Young men. In your other life, you had smoked their cigarettes and made their mothers fall in love with you. They had left wilted flowers stolen from cemeteries on your front porch and slapped your face on a moving train. They had sent you erotic letters, broken into your bedroom. Your bedroom on that cul-de-sac still had a dollhouse in one corner. Dolls were real to you. You felt their eyes bore into you. Some nights, you turned the dolls so they faced away from your bed. That way, you could not sense their accusation. The dolls blamed you for having no agency. For being unable to do anything but be held and stroked and owned and thrown against a wall if it came to that.

You told me you had spent your childhood in a tree reading a book. This was your idea of happiness. No one bothered you. No one interrupted your thinking. You discovered your native thinking. Your deepest, long-form thinking. When you came down from the tree, all you felt was hunger. And all you could feel around you was the hunger of others. The way the young men looked at you. You preferred the tree. But you slept with the young men.

"It was actually only one." I licked your hand, heard a groan come from my throat. "It felt like more at the time because it was new. *I* was new. I wasn't even sixteen. I did it for two reasons. Rebellion, of course." Here, you began to braid my coat.

And?

"Lust, I guess."

Though he was only twenty when you met, The Heavy was not a young man. Had never been. He was not carefree. Not reckless. Not a braggart. He did not know how to manipulate a moment so it went in his favor. If anything, he tried to do the opposite. Other men spoke about sex, speed, and money: "Rig the 390 horsepower alongside the 780, then you'll have yourself one fine rig." The Heavy did not care to impress. He was talked about as rude, grave, unmanly. He was a bad shot, the men said, the worst shot in the territory. While Traps lectured him—"When you see your target, you cannot think of where it is coming from and where it is going. You cannot think of what might be following it"—The Heavy only heard the voices of the animals. He would never kill anything. Traps beside him, wearing dead animals like scarves, presenting their skins as gifts.

We think people look away when they lie, that they add small motions to distract from their lies. You were not that kind of liar.

I have never seen anything killed.

I have never lost anything.

I'm—and then recalling the name of the woman in the popular song, the popular song that, as you approached the territory, seemed to be the only song you could find, despite it being two decades old. You borrowed your name from the radio. You thought it would fit in with the other women's names. You could be her, only her, this invented woman. New start. "I'm Billie Jean." You said the name to The Heavy from the bathtub, where the August before, he had nearly bled to death. "Billie Jean." You repeated the name as much for yourself as for him.

BEFORE YOU SPRANG from the bed that late October evening and ran out the front door, I said, You're stooped and shrunken like a starved animal.

"I am a starved animal."

I followed you down the stairs, and you stood in the hallway with the truck keys in your hand. A cigarette in the other. It was stale, not lit. Pony Darlene was inert on the couch. Telephone receiver against her left ear. Gauze and tape up and down her right arm from the bloodwork. On her T-shirt, she wore a laminated pin that said FAINTER. She had been blacking out lately. She needed protecting.

She had never kissed a boy, never received a telephone call from a boy. But once a week, on Saturday night, she stood on the shoulder of the north highway, in the waitress uniform you stole, and Pony Darlene subsequently stole from you, and she put her beautiful face into the slick lap of that reptilian man, Traps, in exchange for gasoline. She was doing this act for you. But you were grieving, and grief is oblivion. You did not notice your daughter scavenging through garbage at the roadside, looking for money. She was saving up. You did not notice Pony Darlene had a plan.

You told me you lived for her. She was the one who kept you here. The prospect of dying was one you could no longer consider. It was a terrible pressure, motherhood. It had a way of fucking with your options. Life before a child was all miscellany, and in that miscellany, a woman could off herself. Now, there was no way.

Pony Darlene joined you by the doorway. You studied your daughter at length, her lithe body, the faint hair above her lip. She was sorting through herself, and studying you reciprocally—also with horror, adoration. Wanting you, not wanting you.

And then you turned to me. "I had forgotten all about you."

I laughed. This was one of your better lies.

When you kicked your winter coat with your bare foot and made for the door, I saw you were serious about leaving. You lunged for the knob just as Pony lost consciousness. The northwest wind assaulted us. Outside, there was snow. It was cold. Ice fell from the sky. The sky was black, thin, and low.

You drove too quickly for me, Billie Jean. Your motions had taken on a new will, a violence. I could not keep up. I watched the sun rise and set. I lost your scent.

I thought about dying. I thought about my mother.

She had nearly beaten the truck back to the house when Traps's front right tire caught her left hind leg. How he could not have seen her, I do not know, and will never forgive. My mother had told me to stay with the dying man, The Heavy, before she sprinted for help. I did as I was instructed. A human body contains a great deal of blood. If you give it the chance, blood will leave you at a determined pace. Like fire, it was a matter of minutes. After she was hit, my mother could still run to the woods behind the house. That was where I would find her the next day. The birds knew, even in death, to leave her alone. Eighteen years later, her bones are still there. She had told me Traps had a weakness, and that one day, I would find it out. She had told me The Heavy had no weaknesses. She never got the chance to meet you.

You will ditch the truck. As soon as you can, you will ditch the truck and walk in that single-minded way of yours into the forest, and look for the tree of your childhood. The place where everything is clear. Where happiness was once found. For it, you were willing to leave your daughter behind. The Heavy. Me.

How could you leave me behind?

BEFORE WE STARTED to see the boy running, before you timed our runs to coincide with his, you thought, What the hell am I doing? And you looked down at me, keeping pace, and said, "What the hell are we doing?" We are running a band of empty gravel, I answered. And we panted in unison.

Running was like play-chasing. I would watch the other dogs, sprinting at me and then away from me, looking over their shoulders, cueing me, Come on, Come on, and I would tell them, I will chase when I chase. Why would I imitate an emergency? I have other ways to thrill myself. When there is nothing at your back, why pretend there is? But, at your calves, Billie Jean, it was clear I loved it, and you would ask, "Maybe I am doing this for you?" When one morning, the boy ran by on the other side of the gravel, I saw you were not doing this for me.

You sat beside him in the bed of his father's black truck. The truck was what the people of the territory called souped-up. It was perched on what the people called monster tires. The Heavy had to help you into the truck bed; it was so high off the ground. You held The Heavy's hand and stepped up onto his thigh in your territory-issue workboots. I followed.

It was the day we buried Lana's mother. Three years after the big party. You and Pony Darlene wore your matching final resting dresses; later, you would hang the black dresses over a tree branch and sink your bodies into the reservoir. I hated the water. They say every dog knows how to swim. False. Have we not learned the dangers of making generalizations about an entire species? From the shoreline; I would watch you both, I will admit, rigid with fear.

Pony Darlene asked if she could meet us at the Banquet Hall. She wanted to be the last one in the graveyard. Why she would want this was a mystery to me. The graveyard was a bleak place, a rough and treeless expanse, the headstones competing for size with whatever building materials—trailer siding, sheets of plywood, corrugated plastic—the widows could get their hands on. Headstone Saturdays. All around us, heaps of lumber and aluminum, the things not burned in bonfires, were held together with duct tape, the territory dogs frantic and circling the gaudy masses with their snouts in the dirt and rock, barking and whining at the dead. You. Come. Here. Get. The owners shouted for their dogs until they were hoarse.

Pony explained that she wanted to pick up the speeches and the flowers that had accumulated that day. She would put them in a book for her friend. Lana was contemplating her mother's actions. She was gutted, but she explained to Pony she also needed to understand. She was tempted to mix alcohol with pills to feel what her mother had felt. Her last feelings. Get a sense of where she went. Not enough to kill herself. "Obvs, Pony. Swear, Pony. My will has not been broken, Pony." (I could hear Lana's voice through the receiver when Pony was in the living room and I was directly above her on the second floor.) Lana's mother had told Lana that she just loved doing the dishes. The task had such a definite beginning, middle, and end, and this gave her a great satisfaction.

Lana's mother did her shift at the Banquet Hall. She served dinner. She cleaned up. She watched her night soaps. She put on her indoor tracksuit. And then she killed herself in their toolshed. Where her portrait is now rotting between two slats of wood. She made killing herself look so easy. Easy as doing the dishes. Beginning, middle, end. Suddenly, Pony had a sense of mortality. At night, she thought about death. Thinking about sex immediately followed. Death then sex. With Lana's mother's suicide arrived Pony's coming of age. Death then sex. These dark twins spiraled through her mind. She was possessed by dangerous questions. They were like kerosene. She had a new volatility and did not know whether she was haunted or aroused (both, I tried to tell her). When Pony left the final resting book for her friend a couple of weeks later, Lana replied with a postcard in our mailbox. Pony felt it summed up her state and tacked it to her wall immediately. It said, *SIGH!!!*

So we left the truck with Pony and caught a ride with Traps, and over his father's loud music, the boy told you he liked to run. No one else in town ran for sport. It was a motion the territory people did not understand. They left that motion to the animals they hunted, skinned, quartered, and ate.

"I like to run," he said.

As Traps's truck pulled away (The Heavy was in the passenger seat with Debra Marie wedged between the two men), Pony Darlene leapt and waved to you from the headstones, her coltish limbs, her hands white with paper. You lifted yours in response. You felt something turn in your stomach. You had never become used to the love. I have become used to everything else, you would say to me, but I will never get used to my love for her. As the truck gained speed, Pony grew small, and it was when she had vanished from view and all you could see was dust, you knew you needed to get to know the boy beside you.

The thought came on like a spell. You had exchanged words with him in the territory—greetings, mostly. He had stood in the doorway to your bedroom the night of the party. His father, Traps, was referred to as your husband's best friend, but you spent no time at each other's tables. The friendship occurred between the men. It was never extended to the wives, to the children. You were relieved by the separateness; there were only so many faces. The Heavy kept up with Traps out of cunning. (A double note here: one, we were both happy he had some of this in him; two, I had seen some odd pairings in nature—baby rabbits asleep on the slumbering bodies of red foxes, both peaceful and curled like fists—but The Heavy and Traps's pairing was the most unlikely of all.) I reasoned it out this way: The Heavy could not stand to see pity in the eyes of the men, and the friendship with Traps—a man surrounded by trucks, and built like them—went toward erasing the pity.

Whereas Traps took up all of the available space, the boy had an economy to him, a precision. You could not conceive how the boy had come from this man. This filthy peacock of a man. In his cowboy boots. His fur trapper hat. A cheater, a salesman, and (I know this is low on the scale, but it still offends me) an amateur. If you are going to make collages, make *good* collages. You looked closely at your life. Pulled it apart and examined it. There was nothing to drive you from it. When The Heavy walked into a room, you wanted him. Only him. He had a wildness in him. A goodness. On your way north, you had watched herds cross great plains. He was a herd, and he had folded you into it.

But now, in the truck bed, you felt only divided. You worked out the boy's age. Eighteen. You were thirty-two. Fifteen years. Acceptable. Not acceptable. Forgivable. Not forgivable. You judged yourself while you still could. No part of your body touched the boy's. About this, you were vigilant. You kept your shoulders from banging against his. Your legs and arms apart. It was a treacherous road, and in the metal box, you were both rattled and thrown around. The wind rushed at you. And when your hair whipped across it, the boy did not lift his hands to cover his face.

"I also run," you lied.

This was your first lie to the boy. And your last.

YOU DID NOT sweat without purpose. You were calculated. You did not swim the reservoir so much as you completed circuits across it. From one end to the other, from one end to the other. Your tireless body. The way you moved, I wondered if you moved only to punish yourself. To be in motion was to beat something out of you. And even when you did lie on your back to look up at the night sky, it was not without strategy. You knew the worth of floating. You measured it out before submitting yourself to it. Weightlessness had worth, and so you went for weightlessness, and eventually, when you thought she was ready, taught it to your daughter. Your always-willing daughter.

I could not watch, had to look away. Your strong hands supporting Pony Darlene at the neck like it was broken; her body prone on the surface as if on a stretcher. You told your daughter she was a natural swimmer. This thrilled Pony. Swimming was a skill you had brought with you from your former life. At last, she had a piece of it. Got a sense of where you had come from. Pony started to read about the ocean, pictured you living near the ocean. It was a fast-moving river, you wanted to tell Pony, but did not. I would have crossed that river for you, Pony, you wanted to say. I would cross anything for you.

When Pony Darlene entered the Banquet Hall to have her blood drawn and, for the first time, was assigned to you, you had a hard time getting your body to move. She was thirteen, the age a territory girl (or boy) begins doing her bloodwork two or, if her body can handle it, three times a week. "You good?" Rita Star in her pastel dress (they were rotated through the days, pale yellow, pale pink, pale green), seeing your hesitation, challenged you. "You good?" you shot back, and in your powder-blue dress, with your straight face, you led Pony to the cot in the corner, your station.

It was the duty of the women in the territory to draw blood from the teenagers. Only One Hundred, given her poor eyesight, was exempt. The men felt their wives—their sure hands, their soft voices—would be better with the needles and, if required, in offering comfort.

When Pony lay down, you rolled up the sleeves of her shirt to look for a vein and saw on your daughter only bruises. They erupted until they joined. You ran your fingers over them. You could see in Pony's eyes that, even with your light touch, they were sore. How could you not have noticed these? When you spent so many hours just watching your daughter, studying her face and her body, tracking her as she would soon track you, how could you have missed these? You stroked Pony's arms. They were a deep blue from the bloodwork. Glancing from their stations in their dresses that were three sizes too big and always had to be spot-washed after a shift, the women cast their eyes over you. Yes, there was a vein. At her right wrist. By the bone. Thin, but it would work.

Pony loved to nose around the gold-black bedroom, open

any small boxes you had on the dresser, run her hands over the carpet under the bed. You made her sly. You avoided her questions about your past, and so Pony developed other methods of collecting information, getting what she needed—a criminality (the height of which would be robbing a drug dealer at gunpoint). It was the night of your party and Pony was ten and she had been inside your closet, trying on your low blue heels, flexing her toes to make them fit, when she eyed the fur throw stuffed into the corner; behind it, the white plastic bag. She had never seen the bag before. She sat cross-legged on the floor and laid out its contents. She shook the dust from them. The Heavy was trying to zip up your dress— the party one, the slinky one—when Pony came soundlessly down the stairs. A grin filled her face. Her teeth were uneven. She tried to cover them and keep her features slack as a gambler's. In your white button-down and black pencil skirt, Pony was proud. The clothes hung from her frame. I could see her body trembling beneath them. She rolled the top of the skirt to keep it on (later she would make a belt out of duct tape), raised her arms above her head, and spun. You arrowed across the room to your daughter and wrapped your arms around her, around yourself—who you had been so many years before—until Pony pulled herself from your grip. "Let me go."

You told me how you got the waitress uniform. When you were nearly killed in the parking lot of an all-you-can-eat restaurant, the midway mark of your drive north, at the age of sixteen and a half.

You parked at the back of the lot, closest to the highway. In the driver's seat of the stolen Mercedes, you ran your hands through what was left of your hair, then spat into your palms and cleaned your face. You looked at yourself in the mirror. Joan of Arc. Freddie Mercury. Joan of Mercury. Ha. You swung the door open and stepped from the car. Your legs gave out. Don't fall to the pavement. You wore another woman's shoes. You had a taupe purse strung across your body. You tried to make your motions look ordinary, the purse look like your purse.

The restaurant was big and noisy and crowded and terrifically bright. It felt like entering a fever. Everyone was talking. You cannot talk to yourself here. Wait for the car. When you get back to the car, say everything you must. Your mind was dark and fast and difficult to order. You set your gaze so it would not catch another's. The back of the restaurant was a picture window looking out over a canyon that was a mile deep. You could watch the sun move across the canyon. Scenic view. Breathtaking. You found the expression morbid. Especially now.

Above the buffet, there was a shotgun and, around it, the heads of animals. The rich food was under heat lamps. You stood in line and filled your plate. All you can eat. What a proposition. Every time, you switched things up. When you left your parents' large house in the long car some six months before, you did not eat meat. Here, in the roadside restaurant, you ate meat; you ate every kind of meat; you could not eat enough meat.

The diners had thin films of sweat on their faces. A gloss from driving, eating and talking inside the windowed room. They wore cotton shirts and bright slacks. Outside, their motor homes packed the parking lot and had names like LIVINITUP painted above the spare tires. Many of the old couples wore matching ensembles. You felt a sudden and expansive connection to all things. The people, but also the cutlery, the promise jewelry, the maps spread open on the tables. You could hear the chatter of the diners' voices, but you could also hear the conversations they were having with themselves. You could hear their native thinking.

"Ready to settle?" A waitress with tall hair, frosted lipstick, and matching nails filed into darts tapped the check on the plastic tablecloth. You had to reorient yourself. The sun had lowered itself in the sky. Had you fallen asleep? Yes, after five meals, you had fallen asleep. Yes, let us settle this. I will settle this. Myself, I will settle. You indicated to the waitress that you needed a minute. You composed your body, and when the waitress was turned away, you made for the back room. In it, there was a coffeemaker, a microwave, a cat calendar, a deck of cards, a half-full glass ashtray, a stack of serving trays, and spare uniforms hanging from a rolling rack. For a moment, in the room, you stood naked with an empty purse. Then, you put on the white button-down and the black pencil skirt, raised a tray above your head, and walked coolly back through the restaurant, keeping your shoes on, and fast as a fox, lifting mounds of cash from tables. You were really getting away with things now. You could hear shouting behind you. You stuffed the money into your pink underwear. You dropped the tray, had to abandon the shoes sprinting to the car.

You would be dead if, rabid with hunger, you had not left the keys in the ignition.

You had never heard a rifle shot before. The bullet made a humming sound just a few inches from your left ear. You cowered and, from under the dashboard, reversed into a motor home. Please don't let my tailgate be hung up on another, bigger tailgate. Please don't let me be stuck. You pictured your head mounted on the wall, between the heads of the animals. You cranked the steering wheel and squealed out of the lot. You could smell the smoke and rubber from your tires scorching the pavement. Eventually, you remembered to close the driver's side door. Your fine-boned feet bare against the pedals. You looked down at the uniform. The black pencil skirt. The crisp white shirt. It was night, but you could just make it out: a burn mark on the left shoulder where the bullet had seared through cloth—it was still hot and you blew on it—and on the right breast pocket, a word stitched; you read it aloud, "Server."

At that time in your life, those months of driving—in the end, it would be a year of driving—you could laugh or sleep for days at a time. It was the driving that kept you straight. To steer, to signal, to refuel; these basic actions we rarely read into were the ones that saved your life.

In the Banquet Hall, you bowed your body over your daughter's, and inserted the needle into your own arm. Pony—always one for collusion, especially with you—kept perfectly still, and together you watched the bag above her fill with your blood. It had been a long time since you had seen so much of it.

AFTER PONY WAS BORN—holding her, nursing her, changing her, bathing her, soothing her; even when she was not in your arms, you moved as though she was, rocking your phantom daughter—your right arm grew stronger, and your left breast grew fuller. You would fall asleep on the carpet. In a chair. Standing up. You would say to The Heavy, "Motherhood is an inhabitation. My handwriting has changed. Look."

I MET THE HEAVY only after the fire—I was born the moment he was disfigured, in the backseat of a locked truck—so I do not know his features the way I know yours, Billie Jean, but my mother did tell me that beneath the scarring lay the face of an undaunted man.

Soon after you married The Heavy, the women came to the Last House. You had been living there since your arrival in the territory, eighteen months before. In town, you had had run-ins with the women, pleasant enough, but you could see they were still uncertain about you. Your hair was to your tailbone. Your consonants were their consonants. You kept your spine so straight it was as if you had never had to crawl or fight or beg or steal or kill. But, no matter how you answered their questions with their diction, you still gave off the feeling of elsewhere.

The women sat on the padded leatherette chairs in our kitchen. The chairs were beige and brown with a rose pattern sewn onto the backs. We had bought them together at Furniture City. I tried to direct you toward more sophisticated options, but you wanted to fit in, go unnoticed. You knew you were being talked about, and you hated being talked about. You knew that it took a person 170 milliseconds to identify whether another person was in their group. You knew that when ants gathered, they did two things: first, they formed a colony, and then they made a graveyard. You invited the women over for coffee. You would defuse them, be accepted into their group, be absorbed into their colony.

The women took in all of the details of the bungalow. The objects, the arrangements. The mantel, the curtains. The television placement. How the surfaces shone. Beige and brass and black trim. The new couch. Did you make that pillow? Billie Jean Fontaine could needlepoint. Impressive. And that blanket? Billie Jean Fontaine could weave. What else could Billie Jean Fontaine do? (Answer: crochet a badminton net, the women would discover the night of your party nearly eleven years later.) In the kitchen, the shelves were full. The jars faced the same way. In the living room, the carpet was covered in lines made by a vacuum. All around the women was order. It made them feel companionable. Yours was homesteading they could relate to. The women unzipped their coats, loosened their ponytails, and watched closely as you served coffee and, in spite of daylight, slipped alcohol into their mugs. This made the women clap for you. You lifted your eyebrows just so and winked. "Oooooo," the women said. "She's a naughty one."

I want to be one of many. I don't want to be one of many.

I watched you; just behind your eyes were your thoughts. In the woods to the southwest of the Last House, where the sinkholes would form, I had seen the skull of a wolf. This was how I saw yours. Thoughts do not live behind bone. They live inside bone, and bone is fragile. You were always talking yourself into and out of things.

The women were used to tasks. Clearing brush, cleaning headstones, taking blood. Done. By comparison, getting to know you felt slow. They accelerated the process by experimenting with closeness. They told you, the new bride, things about themselves. Secret things. A woman makes herself vulnerable only so another woman will make herself more vulnerable. In hushed tones, the women talked about their husbands, their bodies, and what they liked done to their bodies. The women's heads got closer and closer together around the kitchen table. There were no cards on it, but there could have been. You charted the dynamics of the game, who had the worst hand, the best poker face. The women refilled their mugs and marveled at The Heavy's physical footage. They hoped you would take the bait. You didn't. They compromised their privacy, and trusted you would do the same. It didn't work. You talked, but Debra Marie, Rita Star, Pamela Jo, Cheryl Chantale, and Lana Barbara Sr., her brand-new baby in her arms, heard only omissions. What were you, anyway? The shape of your eyes, the pigment in your skin, that feeling you gave off. The feeling of elsewhere. Did the territory have resources enough to welcome you, a stranger? You would have to prove yourself to them. Prove your worth.

A bit drunk, the women started to warm up to you. They

angled themselves toward you and made offers of intricate hair designs. Hair fashions. Unlimited hair fashions. The women believed that to hold the head of another woman was to know her; to feel the hair of another woman was to read her. They put their hands on your scalp. I was sitting with my dancer posture at your feet—in their new sport socks and house sandals—when the women looked down at me.

"Just because she doesn't bark doesn't mean she won't kill you," they said, and they laughed.

"Kill you fast!"

"Oh God, she's showing her teeth!"

"Will you look at that?"

"Just like her mother!"

And you stroked my head to calm me.

The women took turns. They ironed and twisted your hair, pinned and sprayed your hair, all the while, listening. You told them the plot of the book you had read in the tree. The women loved drama. Your story was better than their night soaps. You concluded it "My parents died in a car crash when I was sixteen," and some of the women gasped. "It was the only trip they had taken without me. My mother kissed me and said, 'We'll be back in a few days,'" you lied. "I would never see them again. I had no other family. I drove north to kill off my grief. If such a thing is even possible." That last part, you flinched, was true.

In the tree, you had read the book so many times you knew you could rely on your consistency. You could recite whole passages from memory. Surely, the women would test you. You needed to satisfy their notion of elsewhere, while stirring up their sympathy. You needed to be exotic, but not too exotic. You needed to secure your place in the territory. More than anything, you could not be found, and returned to the life you had fled.

For the first time, you had more than yourself to protect. You were pregnant with The Heavy's child. You were three months along. You did not want to tell him until you knew the pregnancy would last; he would not survive another loss. You knew she would be a girl. Your daughter would be born in the summer. Summer was a beautiful time here. You would tell The Heavy your news when the women were gone, when he entered the bedroom, emptied his pockets onto the night-stand, and let his jeans fall to the floor. You pictured his reaction. You would stay up all night together. He would tell you his nickname for his sister. You would give it to your daughter. You felt your eyes prick with the thought. The women misread you; they rubbed your back, made soothing sounds. "What was your mother's name?" they asked, wanting more from the book. And when you told the women the name of the mother, your book mother, they said, "Of course," to the seamless story, "of course." You felt the story of the book, the tragedy of an orphan, would be a passport to the territory. You were right. The women put the ends of their sleeves to their eyes. Alcohol functioned like dreams; it rendered them defenseless. The women set about making you one of their own.

You knew the lie was safe; no one in the territory would have read or heard of the famous book. Their tabloid maga-zines were expired. John the Leader had the antennae in-stalled in such a way that the few programs they got on their televisions were outdated. He had warned his followers that if anything happened to him, time would slow to a stop. When you disappeared that late October evening, the people of the territory thought the year was 1985. They hadn't caught up with the rest of the world—and how could they be expected to? Their points of reference were old, and they just kept circulating like stale air.

The truth, you told me, was that your parents simply began leaving when you were fifteen. This was not a shift that was declared. It just happened. They needed to be alone with their agonies and their faults, and besides, you were so capable. Soon, you would be sixteen. What then? You were top of your class. You could cook. You were punctual. You had beautiful manners and distinctive hair that fell thick and straight down your back. Enviable, your mother called it. Enviable hair. You had a job. You were a lifeguard. It amazed you that your parents could speak about you, their daughter, in such general categories. They would list your qualities, list you, and mistake this to be knowing. Look at her grades. Look at her manners. How responsible she is. How competent. Look at her as she pulls children from water and fills them with air.

But you are missing everything, you wanted to tell them. You are missing everything.

They traveled more and more, for longer stretches. When they started to go to Europe for five days, eight days, ten days, leaving the cream-colored car in the driveway and you alone in the large house, you no longer had anyone to impress. With no one there to see your efforts, what was their point? You understood you had developed your talents for your parents, so that they would take notice of you. They would call you in the middle of the night and tell you about their hotel. About their room. Their view. Tell you about the weather, about time.

When our circuit had shortened to be out of the master bed, into the hallway, into Pony's bedroom, and back to the master bed, the house dense with darkness, Pony's sleeping body, but you, keen to solve something, you said, "I guess you're right. When I say my nights are too full, I should ask myself full of what? What are my nights full of exactly?" You told me that night made everything bigger. You could manage your fear during the day, but at night, it became unruly. You could not sleep for fear. You talked to me as a method of survival. "A girl forms herself. How can a mother matter? How can I possibly matter? Maybe it's less about how much time I spend checking Pony's breathing, and more about how much time I spend on fear. Fear is the feeling of being chased. No. Of something approaching. No one tells you when you're growing up that this feeling will go from being exciting to being sinister." You were no longer speaking your mind but ransacking it. "What is going to get her?" You confronted yourself. "What is going to get her?"

You have to try— But you cut me off. "I am trying. I am trying hard, Gena. I am trying so hard. Can't you see how hard I am trying?"

A YEAR AND a half earlier, you got our timing right, and there he was, the boy they called Supernatural on the other side of the empty band of gravel and, upon seeing you, crossing over.

"Hey." A parka and, underneath, a starched white undershirt. The collarbones. The black jeans. His skin was flushed. Yours was too. There were very few pairs of running shoes left in the territory. You both wore the heavily treaded boots. You stood in the road, facing each other, catching your breath. At that point, I was the only one in shape. "Hey," you echoed his greeting. You did not mean to sound so flirtatious.

It was rare to see anyone on that section of the highway—the hunters tended to go east toward the founders' bus and south toward the perimeter, never west because of the sink-holes, and never north because of the reservoir and the people's water phobia—but you were hyperaware, listening for an approach, devising scenarios and excuses in your head should you be caught talking in this remote part of the territory. Though the rule is not written down, you both knew a woman should never be seen alone with a man aside from her husband or father or brother. The boy did not waste his movements. Off the highway, there was an abandoned logging road, mostly grown over. The running was better there, he said. The boy led you to it. I was happy to see he ran alone. He did not bring his dog. His dog was an idiot.

You followed the boy's steps. What am I doing? As if that were the question.

You wore your DAY OFF sweatshirt with a pair of tan panty-hose. You did not have a lot of choice; there was very little in the way of dressing for sport in the territory. You could not wear your indoor or outdoor tracksuits. The women had out-lined their uses very clearly to you. If you had added the belt, the gold eyeshadow, if you had let your hair down, you would be trying too hard. It would appear as if you were meeting someone. As if you were up to something. You had been running for a month, since your conversation with the boy in the back of his father's truck. A few days before we finally encountered him, you keeled forward, put your hands on your knees, and told yourself to stop. Stop this pursuit. Pursuit of what? A boy? An eighteen-year-old boy? What are you doing? "What am I doing?" you asked me in the middle of the highway. "Supes loves to run at dawn, right when the sun comes up," you overheard Debra Marie later that day, in the produce section at Value Smoke and Grocer. You also loved first light.

The boy told you about a diver, a Russian woman who swam out into the ocean, to the places where the water was deepest. One of these places was called the Blue Hole, and there, the Russian woman declared, she would set a record of four hundred feet. No other woman had gone down that deep before, and she would be the first. She would be the deepest swimmer. She would be the deepest woman.

Before she went under, the Russian woman lay motionless on her back and sipped at the air; it was almost imperceptible. She did this so carbon dioxide would not interfere with her dive. You see, she knew when her body gasped, as it would after a minute or so, it was a trick; she could hold her breath for *nine minutes,* just over *nine minutes.* A body floated above a depth of fifty feet. Below that, it became neutral, and at one hundred feet, it grew heavy and began to sink. This was because of our lungs. "I will get to the part about our lungs at the end," the boy said to you; he was in charge.

I found it amusing that he spoke about a woman who could

hold her breath for *nine minutes* when you were both still winded from the run. I found it amusing because I am a bitch.

Above a limestone pit off the shores of Egypt, in the Red Sea (the boy went on) the Russian woman arched her body back and followed a line down through the water. It got colder. It got blacker. Hand over hand, she descended. She did her dive with an iron weight around her neck. She did not wear goggles. Never wore goggles. Always wanted to feel the water against her face, and described the water as thick above and below her body. She barely used her feet to kick. So calm, she appeared almost unfeeling. Here is the part about the lungs. As the Russian woman descended, her lungs halved them-selves, and by the time she reached her lowest point, they halved themselves again. They were the size of—here, the boy looked around—this pinecone or, like, this rock. "The body," the boy said, "the body can do remarkable things."

I don't know that a young man can love the way you love, Billie Jean, I cautioned. Young love may disappoint you. Young love may leave you stranded. Young love is about con-sumption more than anything else. You know only adult love.

"Do I?"

You were fifteen with a thick envelope of money and a long car, you told me. I'm like a gangster, you told yourself. No one there to hear you. On the envelope, your father had written your name in his careful, formal letters. When you know and love someone, your hand relaxes as you write their name. It does not tense. Your father called you twice, and then as the days went on, once a week. Sometimes your mother got on the call and asked the questions a doctor would. About your meals, your sleep, your overall health. Then to say only they were extending their stay. Your father's work demanded it.

Your parents told you the new date they would be home. You circled it on the calendar. You would be sixteen by then. Had they forgotten? Looking out at the car parked in the driveway. They had never taught you how to drive. Thinking of all the things your parents had never taught you, all the things you had had to teach yourself, possessed you. You would learn how to drive. You would practice at night. There was a mall down the street from your house, and at night, the parking lot was empty. Under the dim streetlamps, you would execute your maneuvers. You would do this for hours at a time. You saw driving as a discipline composed of parts, and you would master the parts. The immediate challenge was to get the long, cream-colored car out of the driveway without hitting another car. Done on the first try. You grew cocky.

We started to run every day. Along the empty band of gravel and then off the highway and onto the abandoned logging road, the tracks of which you could barely see. With the boy, we ran in the woods. One morning, the boy stopped you. It was the first time he touched you. He took you by the shoulders. "Lyrics are completely different when they are spoken aloud." And then, "Sweet dreams are made of this."

Other than eardrums bursting and lungs squeezing, what happened most was the diver blacked out. This could occur at the bottom of her dive—the point at which a person is most alone in the world, and will remain so, her contracted lungs, her falling body pulled by the currents—or, more commonly, a few feet from the surface where spectators lay flat on a barge.

The spectators wore goggles and put their faces in the water, lifting them periodically to take a breath, waiting to make out her shape, wondering how the diver could possibly reappear.

"Life is to appear and then to disappear," you said just before we got the lock for the door. You lay down on the bed, Pony secretly under it, recording you and then rewinding the tape. Pony did not want to think about that statement. It brought Lana Barbara Sr. to her mind. Doing the dinner dishes. Watching her show. Dressing for her suicide. Appearing and then disappearing. Lana Barbara Jr. in her bedroom. Lana Barbara Jr.'s father out at Drink-Mart. Lana Barbara Jr. wanting to fall asleep, but not hearing her mother in the house. Feeling scared. Ashamed by that. Calling angrily for her mother. Stalking around the house. Opening the lid to the tanning bed. The sweep of blue light. Why did they shape them like coffins? And then an overwhelming feeling, a voltage through her body, and getting her feet inside her boots, pushing through the snow to the toolshed, where her mother was sitting on the ground, leaning against the wall, only a few minutes dead. "She looked so good," Lana told Pony. "Here's the thing: She looked so good. So relieved. It was like, I don't know" (Lana had the nervous habit of laughing when she cried) "like I got to see her true face for a second."

Just before you die, memories that have thinned and vanished over time come back to you. They shimmer, and then whole reels of activity play across your mind. The deep diver talked about blacking out in this way. She said it was not unpleasant. When she blacked out, she saw women holding out loaves of bread. The ends of their pant legs were wet. There was a river. Children running its shore. And in the woods, men dragging trees behind them to plane into skis. When she blacked out, the diver retrieved the lost parts of her childhood. She was given new information.

Your open mouth went up against the boy's open mouth. It was not even kissing. You could not take off your clothes; by then, it was early fall and too cold to expose your skin. For weeks, it was about how your faces met. And then it was your tongues, and then it was holding each other. Everyone thinks they have to do something with their hands. To use their hands in an exploratory way. To communicate ambition. For your body, I have ambitious feelings. My hands may be here, but soon they will be in an even more windfall position. You and the boy did the opposite. All you wanted was the weight and firmness of his hands. His hands to hold you in place.

"Does your dog always stare like that?" the boy asked.

Looking down at me, standing guard, you said, "She knows things."

All I know is loyalty.

Whenever we lay together on the couch in the living room to watch a late-night movie, the stars of the movie would talk for most of the movie before they got to each other's bodies. They walked. They fought. They ate dinner. They rode on elevators. They sat on benches. And throughout it all, they talked. When it finally happened, the sex was boring. The talking had ruined the sex. We agreed we would have to find other movies. Movies where the talking was significant only as it related to the sex. Watching you with the boy, I felt you had the correct sequence. First, bodies. Then, talking.

"Am I good or am I bad?" you would ask me.

Both. I tried to calm you. Make you feel part of something larger. Humans think they are alone with their actions. If only they would look outward.

"How can I be doing this, doing what I am doing?" The question an animal would never ask.

You did it with your hands. You were used to your parents returning home from Europe in the middle of the night. That was when those international flights landed. "Strange hours," your mother would say, commenting on the travel, summing up her life. It was the night of your sixteenth birthday. You thought your parents had come home early to surprise you. You pictured a candle, some kind of jewelry box. Your father at the piano, your parents singing "Happy Birthday." Such a sad song, your father would say, the saddest song. All of you breaking into laughter. Not bothering with the lights. Pouring you a small glass of sweet wine. Toasting their girl. That's what they called you. Their girl. "How's our girl?" they would ask. When you heard the noise downstairs and went toward it, you did not think to prepare your body for one long fight.

In the tree, you had read about the hunter who killed deer in water using a rope. You had read it a thousand times. The hunter hid his boat in the reeds, and when the deer crossed the narrow channel, he lassoed the animal and pulled it to his boat, wound the slack around the deer's neck, and drowned the deer before hauling it to shore. You did not have a rope within reach, but you thought about the hunter as you sat on the intruder's chest and worked persistently with your hands. That grip. Breathtaking.

You didn't hear any glass shatter. You must have forgotten to lock the back door when you got home from your shift at the pool. You heard the heavy door close. That was the sound that tugged you from sleep. Like a pressure change. You could smell the chlorine on your skin, in the tangle of your hair. You hadn't bothered showering. You tiptoed along the hallway, down the carpeted stairwell, hand gliding against the rail, your eyes adjusting to the pitch dark. All that was familiar to you coming sluggishly into focus. In the kitchen, a far off streetlamp made a ghost light. He stood between the table and the counter, his arms at his sides. Where was your father's suitcase? Where was your mother? He took a step toward you. Then he said your name. Not your father's voice. Not your father.

"When you are a small woman, it takes a long time to strangle a large man," you confided in me first, before confiding in the boy, and then, overwhelmed by the admission, lost your sense of order. "A python is a marvel. How far can I go? The first explorers asked this question and it strikes me as the right one. How far can I go? You do not know yourself until you have had to resort to violence. Violence resets proportions. The assumption is size conquers. Wrong. The one who conquers is the one who can outlast—"

You have always been interested in the limits of your endurance, I interrupted you, trying to lead you back to yourself.

The deep diver used a samurai technique to keep her body calm. If her breath became panicked, she would waste oxygen and not complete her dive; she would either hit an unsatisfactory depth or find, when at her heaviest, she was unable to propel her body back to the surface. Remember, below a hundred feet, a body does not swim. It falls. Remember, the diver had an iron weight around her neck. The technique was about seeing. The use of the eyes. Whereas the eye wants to zero in on a single point, the diver taught it to override the instinct to fixate, and instead take in all of the activity that lay at the borders of sight, all of the small things the eye would normally ignore. This would steady the breath.

The sex was not about what you could give to each other. It was about what you could withhold. Where you would wait to go. The sex was about absence. It was the only time I had seen a species have sex properly.

The boy talked to you about blood. Blood traveled hundreds of thousands of miles. It was the only part of your body that got to circulate through every inch of you. Participate in everything. Your blood carried all of your information. "Blood, come, plasma. The fluids. Sex is the only way I can make my interiors exterior for you," he said factually.

"Do all of the young men know how to have sex the way you do?"

"No," the boy said, still sticking to the facts.

"I may love your body more than I love you."

"That will change," the boy said.

" 'The snow carried her body three thousand feet. By the time they reached her, heart massage was unsuccessful,' " the boy read to you. He did not want to answer questions about himself. He said everyone in the territory was always asking him questions and you, like running, gave him a break from questions. You said, "It's not your answers that interest me as much as it's the sound of your voice. See, I do love your body more than I love you." And the boy responded, "'When Doves Cry.' 'Hurts So Good.'" Fucking him with your coat on, you encouraged him to read his cassette tapes, his truck manual, clippings from magazines, anything within reach. "'If you want something more challenging, do the workout twice.' Side Two. 'Hot for Teacher,' 'I'll Wait,' 'Girl Gone Bad,' 'House of Pain.'" When he ran out of materials, he pulled your coat off you and read the content label. Your coat ceased to be a coat. As it hung on your hook by the front door, you could no longer perceive it as a coat. And when you placed your body inside it and closed its form around you, you felt the boy had taken a match to you.

"You have taken a match to me."

"Night moves," the boy spoke a lyric.

It would be dangerous to ignore each other in town. You agreed the best way was to be like the diver's body between a depth of fifty and one hundred feet. Neutral. When your eyes wanted to see only each other, you had to train them to examine the periphery. You started to visit the truck lot.

Gold eyeshadow, belt, hair down.

You brought Pony with you; it was her presence that neutralized the presence of the boy. But, the frequency of your visits was unusual. In their habit of measuring, the people of the territory started to whisper about you and Traps. In their minds, they drew straight lines between themselves and the animals, themselves and other people. When they had sex, they saw lines appear between their bodies. Between you and Traps, they saw a new line forming.

Of course. Nothing lasted for The Heavy, thought the people. He was not a man rewarded by permanence. And to throw him to the same fate as his father. For his wife to slight him with his best friend. His only friend, the women on Rita Star's leatherette chairs would correct each other, picturing lines, and how now, no lines led to The Heavy.

Your runs got longer and longer, and, not one to give in to suspicions, The Heavy marveled at your body. It was starved when you arrived in the territory. Now, it was the body of an athlete. After he carried you to the Last House, we watched as you moved with deliberate steps from the bathtub to the clean sheets of the bed. On your skin, we saw all of the marks that told us there had been one long fight.

"You don't seem to worry about things," you said to the boy. "To carry them with you."

"I don't."

"You don't seem haunted."

"I'm not."

"I know only haunted people. I married a haunted man."

"I'm young."

About this, I do not need reminding, you thought, looking at the boy who, when he first kissed you, was just eighteen. Four years older than your daughter. What of your daughter? Where have you been? You defended yourself, "You can be young and be haunted."

"I would rather just be young," said the boy, nearly twenty now.

"I love my daughter."

"I see that."

"I live for my daughter."

"I'd be careful with that."

"She thinks I was a waitress. All she knows about me is that I was a waitress, and I was never a waitress." You tried for statements rather than questions, but the boy was onto you, and remained closed. You turned to provocation. "I love two men at once."

"That's superconfusing."

"I am betraying people. You are betraying no one."

"I have no experience with betrayal." The boy was growing terse, you felt. Usually he pulled the pine needles from your hair. He stated, "I don't know how to lie. I am not a liar. I never could lie."

You would go to the truck lot less. Make him miss you.

But, you had no will. "Love cancels you out," you said, lying naked with your coat open in the clearing. The boy had left you there. You were careful to exit the woods separately. When you were away from him, you were mobbed by the chatter of your thoughts. "And it is such a relief."

I know, I said, looking over at you, not blinking. I too live a passionate life. Ask any of the other dogs. But you took no notice. You started to laugh. In your body, you felt only freedom. "The clearing." I felt my ears go back. "Of course, the clearing. We have *really* underexamined that term."

" 'Machine wash cold separately. Delicate cycle. Do not bleach. Do not iron. Line dry in shade. Do not dry clean. Do not twist or wring.' "

The coat that was no longer a coat. The shoes that were no longer shoes. The wallet that was no longer a wallet. To love was to black out. You found yourself floating away from Pony. The boy was only four years older than her. The Heavy would kill himself. He would get his hunting knife, go into the woods, make himself difficult to find, impossible to stop. He would spare you. Only to make you live with what you had done.

You told me you could not remember the name your parents had called you, the name your father had written on the envelope. As you drove north, you emptied your mind of facts. The very first things you learned: your name, the names of your parents, your street address, your home phone number, the name of your school, your grandparents, your neighbors, your cousins, your father's occupation. You wiped them out the way a disease would. You made bright spots on your brain where before there had been none. Height, weight, hair color—the physical description and photographs that would follow you—you would also change, even if it meant adding injuries to your already injured body. Hearing your name on the radio, you thought, I am a murderer. And I have a five-day head start.

"'Get on the main road, one mile, and make a left. There's a small road, unmarked. If lost, look for the blue flagging tape. Follow the flagging tape to its end. Then veer right. When you get out, have your rifle ready. There's a grizzly loose. We call her Killer, and she will kill you,'" the boy read to you. You didn't want him to know you were searching him with your body. You went on. He went on. "'When frostbite sets in, do as the Northern people do and wrap the undressed body around that of the sufferer. May it be my will that my mercy overcome my anger. From the ice floe, the man yelled down to the swimmer, Everything I know tells me this is impossible. All you need is love, love. Love is all you need.'"

"Oh God! Oh my God! Yes!" Love is all you need to make you weak and say embarrassing things, you told me, not the boy, who was pulling on his black jeans—hastily?—you asked me for my opinion.

The more the boy touched you, the more you felt skinned down to your past. It was frightening. You could not seem to get away from it. Could not seem to be this name, this new name that was supposed to make for a new woman.

Nina? Was that what your parents called you? Only sixteen, and already a murderer.

About the dead man, you had choices. You could dispose of the body in any number of ways you considered doable. His dead weight would be much easier to contend with than his fighting weight had been. You had time. About the disposal of the body, you did not need to rush. He was dead. Right? You put your arms out in front of you. Tried to get a breath. Heard a wheezing sound. Could not get your throat to open. Over the two days the man was in your house, you tried to get to the phone to call the police. Several times. You could not move to call them now. You tried to scream over the two days, but could not scream now. Could not get a sound to come from your body. Could not get a sound that would override all the other sounds. The fridge, the power lines, the traffic. The effort of everything. You spat out a tooth. And with that, you got a breath. You looked down at the man. You pushed against his body with your foot and then took a step back before he could get your ankle. Dead. Right? You pictured unloading him from your father's trunk and into the fast-moving river nearby. You would do this alone. Help was past. You had always helped yourself, and this thought sent a charge through you. With it, you tried to lift the man, but could not budge him. How did I ever strangle him? The man looked familiar. Was the man familiar? No. He kept calling you by your name. How did he know your name? The pool? Did he come to the pool? Did you know the man? Did you? Identification, get the identification. Hands in the man's pockets. Dead. Right? Not going to grab your wrists. Your hair. Nice pockets, good cloth. Like your pockets. Nothing. No identification. Nothing with a name, an address, nothing to tell you who he is. Was. No one was waiting for him, this is what you told yourself. No one was waiting for you, this you knew. How different were you, really, from the man you had just killed? Had you done everything you could? Could you have convinced him to let you live? No. If you had not killed the man, he would have killed you, and instead of his body on the floor, it would be yours. When the sun went down, you tried once more to move him. It was impossible. Killing was something that was not *in* you but *went through* you; there, that was the difference between you and the man.

Quickly, you looked away from the body. Your nightgown. Tables overturned, chairs on their sides, curtains torn, rooms that you'd grown up in, but never wanted to walk into again.

"An owl can take a deer," the boy said. "To look at their size, you would think it would be the opposite." And the boy, without paying much attention to the length of his strides and the length of yours, took you to a clearing in the woods, one you had never been to before. There, he sat you down and put a blindfold over your eyes. It was then you knew you would do anything for the boy. If he asked you to, you would leave your daughter for him. Your body shuddered with the ugly admission. Ugliest. Unthinkable woman, unthinkable mother. Take that back. Cannot even keep your wallet straight from your shoes straight from your coat straight from your daughter. You would never leave your daughter. Love had disoriented you. Reorient yourself, and if anything, leave love. How?

"Raise your hand when you hear the owl." The boy gave you plain instructions, and when next you thought you'd feel his body on yours, you heard his footfalls grow distant. You sat there as you had been told. I will hear the owl; I will match the boy; I will win and the only eyes that matter to me will see it.

Many times, you wanted to raise your hand in the clearing, but you could never be sure the sound you heard was the owl. You didn't want to be wrong. To embarrass yourself further. This boy so contained and you so uncontained. You did not even know how he held his fork, what position he slept in. You did not know anything about him other than the order in which he dressed himself, that he liked running, and he disliked questions.

You did not raise your hand once.

Eventually, it grew so quiet you wanted to shout to be sure he was still there, but resisted—that would be giving in.

You knew you could pull the blindfold from your face at any time, so you sat on your hands to keep them from doing so.

When night came and it was clear the boy had played a trick on you, and whatever had happened between you was over, you raged—this was his way of telling you he no longer loved you (if, in fact, he had ever loved you)—and still you sat there as you had been told. They will find me dead. Here, they will find my body. My old body that could not hear the owl. Hearing only yourself, the sudden pitch to your breath, your breath shortening, you saw what your life had become. A woman stranded alone in the woods, left by a boy who had humiliated her into thinking she was loved by him; she was so outmatched. A boy can take a woman.

"Owls are soundless," he said as he lifted the blindfold from your eyes. You saw it was still light out. He had been steps away, watching nothing but you. The boy told you the owl had flown inches from your head a dozen times. He kept waiting to see if you might hear it. He wanted to give you the chance. He thought if anyone would be able to hear it, it would be you.

"I'm pregnant," you told him in response. You felt loved. The feeling broke you and you confessed, "And I killed a man. It happened in another world and another time. When I was sixteen."

You TOLD ME you left the strangled man's body where it was, knowing in five days, your parents would come home to it. When they did, your mother and father searched the battered rooms for you, tearing them further apart, fearing they would find you dead too. Finally, screams came from the large house. Standing over the body, the police tried to make sense of things. There could have been a second man who killed the first man, stole the car, and kidnapped the girl. Though they could find only two sets of fingerprints throughout the house, this seemed most likely, given the girl was just over a hundred pounds. No way she could have done this to the man. I mean, look at him.

Seeing your picture on the news. Standing poolside. Your braces had just come off. You could run your tongue over your teeth. It wasn't a good picture. Recalling it now, you were relieved the boy would never see it. Who you were in that moment. Who you had constructed yourself to be since. It was your first day of lifeguarding. Whoever had taken the photo made you feel unsure about it. It was your father, you remembered. He had insisted on driving you to the pool, and, unused to his attentions, you didn't know what to do with them. When he said smile, you forgot how to move your mouth.

"Wait, how long were you in Europe?" The police questioned your parents while they worked on identifying the dead man, establishing the time of death and the location of the car. They were sure if they found the car, they would find you.

The police asked the public for help. A sixteen-year-old girl has gone missing, they said on the news, and then spoke your name. When you heard it, you knew you had already separated yourself from your original name. How easy it had been to do. Appearing then disappearing. Driving north, you tried out a different name with every encounter. Scissors furious through your hair, cut so short, when you stole a suitcase from the back of a car at a rest stop, a man hundreds of miles later thought you were a choirboy going to a wedding in your white three-piece suit. All your thoughts were survivalist. What to eat, where to sleep, how to get water and gas. You had to be inventive. Sometimes you found leaks from the valves of the gas pipelines along the way. Sometimes you were forced to make a bodily trade.

As a lifeguard, you had had to save someone only once, and despite your instinct to rush to the drowning boy, you did as you were trained. While he took in more and more water, you did not go anywhere near him. You pushed a flotation device at him and kept your legs straight out in front of you should you have to kick the boy away. Your eyes fixed on each other, you asked him factual questions. Get the name. Your instructor had told you it was critical to get the name, get the name of the drowning person, and use it like hell. "What is your name?" you kept asking the boy, and when he hurled it at you, you used it like hell.

It was the boy's father who had attacked you. You made the connection when you were painting the Mercedes sedan in the empty parking lot of the mall. You remembered him from the pool. The other lifeguard made teasing comments about him: he was always staring at you; he was obsessed with you; he didn't come to the pool to watch his son; he came to watch you—in your bathing suit with your whistle looped around your neck. He just wanted to get you alone in a room. Be saved by you, the other lifeguard taunted. You shrugged it off. You took no notice of the boy's father. To your eye, he was old. He was a different species altogether.

You had not chosen the territory as a destination. Had never heard of the territory. What guided you was a graph in your head: physical space versus physical bodies. You wanted the axis where the lowest number of human bodies occupied the highest square mileage of open space.

As you drove north, you refused to mark time the way you had before. Instead, you watched the weather. You could see a storm approaching long before any warning on the radio. With your windows rolled down, you measured the temperature, the wind, the snowfall. The ice formed on the roads and then the snow made them impossible to pass and then the rains came and, with them, higher speeds. You covered so much ground in the spring that by the time you fell from the driver's seat, wearing only the black lace underwear and the knee-length white suit jacket, onto the territory, you could barely walk. With your gas tank nearing empty, you made out the shape of a low building and a man walking toward it. A body. Space. Vast amounts of space around the body. Your axis. You had found your axis.

After being in a single, seated position for such a long time, you had stopped using many of your muscles. You spent that first summer in the territory being reintroduced to them. While the women talked about the mud on the ground, and the men constructed boardwalks between the bungalows, The Heavy devised exercises for you and, with you in the Last House, felt fulfilled by nursing. Felt fulfilled by you.

THE BOY CALLED IT forensic when you gave him the gift of a thick strand of your hair, and the secret name you had always wanted for yourself on the envelope. Loosely handwritten.

The question of faces. "I will never be able to convince

The Heavy that the baby is his." Everyone in town remarked upon your skin. And your hair. What had been a fit body took on a formlessness, but this was the pattern for wives and husbands. The women had wondered when it would be your turn to stop wearing a belt. You wore your winter coat long after the thaw, but while the people scrutinized you, no one thought it was odd. You were from elsewhere. When they were hot, you were cold.

In the bedroom, you threw up a fencing around your body. You came to admire The Heavy for a new quality; he was, at that point, an unsuspecting man.

When the pain came on, you went to the clearing in the woods as you and the boy had planned. It was daytime, which concerned you. Not what you had pictured. You had pictured nighttime, nighttime, which is trackless. You could not take the truck. You would have to walk. "Taking the dog for a run," you spoke hurriedly to the man and the girl who watched you pull on your coat. A face that was pale. Why a coat when it was spring, so fleetingly spring? But they did not read into your actions; time will do that to relationships. We walked the band of empty gravel, but we had to do this very slowly or it would have happened there. This was fast, you told me. Faster than Pony had been. I know the pain. I know the pain the way I know an enemy. You worried you would not get to the clearing. We paused when we had to. You took deep breaths and urged your body forward. You trained your eyes to examine the perimeters. You could not make any noise; close by, an entire town was awake. We stepped onto the abandoned logging road, and you fell to your knees and crawled toward the clearing. I stayed right by your side. The forest was at its most perfect. Dense with life multiplying all through it. Undisturbed by men. You pushed your face into the ground to scream. The boy intercepted us and he carried you the rest of the way; in his arms, you thought, he is ready. But then you looked up at him and could see he was frightened. This boy who had been steady and had fascinated you appeared scared, gangly—had his complexion always been so flushed, so uneven?—and his child was descending rapidly through your body. Your eyes went back to the perimeters. The boy said things to you, sympathetic things, but you thought, What is sympathy? Is sympathy even feeling? The boy reaching for you, and you, suddenly unreachable. And cold. You felt only cold toward the boy. You understood now he thought birth would be romantic. Birth is fast and bloody, you wanted to tell him, but could not. Of all things, birth is most like slaughter.

"Hand me something I can break," you hissed at the boy.

"A woman's body knows just what to do," said Debra Marie in a conciliatory tone, when she stepped from the woods into the clearing and stood with the boy over your body. She got down on her knees and placed a damp cloth on your back. "Get the fuck away from me," you may have said to Debra Marie, her workdress stuffed with owl feathers and foam. Her pregnancy keeping time with yours. You too had listened to the girls on the CB. You too would have the baby. Hand over the baby.

Part Three

———

BOY

7:00 P.M. October 24, 1985. Thursday. Billie Jean Fontaine runs out the front door of her bungalow with her truck keys and a cigarette. (Unjust. Not the plan. Searing pain.) Truck departs. Truck has not been recovered. Color: matte black. License plate: FONTN.

Dog follows Billie out. Dog returns the next night. Exactly twenty-four hours later. 7:00 P.M. October 25, 1985. Friday. (I was in the woods behind the house with a decent view of Pony Darlene in a red ski jacket, tan dance tights, and yellow hunting glasses holding my father's rifle between her shoulder and jawbone, the way you would a telephone receiver. And behind her, the women of the territory carrying out a full-scale extermination, then incinerating all that remained of the Fontaines' life. Okay. Pony's hoardings.)

The dog's return tells me the truck cannot be that far away. Adjacently, Billie cannot be that far away. Say it again. Billie cannot be that far away. Billie cannot be that far away. Reason to live. Last reason to live. Only reason to live. Still. Reason to live. The dog's snout is drenched in blood. The dog is known to be gory, oversexed, and a recluse. The dog is known to be of violent extraction. The people cannot decipher whether the blood is human or animal, and, though of a spectacular intelligence, the dog will not say a fucking thing.

7:00 A.M. October 26, 1985. Saturday. The present. The second morning Billie Jean Fontaine has been missing. Yes, that is the word the territorials are using now. *Missing.* When she left, she was dressed in nothing but a tracksuit. Grave concern. Temperature below freezing. Sky the color of steel. Snowstorm possible. Word is circulating The Heavy kept spare outerwear, workboots, and fuel in the cab of his truck. Three to five jerry cans. He cannot recall the exact amount. It's five. He also has an aluminum supply box bolted to the truck bed. It is single-locked, and contains a rifle, spare ammunition, a set of flares, a bottle of lighter fluid, a pack of matches, and a wineskin filled with water. The Heavy installed this after his last truck was totaled, and he began to think in emergency scenarios.

I heard the squeal of the tires that July evening as Billie cranked the wheel then sped into the stand of trees that obscured the clearing. Our clearing. The crash was loud as gunfire. On the truck lot, the men looked to the sky to see what might fall from it. Even from a mile away, I knew the crash was Billie's doing. My father ordered me into the passenger seat of the Fully Loaded tow truck to bring what was left of the Fontaine vehicle back to the lot for scrap. A few days later, he gave The Heavy the most minor discount when he came in to buy a new truck, saying there was barely anything salvageable from his old one. The Heavy didn't fight it. My father took his money.

And me, standing beside my father, behind the metal desk because that is where my father likes to have me when deals are being carried out. Desperate for news of Billie's state. Wondering if the crash made her confess to everything. Trying to stay cool, but instead growing parched and attempting to swallow without making a sound, failing at this, and so, overtall and glottal, pulling down my ball cap and adjusting my hood. The Heavy told my father Billie Jean was on the mend. "Just a scrape." He downplayed it. Nothing about a tormenting affair that made you want to drink poison. Nothing about a love child.

The men of the territory converge on the front yard of the Fontaine family bungalow and break into search teams. Team Fur Thumb, Team Hot Dollar, Team Sexeteria, Team Neon Dean. Team Traps. Trapezoid, the Trapper, the Trapline. Go, go, go. Let's do this. Bring it. Between the men: a current of competition. In their heads: advanced sexual positions and future sandwiches.

I am not a team man. I am not a man's man. And when Billie said, "Well, then what kind of man are you?" I lowered my mouth into her body and spent time with the question, distancing her from the question.

Billie + Will
Doubtless as math.

"Supes!" Overenthusiastic for a search operation. Tone it down, Hot Dollar. Approaching me—"Hey, Supernatural"—

the men remind themselves to be somber. Wide-stanced and wood-grained, they look like their chainsaw art. They are not wearing underwear. They are missing small and large body parts. "Supernatural, hey."

"Hey." I keep my hands in my pockets. Waving is for other, friendlier people.

"'Sup, Supes?"

"'Sup."

"You know how hard that is to say?"

"No."

The men are looking at me. Am I wearing pants? Check, check, one, two. I am wearing pants. They turn to me. "Supes is here." And then to each other. "Give Supes a team."

"Yeah, give a team to Supes."

"Team Supernatural."

"Sign me up."

"Team Supes."

"I don't want a team."

"All the way."

"Not all the way."

A founder thing, apparently. A John the Leader thing. "All the way" is a favorite expression of the people. It is written in large letters across the back wall of the Banquet Hall—if you can even call it a wall given the Banquet Hall is a dome, which due to underengineering is badly caving in on itself. When you enter the Banquet Hall to mourn or be drained of your blood, it threatens collapse. In visual effect, this would not be unlike the Upper Big graveyard, where, despite the widows' efforts to make it appear otherwise, bloodless bodies lie under rubble. At final resting, when you stand before the portrait or the black square, propped inside the plastic garden of Fur Thumb's Flowers, under the repositioned medical lights, you are also looking at ALL THE WAY. Now just WAY.

Dead? No way.

WAY.

FIFTEEN THINGS shortly after 7:18 A.M.:

1. The product, when it was introduced five years ago, in 1980, was called Human Blood.
2. It was recently rebranded Teen Blood™.
3. In a campaign led by my father, the product's new slogan became "Younger. Hotter. Faster."
4. The product's guarantee: No blood older than twenty.
5. The soundtrack for the territory-wide infomercial (okay, propaganda) is electronic keys with the recurring refrain "Teen Blood, all the way."
6. A young girl from the territory sang the refrain in the cavernous trailer of the Delivery Man's eighteen-wheeler after having three-minute front-seat sex with him, and still getting pregnant. When the song became extremely popular, the Delivery Man claimed the girl's voice to be his own, and his vocal range bigger than that guy. You know. That guy. The one who sings "More Than a Feeling."
7. Neon Dean wrote the music for the infomercial. He

paid the Delivery Man in drugs for the recording of the girl, who would, they agreed, in any other place, be a total star.

8. The girl was Pallas Jones. Drunk one night at Hot Dollar's Hi-Fi Discount Karaoke, she held the microphone like it was a grenade, said her stage name was Deluxe, then, under a mirror ball, covered Nazareth's "Love Hurts." Neon Dean, at the back corner table dealing pills with his associate, Peter Fox St. John, fell for her in that moment. Hard. Even though it was clear to me Pallas was singing the song to her brusque roommate, Future, who was mouthing the words to me.

9. In 1980, I turned thirteen. I was the first person in the territory to do bloodwork. My father volunteered me and then took pictures of the moment I was led to a cot and injected with an IV needle. He has the pictures paper-clipped to the visor above his steering wheel.

10. I still don't know how to smile.

11. According to my father, who manages the finances of the territory, product sales have boomed since the rebranding.

12. My father recently bought himself a ring for his pinkie with a gemstone in it. Onyx, I guess. When he first slipped it on, he said, "No big thing."

13. The north highway is in major disrepair. There is a territory-wide black mold issue. At Value Smoke and Grocer, a carton of milk is just over ten dollars. If you

can get it. Sometimes, Neon Dean has extra cartons of milk, but he has to charge double given the space the milk takes up in his fridge. The Banquet Hall is still falling down. Our pay for bloodwork has not gone up in five years. It's still $9.50 per pint. Can't buy a carton of milk. No signs of the boom, et cetera.

14. Does my father inject himself with my blood?

15. Not even my darkest question.

I watch The Heavy pace back and forth and back and forth across the same small quadrant on the Fontaine front yard like a tiger in captivity. Freshly showered, camo outerwear, their boots blackening with soot, the men of the territory pen him in. Each of them will have already downed a raw egg, lit a cigarette off his stove top, singed his eyebrows, and brushed his dog. "You don't want to do this, man."

"Trust us."

"Leave it to us."

The Heavy wants to join the search for Billie. Because the FONTN truck was not seen in town or on the north highway exiting town, the current thinking is that Billie has taken one of the hundreds of abandoned logging roads and driven the truck as deep as she could into the woods. To clear her head.

"Let me give you the lay of the land."

"Seriously, man."

"We're serious."

"You stay here," and Team Man Store claps The Heavy's shoulder hard. Wrong motion. The man has lost something, not won something. Did I say this out loud? Possible. Because

The Heavy looks over and catches my eye. And my heart exits my body, though to chase it across his scorched yard (the bonfire made by the women last night was intense) would only prolong this moment.

Unlaced workboots, easily a thirteen. Custom denim. A coat. Pause. That's Billie's coat. Rewind. The Heavy is wearing Billie's winter coat. On him, it is more of a vest. A current passes between me and The Heavy. Ancestral? Celestial? Spectral? Coincidental? I don't know, but I see his eyes are the same as my eyes.

How have I never noticed this before?

What you observe when you have not slept for days. Yes, the green, but also the deep blue sockets, and that look, what is that look? Desperation. No. Fear. Yes, fear. Me too, I want to say to him, I am also sick with fear.

"I CAN BE chronological for you," I said to Billie one morning in the forest.

"What does that even mean? Like obey the laws of time?"

"Yes. That is something I can be for you."

"Thanks a lot," she said, turning away her large, naked body. "About chronology, I do not need reminding."

I am trying to find the things I can be rather than the things I can't, I didn't say to Billie, who was winding shrink wrap around her midsection, making it clear she wanted no help.

7:29 A.M. The Heavy turns his broad back and closes his front door behind him. Billie's coat is splitting along the seams. The Heavy has trimmed his large beard and brushed his thick, shoulder-length brown hair off his face. "An ugly man made uglier," I hear one of the men say. Through the picture window, I can make out the colossus of The Heavy's body as he transits his bare living room. Nothing but a television on a television stand. No table, no chairs, no couch. The mantel is intact, and Billie's framed portrait the only thing on the wall above it. In it, she is wearing the long and tight and silver dress she wore at the party. Rhinestones around her eyes. The Heavy leaves black tread marks on the gold carpet. They look like dance instructions for one. He enters the glassed-in part of the bungalow and, in plain view, crawls into a black recliner. The recliner is hooded. At the base of the hooded recliner is a kick-out footstool. The Heavy kicks it out, lays his rifle on his chest, and pulls the hood down over his face. When an aching man wants to hide, he does not want to have to get up to do so. When an aching man wants to hide, he wants the easiest chair. The Heavy should call the chair the Easiest Chair, but it's not like I will ever tell him this.

"Team Supes!"

"Not Team Supes." I walk down the unfinished driveway and onto the north highway.

The men of the territory love me, and the love is undeserved. Billie loved me, and I waved to her. Dumbly, I waved. Struck down, I waved. When she would arrive in the clearing, my hands would float up like I needed rescuing and go straight for the zipper of her coat. I want to make you something. A boat, a cabin, a flying device, a new genus. I want to name a meteor for you, a storm. A child.

"Do all of the women know how to kiss the way you do?"

"No," Billie said.

I would die 4 U.

Love made me tacky. Love made me abbreviate. Abbreviating is for rushed nonreaders. I was never either of those things. "You move like sea life," Billie told me. U R the only 1, I did not tell her. How you don't have time for the full sentiment because in your head there are too many sentiments. U + me = 2night. And the sentiments are hurtling at you and begging for expression, and so, if you are like me, Supernatural—Super Unnatural—you get fully overwhelmed by the noise in your head and you say nothing. I said nothing to Billie. When it mattered most, I said nothing. Not true. When it mattered most, I did not say enough. True. I love you. I felt those words, but never spoke them. Billie did. Question: Would those words have made a difference? Answer: You know the answer.

I look up to Pony Darlene's window. Where are you, Pony? The black bedsheet Pony used for a curtain, the one with the YO on it—which she told me was actually BEYOND, which was where she intended to go, "Beyond the territory," she told me her plan—has been pulled down and torched like everything else. Now her window stands empty.

Where R U, Pony? I have six topics I would like to introduce to the conversation we swore we would continue (Friday, dawn). Swore.

1. You're right. A numbered list can help a person tortured by the black swarm of his thoughts. No need to name this person. Yeah, totally me.

2. Why didn't we ever talk at the Lending Library? Like,

in a respectful whisper. I saw you there almost every weekend it was open. I don't have a name for that moment when two people who see each other regularly decide to start talking, and it's as if they've been talking all along. Do you?

3. Kinship? Weird. Nice.

4. Nightmare. What about daymare?

5. Undying love. What about dying love?

6. You know how there are striking names for groups of animals? A brood of termites. A cloud of bats. An earth of foxes. A cry of dogs. A band of coyotes. An obstinacy of bison. A sleuth of bears. You know how there are no striking names for groups of people? A mess, a mob, a crowd. We need to rethink this, Pony. We need to rethink this so it's individual. A complaint of Trapses. No. A deception of Trapses. A telepathy of Ponys. No. A secret of Ponys. A confusion of Supernaturals. A solitude of The Heavys. And Billie. What would Billie be?

A heartbreak of Billies.

"I GET YOU," Pony said to me, after she robbed the Delivery Man while I watched within fighting range from the ditch, then unfortunately startled her when she kicked the passenger door closed with her combat boot while still pointing my father's hunting rifle up at the Delivery Man, and I soundlessly put my immense hand on her shoulder, not heeding the words Sharpied across the back of her outerwear, CAN'T TOUCH THIS.

"Sorry."

The Delivery Man peeled off. He drove a refrigerated truck with the words HUMAN BLOOD on its side. He reminded Pony of Bon Jovi yet ailing and poor. He had medical alert bracelets up both arms, which were stolen and covered a mess of tattoos. We agreed the Delivery Man needed at least one new organ. Pony said he wasn't all bad.

"You know how on Free Day," Pony said, "people put stuff out, and they label it AS IS."

"Yeah." I didn't want to say Free Day was garbage day.

"He's as is."

Pony said all she had to do was keep her finger on the trigger of my father's Lee-Enfield. The Delivery Man told her that, to get here, he has to fly into a small town. Doesn't even have a 7-Eleven, he said. A 7-Eleven is a convenience store where you can get gas, cigarettes, magazines, and soft drinks in one go. We're surrounded by water. He said the territory is in the middle of a massive island, but the island is getting smaller. Water levels are rising. He said it used to be a straight shot north, but then everything warmed up. The flight to the small town is seven hours long. Supplies are flown in ahead of him on some kind of cargo plane, then loaded into his truck. He drives to us only because he gets paid a way above average sum of money by the company that buys our blood. And he gets a dental plan. He said the drive takes him two days. The planet is huge. We know only a fraction of it. Might as well be outer space. He said David Bowie is dead. He said he worked danger pay into his contract. Coming to an isolated northern community carries significant risk. He is a slob but he has dreams. He has a really bad pill habit and needs a root canal. He said he has a safety-deposit box with his mother's ashes in it, stacks of cash, and Bruce Springsteen's guitar pick. *Born to Run.* Great fucking album. We'll all be outlived by that album. He said it's not the blood that's valuable but the plasma centrifuged from it. Fast-growing plasma market. It's used for transfusions, but more, he said, it's used in pharmaceutical products. Drugs. Drugs for new diseases. New diseases every day, man. He said plasma is the color gold. He said he is going to retire off our plasma and live in a room in a roadside motel with a hot tub and a hot plate and a great cable package within walking distance to a hamburger joint and a strip club.

I ran alongside Pony as she rode her bicycle home. Her tenspeed. Both of us cutting through the dry cold. Our faces in the wind. "I get you," she said. It was the longest conversation I have ever had. Longer than any conversation I had with Billie. We were always rushed, clandestine, but also, I should have talked more. Told her more.

WHEN MY MOTHER took our baby, there in the clearing in the woods, her motion was swift. She had to get back to our bungalow with the baby hidden in her arms, and when my father came home from the truck lot—"Why didn't you call? Why didn't you come and get me?"—my mother had to lie: "It all just happened so fast." She had to burn the foam and the owl feathers before he arrived. She had to hold the damp cloth to her face and give herself the face of exertion. Do I stay with

Billie or do I go with my mother and the baby? Do I hold the baby? Do I carry the baby for my mother? I don't even have a parka or anything to hide the baby. It's May. My parka is in storage. I didn't think through blankets. I am not a covert thinker. Wait. I have just had an affair for a year and a half. Am I who I think I am? Not the time. Do I walk Billie home? How could I possibly walk Billie home? How could Billie possibly walk home on her own? This part of the plan we never discussed. We got only as far as handing over the baby. We had pictured the whole thing happening in darkness, when the other questions wouldn't be ones we'd have to ask.

"I don't know what to do now," I said to Billie, and, lying on her side, she thought this was hilarious. Billie laughed until her laughter gave way to something else. It was the sound of her breaking. I tried to join in, to undo the breaking, but when she could speak again, Billie pushed against my shaking arms and said, "You too. Get the fuck away from me."

Running home, I passed a man—Visible Thinker? Hot Dollar? The Heavy? It was The Heavy—and he said, "You all right there, Supes? Should I get the nurse?" And he pointed to the blood on my hands and arms, my shirt. In the clearing, I must have held the baby at some point.

I made something up about hunting, which I was unskilled at. Run, Billie, The Heavy is not at home. Run. Pull yourself from the clearing and walk in that single-minded way of yours back to the house, and get into the bathtub. You have done harder things. You have done no harder thing. You can make it before he gets back. Wait, am I being a decoy? I have two strengths, and being a decoy is not one of them. Do I just stand here and prolong this conversation so she can get home? Again, not one of my strengths.

"Was just on my way to see your father."

"Oh. He is at the truck lot."

"On a Sunday?"

"Yes, sir," I said, and I pictured my father, covered in black paint, talking to the air.

"You sure you're all right? You're awfully pale."

"Yes, sir," I said to the man whose wife had just delivered my child.

"What did you kill?"

"Sorry?"

"You said you had been hunting. What did you kill?"

And while I had the word *rabbit* circulating through my mind, I could not get it to exit my mouth, but instead wondered if The Heavy knew Billie had killed a man when she was just sixteen, strangled him with her bare hands, the man was the father of a boy she had saved in a public swimming pool, she had worked there as a lifeguard, and the man had formed a fixation on Billie and had broken into her house, it was the night of her birthday, when her parents were thousands of miles away, always thousands of miles away, and then some fifteen years later, she had fallen for me, that was the word she used for the feeling, *fallen*, and fairly soon after, only a matter of months, was pregnant with our child—was it a girl, was it a boy, in the low beige house behind me, did I have a daughter or a son?—and on the empty road, The Heavy and I stared at each other, one of us covered in blood, one of us not, two men who could not lie.

———

7:39 A.M. The whole territory has come out for the search. Matte black trucks are crowded along the shoulder and parked with forethought so no one is boxed in. Everyone has a personalized license plate. For an additional two hundred dollars, my father will "hook you up." NDEAN. HOTDLR. FURTHB. LADY-GLD. VTHINKR. Some of the trucks have moose antlers rigged to their grilles. Some have horseshoes, bells, strings of lights, fluorescent duct tape shaped into cobras, mountain ranges, naked women. Others have extended their truck beds with wood frames and metal banisters, the hulls of wheelbarrows. One truck has a black tarp over its bed, and the rotating blades from fans drilled into its sides. Shona Lee, her defender's body, her hot-rollered bangs, steps down from this one. Lip gloss, Kodiaks, widow. WISHBN.

"Morning, dear."

"Morning."

"Hard day."

"Yeah," I agree with the woman who, just eight months ago, lost her husband to a self-inflicted rifle shot to his heart. Three shots. The first two did not kill him.

Their son is asleep in the back of her truck. He is not named after his father as is the territory way. His father knew he was coming and still blew a hole through his chest. Shona Lee has not come to accept this. An outrage of Shona Lees. "Hard day," I say to her, as she wakes her boy.

I would like a panic button. I would like to be looking at a mirage. I would like this conversation to be more with God and less with myself. I would like to see Billie again. Even if it

is just one more time. "Like our Fully Loaded, isn't it, Son?"
And my father swings his keen, ropy arm high up around my
shoulder, trying for something, trying for peace. He gazes over
the hulks of the assembled trucks. "That's our work, Son," he
says, and he speaks the slogan of the lot: "Giving motion to
men." I slip from my father's grasp without looking at him.

Did you do something to Billie?

Not even my darkest question.

YESTERDAY, I searched the clearing. I searched the truck lot. I
unlocked the trailer door and pulled the string to turn on the
overhead bulb. Billie was not hiding beneath the metal desk,
not lying on the ground, not throwing a match into the woodstove. All of this I have checked and checked over the last
thirty-six hours. I ran the band of gravel, the abandoned logging road. I went to all the places we used to go. Where Billie
lifted her workdress, and I read to her.

" 'There is no obvious care toward appearance. The teeth
are browning and in some cases, broken' "—I loved her body,
could not get enough of her body—" 'The hair is unbrushed,
and the whites of the eyes jaundiced to indicate a general lack
of health. The skin of the face has taken on years. Given the
slight contraction of the diaphragm, the voice is nearly inau-
dible,' " and I went on because Billie commanded me to with
her hips though it was not totally straightforward to read this
longer text aloud—I had not banked on reading the whole
thing—while having sex with a woman who was extremely, if
exclusively, pregnant.

Okay. And the material was regrettable. I had started with

the previous chapter, which was all about love, and how love changes us. I thought it would serve as a way of articulating my feelings for Billie. I never thought I would get to the next chapter—when the *absence* of love changes us. Okay. Kills us. "'The physical withdrawal of the body is typical of reality contact impairment and severe alienation. Other symptoms include shortness of breath, nausea, and a fixed visual focus.'" I was definitely wishing for a break from the reading part by this point, but did not want to throw Billie off. "'When interviewed, the brokenhearted asked their examiners to provide a reason to live—'"

"Oh God! Oh my God! Yes!" She always said this before her body fell onto mine, and I knew it embarrassed her. It just wasn't even close to how she talked. "I sound like one of those tanned girls in town," she would say and laugh it off. Join in. Especially at this bodily moment, join in, but all I could think of was my father and how he laughed in his sleep. How his laugh was the loneliest sound, the sound of a man in the woods separated from his people.

7:52 A.M. Almost daylight in the territory. I make my way back to the Fontaine front yard and look up at Billie's bedroom window. Don't look up at her window. I can't help myself. She is not there. If you say so. Stop looking. That's superhard. Look at the ground. Looking. Study the ground. Studying. When the men and women try to trick you into saying "Billie" or even "Billie Jean," say "the Fontaine mother." I will. Say it. "The Fontaine mother." Swear. Swearing. On Billie's life. Hold up. There is darkness and then there is maximum darkness. On Billie's life? "Why must you always go for maximum darkness?"

"You are totally talking to yourself, Supes." A girl—Lorraine, I think, or maybe Tristan, no, Rochelle, no, Tiffany, no, Tina, no, Future, yeah, it's Future, I'd be so fucked without the necklaces—pulls me aside, unzips her outerwear, pulls over the strap of her sports bra, and then the thinner strap of her other, inner bra, and then pulls down her tube top to show me a red heart painted in nail polish. In this moment, I hate intimacy and all it asks of you. "Once my tan is perfect," Future says, and she smells of sweat and coconut oil and sugar cereal and closet floor, "I am going to peel the nail polish from my chest and I am going to show my real heart to you, Supes. And you are going to make me your wife. I mean, we're nineteen. Nearly twenty. Last year of bloodwork. It's time, Supes. I'm your future." And she tries to touch me. "Get it?"

Your father is Neon Dean's father, I do not tell Future. Your father is dead. Your mother, Rita Star Roulette, had a one-night stand with Dean Harvey Sr. after the final resting for his younger brother. Rita Star was engaged to marry the younger brother, but he died when he got his leg caught in a bear trap and bled out before anyone could reach him in the blizzard. Killer winter, everyone said. He was stored for five long months in the Death Man's shed. After he was buried, Rita Star and Dean Sr. got drunk. In their final resting clothes, they had wasted-mourner sex behind the Banquet Hall. You were the result. Your mother called you Grace. Easy to read into.

Your mother refused to name your father. When you were old enough, you stormed from your mother's bungalow to live across the street. You shot arrows into the small bodies of grouse from Pallas Jones's bedroom window. You cooked the grouse over an open fire in her yard and then brought the cooked bodies to her bedroom. You ate them on her twin-size bed. You stole her mother's cigarettes, her father's liquor and barbecue sauce. You spread Pallas's blankets on the floor, and pretended they were a lake. In your bra and underwear, you slid across the blankets. You hung fly tape like streamers. You had your birthdays there. At night, you lit sparklers and sprinted around the Joneses' property, making circles with the light before it burned out, spelling your name, the names of the boys you loved, while Pallas wrote *Grace* as fast as she could, over and over.

Rita Star wanted you back. She put up a sign in her picture window,

Rita Star's Tanning Emporium, Fitness and Palmistry

She had no intention of starting a business. She thought those were your interests, and the sign might work as a lure. It didn't. Whenever you saw your mother enter or exit her bungalow, you lifted Pallas Jones's cracked bedroom window and you screamed, "Give me a name! I need a name! Without it, I'm only half-alive!" Your mother left you that way. "Spill it!" She wouldn't. One night, Pallas Jones consoled you. "You have to get free of your past." Taking this comment to its end, you did what no woman in the territory had done before. You renamed yourself. Future. No last name. No family name. No family.

"Oh God! Oh my God!" someone is yelling at me. It's Future. She is zipping up her outerwear. "Are you even listening to me?"

"No."

"Ugh!" Striding away from me, Future has to adjust the plaid blanket she has cut and belted for a kilt. The hem of her kilt is stapled. On the back of her jacket, she has written STAY UGLY.

Dean Harvey Sr. That's who you are looking for, I do not tell Future.

ELEVEN MORE THINGS I do not tell Future shortly after 8:00 A.M.:

1. I will never marry you.
2. Even though your mother has offered my father a share in her thriving business. A majority share.
3. And my father has been pressing me, waking me in the night—"You'll be set for life; she's a pretty girl, a real firecracker"—I will not marry you.
4. I will never marry.
5. I will never love again.
6. Love kills.
7. I am the last Linklater.
8. I would like a sister.
9. More than anything, I would like a sister.

10. A sister I can die with.

11. The last Linklaters. Plural.

8:13 A.M. The search teams step into the north woods. The same woods the Fontaine dog lunged from the night before, her snout bloodied and, for the first time, barking. I watched Pony as she clamped the dog's snout with her hands and barked back, "What happened? Tell me, Gena Rowlands, tell me," and then unclamped the dog's snout, held her hands to her nose, and inhaled the scent of the blood.

As the men enter the forest, the territory women hand them flyers. Pregnant Denise, married to Lana Barbara Smith's father, Visible Thinker (complexion like sandpaper, boring in more than fifteen ways, basically Phil Collins, the defeated owner of Furniture City, where Denise worked as a cashier-in-training without ever making it to cashier), hands one to me. "Too bad," she says through her overbite. Then she looks at my mouth, the gash through my top lip. Before I can stop her, she touches it—"Hot. Superhot"—and then blows on her fingertips. I haven't been touched in three months.

BILLIE JEAN FONTAINE
MISSING

And below, Billie's portrait. The rhinestones, the party dress. The one I watched her pull off her body. She had to do a slight contortion of her hips. She left the dress in a silver pool on the floor of her bedroom. She had her back to me.

From the half-open doorway, I watched her with a boner I can only describe as aerodynamic. Was I breaking physical laws? Could I even blink? Who was this woman? How could I get her to take notice of me? Questions I would ask myself later. She stood in her black lace underwear and low white heels. Her hair hung down to the band of her black lace underwear. She wore stockings with a shimmer in them. They had lines that ran up the backs of her legs. The lines *and* the stockings ended at the tops of her thighs. At the crease. I was thirteen. I would never be the same. I had done my first bloodwork that day. Inside my father's flashbulbs. With a violent hangover. It was 1980.

The night before, The Silentest Man had motioned for me to come into Drink-Mart Infirmary. I thought I would find my father drunk and have to arrange his limp though laughing body across my handlebars and ride him home (not easy). Instead, The Silentest Man put his hands on my shoulders and said the word *supernatural.* The men of the territory drew closer. Their weekends were for hunting. They had their shows. They had their drinks. Their meals were hot, their lunches packed. They had their jokes with the other men, and these were verbal patterns the men knew to repeat with slight variations every time. The ante. The men agreed to up it. They took risks. They knew what it was to be scared, and they sought that out. They wanted the rush. Stalking an animal, a woman's legs spread, the crack of a rifle, a window rolled down, a song played so loud your dog could explode. They understood the headbang. The power of it. How it made you dizzy, and that dizziness had a lifting effect. Speed metal was the savior. It would carry you up. If you moved your neck fast enough, you would lose the horizon. In his rough and hyper sentences, my father talked about these things. Went on talking about these things. He did not notice The Silentest Man's hands on my shoulders. Meaningfully on my shoulders.

My father drank more, grew maudlin, started to throw the word *love* around. Looking at the nugget of gold in the square glass case behind the bar, he talked about the days when the mines were still operative, and the men spent more time underground than above it. The blast every afternoon at four o'clock, and one shift of men would come up, and one would go down. When you surfaced, security would check your pockets, your boots, the hoods of your outerwear, your work gloves, under your tongue. Make sure you weren't going home with any gold. "I have my gold already," my father said. And the men, having heard the story so many times before, shouted in unison, "Already got my gold at home!"

All I could hear when someone approached me was the sound of sirens. All my father could hear was himself. My father was a deep participant. Into all moments, he inserted himself, and was at ease only when dominating. Growing up, I looked for someone to be like. And the only one I could find was The Heavy. When I was a child, he let me run my fingers over his face, the scars from his burns. They were hard. I understood the human body this way: hard parts protected by soft parts. The Heavy was inside out. He did not hunt. Did not make jokes. Had long hair. Used a fork to part it. Did not drink. He was not at Drink-Mart Infirmary. Never came to Drink-Mart Infirmary.

"Supernatural."

"Supernatural."

Even my father got quiet.

"Supernatural," The Silentest Man said one last time, and the men started to bat the word between them, abbreviate the word. Only when they bought me bottles of moonshine, put cigarettes in my mouth and lit them, hit me on the back like I was choking, I might have been choking, did I understand I had been named. "Supernatural." The men wanted to shake my hand. This, I ignored. I kept my hands in my pockets. My immense hands, would they ever stop growing?

"Supernatural."

"Supes, for short."

"Yeah, Supes."

"Supes."

All around me, a great noise erupted. It was my new name, and from the mouths of the men, from the mouth of my father, it came at me like sirens.

Approaching the Fontaine property the next night, the night of the party, my mother and father in the front seat, and me, a dread of Supernaturals, in the truck bed, I could see lights strung across the yard and a net of some kind. Later, I would find out it was a badminton net. My father would spend most of his night on one side of it, winning. From the house came loud music. My mother had made a cake. This was at the time of her primary sadness (I will get to this). The cake was small, and in her anticipatory hands made smaller. Billie in her silver dress with the little silver squares around her eyes immediately led my mother in her stocking feet up the stairs.

Seeing only adults, adults who wanted to talk to me and ask me questions—remember, I had been named the night before, the wrong name, a name that did not fit me, did not *get* me— I pushed my way through the crowd to a room in the basement. There was one bulb on the ceiling, and someone had unscrewed it so the light was strobing. "It's a disco," Peter Fox St. John told me. He stood at the door with his arms crossed, pretending to be a bouncer.

"You eighteen?"

"No."

"You got ID?"

"No."

"Money?" Then he called after me, "Yeah, that's right, Will Jr. Walk away! Just walk away! Like you always do!"

In the next room, the younger kids were wrestling. Pony Darlene was duct-taped into a black skirt and a white button-down with the word SERVER stitched on it. Her hair was high and curved around her head. She watched the boys of the territory throw themselves onto a stack of mattresses. "Heads up!" The boys tore their shirts off, and their vapors filled the room. They found a roll of yellow flagging tape and tied strips around their necks. Called them gold chains. Said they were miners. Lana Barbara Smith flung her arms wide and told everyone she was a psychic. "I can read your mind," she said. "I know who you love. The one you love is the last one you think about at night. When you're falling asleep." In three years, she would be motherless. Her purple blouse with the high collar and the ruffles down the front, and over it a territory-issue corduroy dress. Her hair was auburn and wide as a halo. A group of girls braided their ponytails together. One wore an eye patch. Her brother had recently half-blinded her with a BB gun. She wanted to play Truth or Dare. Pony had no idea where to place herself. Who to talk to. What she would say. A loneliness of Ponys. No. A loner of Ponys. Big difference. I went back to the disco.

Peter Fox St. John patted me down. Confusing, but the beginnings of the boner were then. "For fuck sakes, it's Supernatural," Dean Jr. (soon to be Neon Dean) said from inside the disco, puffing his chest. "Let him in!"

Someone had set up a Walkman with speakers, and music was playing. "Video Killed the Radio Star." I loved that song. The floor of the room was piled high with coats, and the girls were stepping over them, lifting the ends of their dresses up to their hips like they were walking through deep snow. The coats were moving. I watched the girls' thighs, and my boner went from recreational to serious. I wanted my tongue to make contact with the thighs. My face to make contact. I needed to make contact. The light flickered. Sounds were coming from the floor. Effort, I guess. A girl—Lorraine or maybe Rochelle, this was pre-necklace, Future when she still went by Grace?— came toward me wearing one of the men's coats. She stood in front of me and unzipped the loose camouflage coat like the zipper was stuck. When she finally got the zipper down, she pried the coat open as if it too were made of metal and she was bending the metal back. Metal is so difficult. Won't you help me with this difficult metal? Oh, I can do it after all. Beneath the coat she wore white underwear and white sport socks with blue lines around the tops that she had pulled up and over her knees. I took a step toward the underwear. The girl closed the coat. I waited it out. She opened the coat. I got in.

Even when it promises sex, I have a hard time with any group activity. I am not a group man. The way I am not a contact sport man. Or a private club man. And what was happening in the disco was basically a contact sport in a private club. I was first to leave.

"Too good for us, eh?" Peter Fox St. John said.

"Not even close," I said to myself.

I made my way upstairs. "Supernatural." The adults took notice of me, came toward me. Some of them were dancing. My father had a Player's unfiltered hanging from his bottom lip, his arms in the air. The glint of his belt buckle, a rock to his hips. His pressed jeans, his polished boots. He was in the middle of the living room; Rita Star, Cheryl Chantale, and Pamela Jo circled him and pulled the pins from their hair. Turtleneck sweaters. Complex earrings. A sheen to their faces. Eyes roving the room then catching on me. Sharks to a kill. "Supernatural." The women put their glasses to my lips. I had thrown up the night before. I had slept on the tiled floor of our bathroom. My body in a sprawl. Smelling badly of fermentation. My mouth at the base of the toilet bowl. Legs jutting into the hallway. My father stepping over them. I would never drink alcohol again. I would be like The Heavy. I dodged the women and continued up the carpeted stairs to the second floor of the Fontaine bungalow. I had never seen The Heavy's bedroom. I pictured the cell of a monk. Not Billie Jean Fontaine in her black lace underwear and low white heels. Swinging her hair to one side, careful my mother would not see the marks across her neck and back that told me there had once been a fight. One long fight.

2:00 A.M. March 14, 1980. Friday. The night I was named Supernatural. Before the bathroom mirror, my father propped me up by the elbows, then by the armpits. "Easy," he said as he placed his much smaller body behind mine to keep me upright. "Easy." I could feel him shaking as he identified all that was the same in our faces. See, the bridge of the nose. See, the sharpness of the cheekbones. See, that cleft in the chin. My head fell this way and that. The room spun. My eyes, green, were mostly closed, and, despite my height, my father, on my bicycle, had found a way to ride me home.

His gold.

10:33 A.M. October 26, 1985. The present. The number of places Billie could be grows proportionately to the number of places I have looked. And the time she has been gone. Thirty-nine hours, thirty-three minutes. The men of the territory are tracking Billie with their dogs. I have managed to outrun them. To search alone. "Hold up, Supes!" No. Not holding up. I climb a ladder to a hunting blind for a clearer view of the forest. The blinds are scattered throughout the woods; some are simple platforms made of pallets, chipboard, whatever the men can get their hands on. Others are the bodies of old trucks raised on thick logs, the husks of trailers, and in the distance, I can make out the founders' bus. Twenty-seven feet off the ground. OR BUUST. The letters of the stolen TOUR BUS rearranged.

Below me, the men advance in formation, keeping just

over five feet (Billie's diminished height when she disappeared) between them. They have their headlamps in their outer-wear pockets and dig for them now. They know what it is to have their headlamps burn out at night in the woods, but not when there might be a woman in those woods who is lost and could be difficult to understand. Could grab their shoulder, touch their face, run at them. The men stop in their tracks, pull off their work gloves, dick their hands, wipe them down, and test their headlamps. Shine their beams at the ground. The accumulating snow. Almost three inches. The men look to the sky. Eyebrows and eyelashes gathering frost. A sting in the air. A northwesterly. The creak of the trees. Five and a half hours of good light left.

I pull out my father's binoculars. I swiped them yesterday from the top drawer of his metal desk. He keeps them there alongside his personal effects, which I try to avoid looking at too closely. (Mouthwash, cologne, Band-Aids, tin of chew, extra padlocks, tire studs, electric razor, various phone numbers, and a backup pair of underwear. Killeth me noweth.) My father loops the binoculars around his muscular neck after I have washed down all the trucks in the dealership, and he goes from row to row inspecting them. Talking about how the air is dangerous. The air is gasoline. Our people are not meant to live for long, Son. Our people are meant to live for short. I hold the binoculars up to my eyes now, and try for the qualities of an owl. Let's admit. This human form is lacking.

Around the many sinkholes that have appeared (there are mineshafts throughout the territory that were boarded over five years ago; they tunnel outward two thousand feet below us and have made the ground "unstable"), mostly in the area known as the west woods, but increasingly close to town, fences have been staked and strung with flagging tape. Bright yellow, bright blue, bright green. At the bottom of one crater is the lawn chair of One Hundred. At the bottom of another, the St. John family bungalow. At the bottom of the most recent crater is a truck.

Sexeteria was not in the truck when the ground gaped open ten by sixteen feet and swallowed his rig whole. He was in the back room of Home of the Beef Candy with Shona Lee. A rapture of Shona Lees. When my father said "Let's give it a day," then went by the diner to console Sexeteria, and offer him a deal on his next truck, Sexeteria told my father he had decided he did not want to replace his truck. He was never really a truck man. My father threatened to torch himself. He held a lighter to his FULLY LOADED belt buckle. Then to his gold tooth. His blue thumbnail. The scar on his forearm. His necklace of keys. Sexeteria told him to cool it. He was the first in the territory to say "chill." Sexeteria then made his own wide-plank skateboard and spray-painted it hot pink with the letters of his former license plate, SXTRA, and started a craze, selling SXTRA decks out of his restaurant to the boys and girls of the territory who got whatever part-time work they could at The Man Store, The Woman Store, Deep Space Tapes, Drugs and More Drugs, and then built ramps on their properties. My father griped that Sexeteria was damaging our business by corrupting the next generation. He still went to Home of the Beef Candy for the lunch special, but now he ran his Zippo along his jeans and stood in line with a high flame.

11:01 A.M. A makeshift tent has been set up on the Fontaine front yard for the search teams to rest under and shield themselves from the turning weather, but no one will take a break. Inside the tent, there is a foldout table with a plate of oatmeal cookies, baked by my mother, and a tray of sandwiches wrapped in wax paper, donated by Home of the Beef Candy. Margarine, yellow mustard, lunch meat, a lettuce leaf, a cheese slice. Brown bread or white. Always a sense of surplus the day after Delivery Day. Beside them, the leftover flyers. A rock to weigh them down. BILLIE JEAN FONTAINE. MISSING.

The women have built a small fire and huddle around it for heat. Neck warmers and earmuffs, a transistor radio crackling some sort of country music. There is a silver pot filled with coffee, a ladle to serve it. My mother serves it. The women hold their mugs to their chests and blow into the steam, making ghosts. "I am sorry to say this aloud, but won't her feet be giving her trouble by now?" Rita Star asks. "They might be giving her trouble," Cheryl Chantale responds, and the women look out to the woods and picture Billie, the flurry of Billie, her bare feet coming down against the sharpness of the clay and the sticks. The mean cold of the snow. They were never true friends to her. The tarps above the women snap in the wind.

My father told my mother that Billie Jean Fontaine left bungalow 88 without her boots. Without her socks. Her mitts. Her hat. Just her tracksuit. The indoor one. Without her coat. Damn it. 7:39 P.M. October 24. Thursday. It was Rita Star Roulette who called it in first and described what she had seen. The Heavy, oblivious with his snowmobile goggles and hearing protection on, and that daughter of theirs, also named for tragedy and herewith fated for it, slumped unconscious in their front hall, and that ancient lesbian killer dog nearly getting clipped as Billie hightailed it out the driveway. Couldn't tell whether the hound got in or not. What with the night. What with the wind. Not like we got streetlamps here. The moment my father hung up, the phone rang again. We all jumped. "Linklater residence." This time, it was The Heavy. "She said she was going into town." I could hear The Heavy's voice, clear as if he was in the airless room with us, in the kitchen of bungalow 1. "She took the truck." A pause. "Nothing to tell me, eh, friend?" My father cast a quick glance at my mother. She was doing the dishes. The Heavy went on, "I need your truck. I need the fog lights. I need to find Billie Jean."

My father is not a bad man. I heard the worry in his voice when he hung up the brown wall phone and told my mother the details of Billie's disappearance while grabbing his outerwear off the back of his chair, directly across from my chair, and pretending I was not in the room. The shrinking room. Completely avoiding my face. Forgetting his hunting rifle by the side door. How could he forget his rifle? I would take his rifle. And Pony, in the graveyard, later that night, would take it from me—"You think I could borrow that, thank you"— then riding off to rob the Delivery Man. "I won't be able to come back here," the Delivery Man said to Pony. "You know I won't be able to show my face ever again."

My father loves to help people. Loves to get calls. Trucks in sinkholes, legs in bear traps, rifle shots to the chest. My father does not love to help me. My mother listened to my father, but she did not lift her head once to meet his eyes. We had had a casserole for dinner. We always had a casserole on Thursday nights. My mother nodded while she attacked the already clean dish with her steel wool.

12:22 P.M. How will she survive without her coat? I picture Billie coatless at the bottom of a sinkhole. Billie motionless and fixing her gaze up at the sky, waiting not for me to peer down but for death. U + me = 4ever. Don't picture it. Won't. Swear to it. Swearing. On Billie's life.

ALL THROUGH THE BUNGALOW, my father had been preparing for the baby. He painted our spare room and built a crib. It was a beautiful crib. He spent hundreds of hours on that crib. He told me that, when I was a baby, I slept in a drawer pulled from my parents' dresser. It was on the carpet beside their bed. It had a fur throw in it. Coyote. With a satin backing. I was a bad sleeper, my father said. "Your mother and I lost years." He laughed.

My mother, her hands working fast, knit small sweaters and small pants in whatever color yarn she could find in town. One Saturday night when my father was out at Drink-Mart, my mother, nearly finished with a blanket, nearly due, rested her hands on her round stomach and, aglow, said to me, "This is the kindest thing anyone has ever done for me."

Six months before (last November, when Billie was just over three months pregnant), Billie and I talked about it and how, regarding options, we had none. She said we had to be practical. Be practical thinkers. "We have to have a plan,

Will," she said. She lived for her daughter. Billie told me this countless times. I finally understood this feeling. Recently. You see, briefly, I was a father, and about my pain, Billie seems to have forgotten. She is not the only one who would like to lock herself in her bedroom, pull the curtains closed, and speak solely to an animal. Lose track of time. Lose track of weather. She is not the only one who wants to be in a black truck driving headlong into a deeper blackness. I too look up from a crater and see a sky that is mostly ice.

Billie would have the child and know the child remotely. This, we decided, was the only way forward. The child would be in my home, and this gave Billie comfort. The woodstove, my hands, my voice. I cared. I was the most caring human. Billie's words, not mine. At least I would be near our child. Day after day, for this was how we saw the world then—as an ongoing enterprise—I would get to be with our child. She could not leave her own home (nor did I want her to). Pony Darlene, The Heavy. While she loved me, she also loved him. The loves were not opposing, but simultaneous. "I loved him," she said, "and then you just happened to be there at the same time, and I loved you too. First the atmosphere, then the sun. First the sun, then the atmosphere." Okay. Am I the sun or the atmosphere? I wanted to ask Billie, but did not. "Love is not finite," she told me. Yeah, I know that. Infinity is something I have totally come to know.

Love = infinite.
Pain = infinite.
Billie = finite?

———

I STEP OVER the flagging tape and stand at the edges of the craters, look down into the hollows. Going methodically, sinkhole after sinkhole. 1:16 P.M. In the clearing, I lift every branch, move every rock, again, again. Why did we even call it the clearing when it was crowded with boulders and fallen trees and brambles and nests, and barely findable? Billie always had pine needles in her hair. I would make her sit still while I pulled them out, raked my fingers through her hair. I knew she felt cared for. The truth was I didn't want to get caught. I was so frightened of being asked a question I couldn't answer. I knew Billie could handle any question. She could lie.

The story she had told the women to gain their trust was about growing up in a small town and then moving to an outpost. On a great body of water that froze in the winter. You could drive across it. Her mother taught her how to needlepoint. How to crochet. Her father was a deer hunter. Her parents died in a car accident. Driving across the ice road and hitting open water. The story had just enough for the territory women to relate to. They felt Billie's life could have been their own.

I am not a liar. I never could lie. Okay. One lie. I don't like to run. That was my first lie to Billie. And my last. I had read about being casual. About how to start a conversation. I had so many lines in my head, but when one came out of my mouth, I yelled it. "I like to run!" I don't. I don't like to be further inside my own panicked breath. Blood filling my boots. My lungs burning. I did not lie about the owl. It would have been easy, but I did not lie about the owl.

I look back to the Fontaine bungalow. Pony Darlene, blocked from the ground search like The Heavy, sits on the slickening roof in her red jacket and hunting glasses, now on top of a black ski mask, her knees folded to her chest. The window she climbed through hangs open, Billie's bedroom filling with snow. 1:53 P.M. A couple of hours of good light left. I wave to Pony. Pony catches sight of me. She is waving back. No. She is pointing at me and then pointing wildly in the direction of the reservoir, and nearly slipping off the roof as she pulls her body through Billie's bedroom window. 1:54 P.M. I am close to the water, running to the water.

IT WAS A LATE August night when Billie first led me into the reservoir. I waited for her near the shoreline as we had agreed that morning. (I was always at least ten minutes early for every encounter. An anxiety of Supernaturals. Chronological. Not chill.) I could hear her footsteps approaching, then her body exited the trees. Her amphibious body. Swift limbs, bare feet. She stepped lightly onto the black mud and looked around. She did not see me. I chose not to announce myself. I watched her strip off her nightdress, hang it from a branch, and enter the water. She did not pace herself. Had no patience. She wanted things immediately. Sensations, revelations. To die during a storm.

I watched Billie propel herself out and into the center of the deep blue hole. Her motions were fantastic. Her weightless body terrifying. I had asked her to describe swimming. She refused. Said I had to feel it for myself. Said, "Meet me at the reservoir at 3:00 A.M." "Or what?" I said, trying to sound like the bold person who would ask that question and with any luck, become that person. I did not want to remind Billie that my only experience of water was to rotate my stooped body, six and a half feet, in the shower every morning after I went running and before I went to the truck lot.

I rolled the cuffs of my black jeans. I stepped into the dark water and heard a faint sound leave my mouth. "Ah" or "Fuck me." Leaves drifted from the trees. The leaves coated my shoulders. They fell on my head. I had just stopped shaving it and had a down on my scalp Billie loved to run her hands over. The water was up to my ankles when Billie saw me and came toward me sleek as a torpedo. The ground beneath me was soft and cold, and consuming my feet. Some bodies don't float. Would my body be one of those bodies? I took another step and could not believe the resistance.

I had read about John the Leader's death. He went for a swim one night, a year after he founded the territory, and never came back. I could imagine his followers standing where I stood now. They knew he had drowned but could not accept it. He was an excellent swimmer. His followers looked out over the surface of the reservoir and pictured beneath it forces at work, currents and animals they could not see. And then they pictured their leader. His untamed head of hair, the way he switched between languages depending on which was closest to the thought he so urgently needed to express, no, expel, and they saw the same things operating beneath him. Forces, currents, animals. Yes, that was it. The drowning had been intentional. No one in the territory swam again.

Until Billie.

I have circled the reservoir many times over the last nearly forty-three hours, but now when I reach it, the pump at one end, and the hoses running from the water to the pump, in the center of it, about thirty feet from the shore, a shape floats. A human shape. The shape is partly clothed. The shape has no shoes on. 1:59 P.M. I look back to the roof of the Fontaine house. Pony is gone, the window left open, pushed back and forth by the northwest wind. Snow will be collecting on the dog, burying the dog, and the dog, so morbid, will be pleased. The northwest wind picks up. Just when you want tenderness. The window bangs against the house. The window breaks.

One of the territory girls catches up to me, pulls off my father's binoculars, and looks out over the black water, the white arms, the long, loose hair. "She was such a good woman, seriously. So kind. She was always giving us things. She was so generous that way. See this throw? She gave this to me. This fur throw? This was her fur throw." And she holds it to my face. "She *slept* under it." Then the girl with the DELUXE necklace in the good gold, the last of the territory gold, Pallas Jones, hollers with her incredible pipes, "Body in the reservoir!"

ONLY ON SATURDAY NIGHTS did my mother and I have time alone. My father would manage to get home from Drink-Mart, unlock the front door, and close it behind him before falling to his knees, then to his face like a man shot in the back. My father had a compact body. Dragging him along the hallway by his boots, my mother could handle him. "Let me," she would say as she pulled him into their bedroom. Two single beds with pressed black bedcovers, turquoise and brown throw pillows, and between them, dustless, and hung too high, my portrait.

In it, I am squinting, glaring at my father's camera, but half–turned away. My hands are in my pockets. I look like something is flying at me. Him. "It was the best I could get, okay?" my father defended himself to my mother, bending the nails on the back of the wood frame, then positioning the portrait on their wall. In the dark square left by my old portrait. Fifteen, and just as reluctant, but spattered with acne. Now wrapped in a black bedsheet and stored in the crawl space. "It was the only one where the boy's arm wasn't over his face," he lied. "Okay?"

Training his lens, my father said, "We need a new portrait of you, Son. Never know what's gonna happen here," and I pictured him stabbing me in the neck. I was standing in front of my father's truck. His fog lights mounted on the roof and, above them, the galaxy. I was eighteen. It was night. The earth spinning at a thousand miles an hour and my father telling me to hold still. "You sure aren't *that* boy anymore," he said, conjuring my old portrait, the one that needed replacing. "You're a man now." *Flash.* Am I? Am I a man? Okay. I'm a man. What kind of man? I wanted to ask my father. *Flash.* The affair with Billie had just begun. Did he know about the affair? *Flash.* Is that why he considered me a man? A cheat like him? Impossible. Billie and I were traceless.

My mother had tried to have more children—for nearly two decades, she had tried—and I knew, of all her sadnesses, this was her primary one. I, in my singleness, was her primary

sadness. No one in the territory knew about it. Like a dangerous animal, she kept it confined to the bungalow. She had to
keep it in line. Keep herself in line. "You have to go to bed," I
would say to my mother, polishing the silver, scrubbing the
shower, stone-faced, her hands raw. "You need to get some
rest," I would say, and she would look at me like I was ruining
something for her. And then she would place me and tell me I
was right. "What am I doing?" She would pull herself to
standing. "What am I doing?" she would ask, not wanting the
answer.

Despite my status as some kind of phenomenon in the
town—remember, undeserved—my mother felt inferior to the
other women of the territory, all of whom had multiple children, were laden with children.

SEVEN THINGS:

1. Except Billie Jean Fontaine. She was not laden with
   children.
2. But she was an outsider, a newcomer, and this was a
   kind of defect.
3. Having the one child fit her defect.
4. Even though my mother wore her low blue heels every
   day for five years, Billie was never invited into our
   kitchen.
5. Billie would say, "A woman does not love her friends as
   much as she is haunted by them."
6. I listened to the women in our kitchen try to talk about
   something other than Billie, and not be able to.

7. "Who has a dog that obeys like that? A dog who does
   not tear at her dress when she is dancing like that?
   That is a woman who can speak to animals and the
   animals will listen."

For eighteen years, as the other women made and delivered babies, my mother was the one to lift the heavy objects
around them. "I'll get it," my mother in her starched workdress would say. "Not in your condition. Let me." Some days,
unfolding cots, setting up medical lights, lugging coolers filled
with bags of blood, pushing them forward to the loading dock,
she felt like an invisible servant.

"'The broken-hearted are always cold,'" I read to Billie.
"'While they will never ask for warm liquids, they may ingest
them if presented. Though not considered fatal, heartbreak
can kill, if indirectly.'"

Billie and I had considered lying to my mother. A few of
the young girls in the territory were pregnant with the sons
and daughters of the Delivery Man, and I could protect Billie
by withholding her name and offering up one of theirs.
Tristan, Lorraine, Rochelle. I would see the girls staring into
the bonfire at the graveyard. They would ask each other,
"Does the search for warmth explain, like, nearly every action
here?"

"Yes."

"Is that the same thing as love?"

"No."

In their heads, they would mix up *embryo* and *embargo*. They
would toss the Delivery Man's amateur wood carvings into the

flames. "Total former inmate," they would say and watch his efforts burn. For the boys, the bonfires were smoke signals. They wondered whether a satellite might see them. Whether something might land here. A spacecraft. Opening its jaw and flooding them with light.

10:45 P.M. November 17, 1984. Saturday. Sitting across from my mother in our silent kitchen, the waxed floor, the pressed dish towels, and me, her primary sadness, I could not lie. It was a risk after a long series of risks. My mother could have threatened me: Why would I do that? You have been so dishonest. Why would I cover for your dishonesty? I wanted to give something to my mother. To lift something heavy for her.

I proposed the Mother Trick. I told my mother Billie Jean Fontaine was carrying my child and was, we thought, about three months along. Then, in the long quiet that ensued, I tried to read my mother's face. On it, two things were happening: She could see how, pregnant, she would shift upward in the esteem of the women. This feeling in my mother, I did not want to see. A shallow feeling when I had lost track of how to have shallow feelings. Had I ever known how to have shallow feelings? Yes, don't oversell yourself. I had layered three shirts when I first started to run to make me look older to Billie. I had tried to lift a bag of concrete and could not. I had held a pelt to my jaw and deliberated myself with a beard. Am I who I think I am? Not the time. And then something else crossed my mother's face: she sensed a fault line in Billie's marriage to The Heavy, and was happy for it. In fact, it seemed to make her shine.

After taking blood at the Banquet Hall, the women of the

territory would gather in Rita Star's kitchen. Some evenings, they would gather in ours. Brown, turquoise, spotless. Here, have some citrus, here, have a rest, now you lie on that cot until the black spots go away; in their unzipped jackets and matching dresses, the women performed their days for each other. How could they be tanned and pale at the same time? The women were confused by the teenagers, but went on draining them. These girls and boys with their big hair and their bad teeth, inching up their shirt sleeves, were the only things keeping this town alive. The women watched the hospital dramas and knew in other places the IV lines worked in the opposite direction, but whenever this point was raised, the women countered it. They stirred their instant coffee. "Blood is renewable," the women reminded each other. "The *only* renewable resource," they quoted the infomercial. "And besides," they reasoned, "how else would we feed our kids?"

When I came back from the truck lot, wanting only to be alone, the women grabbed at my cheekbones and my chin, held my shoulders, ran their tired hands over my face. "Look at him. Look at Debra Marie's beautiful son, her fully loaded son with all of his limited edition and discontinued features." And my mother, the primary sadness having left her body and been replaced by purpose, superlative purpose, announced, "I am pregnant." The women took their hands off me and held them to their mouths, and then ran them over my mother's stomach. At that early point, just foam.

I watched my mother step down slowly from her truck and put her hands to the small of her back. I watched her as she arranged her features at will. How she had one face and then, as she needed, summoned a different one. When the other women decided whose kitchen to meet in after taking blood at the Banquet Hall, my mother spoke of her exhaustion. The other women grew nostalgic for their exhaustion. Two, three, four, five kids, they lit each other's cigarettes, widened their eyes, and warned my mother her whole world was going to change. "When you have only the one kid, you still have something left to say," the women told her and they laughed. Together they were jovial, understood. "The thing is," my mother confided in me later, "I really do feel exhausted. I really do feel sick. The strain on my back is real."

In our bungalow, my mother sewed small clothes for the baby and large clothes for herself. Her body bent over the kitchen table, the lone, dim light above her. If my father called to say he was staying late at the truck lot, she did her sewing with the beige mound, her pregnancy, beside her. To give her skin a rest. She prepared the duct tape in advance. The silver strips hung from the edge of the kitchen table should she suddenly hear my father's engine approach. She was agile. Going from one state to the other.

I watched as Billie did not put her hands to the small of her back, and never spoke of her exhaustion. She had one face. The same face. In town, she made sure she still had something left to say. In town, no one ever asked Billie how she was feeling.

After we swam, and I was just so relieved to be alive—min. darkness, max. luv—Billie would say, "Wouldn't it be nice to have a fire, build a little fire on the shoreline? Warm our bodies and be dried by the fire?" But I wouldn't build a fire for her.

I wouldn't take the risk. I thought it was greedy, her wish for a fire. When we were already getting away with so much. When her house with her husband in it was only three hundred steps away. And Billie would say, "You are so young. Where's your stupidity?" I didn't want to say I was looking at it. I was looking at my stupidity. All the death-defying things I did to impress her.

2:07 P.M. The water of late October seeps into my steel-toe boots, then fills my black jeans, and weighs down my hoodie and my parka. I already see death when I see water, and now I am traversing the frigid reservoir, high and churning, to recover a corpse. In my head, I hear my father's voice. He is talking about the rush. Wanting it. Seeking it out. It tells you that you matter. You have an effect, Son—my father would spear me in the chest with his finger—you can change the course. No I can't. There are forces more intelligent. Forces more mighty. Forces we might perceive, but cannot understand. A force. What would you call it? Do you have a name for it? You must have a name for it. Tell me! Tell me what you would call this because I don't have a name for it—and though I am careful to keep my head up, I inhale a mouthful of water arguing with my father, no, I am arguing with myself, and coughing, I wrap my arm around the shoulder of the corpse, which, given the hair, I will guess is female, but if I look at her closely, I will drown, which I have heard only great things about, that it's basically like taking a tranquilizer, and, though I am tempted, I tilt my head up toward the sky, which is colorless and, by me, unmoved.

I watched my mother hold the damp cloth to her face and her neck. "Don't just stand there. Take a shower," she said. I took a shower, and at my feet, the water rose pale pink. The bathroom mirror was fogged and I saw how low it was. Too low to capture my face. The mirror stopped at my shoulders. My shoulders, which were broad and just framed by the mirror. I burned my bloodied shirt with the owl feathers and the foam and spread the ashes over the dirt of our backyard. I didn't know if Billie had made it home. I didn't know if Billie could walk. I didn't know a body could bleed that much. When my mother lay back in her bed with her hair design pulled out, I asked, "What about the blood?" and what I meant was what about the blood that had come from Billie's body, will Billie be okay with that much less blood? And my mother, looking up from the baby in her arms, ordered, "Take the black sheets from the linen cupboard and put them all in the wash. Burn a tarpaulin in the yard." And when my father parked his truck in the driveway, I waited a few minutes before I slammed the back door. My father met me there and, his eyes glistening, said, "It's a girl."

He wanted to smoke with me outside. Smoking was one of the ways we spent time together. I hated smoking. I smoked with him, and, when he'd finished his cigarette, he said, "We'll call her Debra Marie Jr." The tarpaulin still smoldering, I scanned the yard for owl feathers, and my father put his arm around my shoulder. I let him. His voice wavering, he said, "The baby looks just like you."

I drag the corpse onto the embankment and lie down beside it. Above me the mouth of the girl in the fur throw—

which has been cut up the front, and sleeved and collared with safety pins and duct tape for a coat—moves rapidly. My heart pulses in my head, my stupid heart. The majority of the girl's outfit is broken. Her ripped daypants, dyed and eaten away by bleach. Streaked with bicycle grease. I can see her bluing legs, her white underwear. I look away from the girl and down at the ice casing my boots, my jeans, my parka. Casing my ball cap, my hood. I look like I am in a hazmat suit. No. A body bag. Yes. Winter, like death, when we are left alone with our questions. Why, Billie? How, Billie? What, Billie? Should I have built a fire for you? Told you I loved you? "What could I have done? You know the answer."

"He is totally talking to himself," says Deluxe from inside many coyotes. "Maybe he has hypothermia?"

Again, have heard only the best things.

Around me, the search teams gather. They have never come this close to the reservoir. They look down at the spill of long dark hair, the nude body, mostly preserved in a rectangle of ice. Their sons and daughters give each other boosts and shimmy silently to the tops of the pine trees, thin and new, that ring the water. They have never seen anything dead. They picture their faces serene against satin. No.

My father breaks the silence. "John?"

"Not much left of the face."

"But a man."

"Obviously."

"Must be John the Leader."

"Must be."

"He finally surfaced."

"John."

"Wow."

"It's a sign."

"Yeah, but of what?"

Then, turning their eyes on me, "The boy can float."

"The boy can fucking swim," the men say in disbelief.

"Supernatural, all right."

"Super Fucking Natural."

"Super Almighty Fucking Natural."

I DID NOT KNOW how to figure out whether Billie had made it home. I could not leave my bungalow again to check the clearing, or to watch for Billie in the windows of her bungalow. My father had already asked me where I was that day. Why I wasn't at the truck lot. How no one can sell a truck the way I can. I barely have to speak, and the truck sells. All I have to do is walk around the truck and, shortly after, my father watches it drive off the lot. If a territory man sees me sitting in the driver's seat, even of the most featureless truck, I sell it to the man. Of late something seemed to have gotten into me. I wasn't selling as many trucks, and today, I didn't even show at the lot. He needed me. The family needed me. I had a sister now, a little sister, and my sister needed me. I had to come to the lot and sell the trucks off it. My father selling me on selling until he left the kitchen and in his sock feet paced the hallway with the crying baby. Not a bad man. Both of them making noises. Years old. Hours old.

When the bungalow was finally quiet and my father had closed the door to the spare room, the baby's room, and then closed the door to his own, I called Billie's house. I had never done this before. I wouldn't take the risk. This time, I knew if The Heavy picked up, I could apologize for the late hour and explain it away with news of the baby. The happy news. The baby that was his wife's baby. The baby I couldn't bring myself to look at. It was Pony who picked up. Her voice quick and hushed and matter-of-fact. "The Complaint Department," she said. "Tell me what's troubling you."

"I get you, they say this in town. I get you. The men say it during the day at the truck lot, and the girls say it at night by the bonfire. I get you. I totally get you. You don't get me. No one gets me. Even the one person I want to get me, the person I am closest to, doesn't get me and I don't know how to get her to get me. When I am not selling trucks, I am having my blood drawn. I have my blood drawn more than any other boy or girl in the territory. I can watch my face change in the mirror. I am both elderly and of the future. Is that even possible? Do you know what I mean? Do you get me? Am I allowed to punctuate my questions? No. In the territory, no man is allowed to punctuate his questions unless he is telling a joke. I don't tell jokes. I am not that kind of man. I am my own man, but even this is a line I borrowed from a night soap. From watching a night soap through the window of the person I most want to get me. Get me is all I want to say to this person. Get me. I hate to smoke. I hate to hunt. I hate to kill animals. I hate to eat animals, and then smoke after I have eaten them. I am quiet. This is my only hunting quality. This is my only smoking quality. I hate trucks. I am scared of needles, but no one can know needles frighten me. This is not acceptable here.

In fact, blood frightens me too. Many things frighten me. Sleep is agony. Make a fist, the women say, and I feed the lines my blood. Sometimes, the line has not been put in properly and the blood makes my forearm swell. Sometimes, the line will come out and my blood will shower the woman standing over me. I am constantly generating new blood and then giving my new blood to plastic bags. I have bruises all over my arms and legs. The women try to find new entry points to me, but sometimes they have to resort to the old ones. Looking for entry points, they say as they prick and stab me. I have control over my reading materials and my cassette tapes, but I do not have control over my blood. I do not have control over my body."

"They might as well make vests out of you," Pony says.

"Yes."

A not uncomfortable silence, and Pony asks, "Is that the extent of your complaint?"

"No."

Then The Heavy's voice comes on. "Who's this?"

That night, I take the baby from her crib and bring her to my bed. I put her on my chest without looking at her face. My daughter's face. My daughter. "I'm a father. Do you hear that, cold world? I'm a father. Do you hear that, you perfect tiny girl?" I whisper, the two of us together in the black room. "I'm your father. I'm yours."

THE LIGHT IN the territory is nearly gone. The men turn on their headlamps and aim them at the corpse of John the Leader, rolling the rectangle of ice that contains him, on the count of three, to a tarp, and then roping the tarp closed. Not taking note of the path worn from the water to the Fontaine bungalow, the men follow it, up and through the woods, carrying John's leaden shape on their shoulders, the way they do a coffin. Pony and I are close behind. She leads me as if I am blindfolded. The gentle push of her hands on my back. "Watch your step there, a big root there," she says, though she does not have to. I know the path well.

Fur Thumb, Hot Dollar, and my father carefully lower John into the back of my father's truck. DEALR. They decide Fur Thumb and Hot Dollar will ride with my father to the Death Man's trailer. Their wives, Cheryl Chantale and Pamela Jo, can drive the FURTHB and HOTDLR trucks home. My father reaches for the ignition and turns his truck keys, unleashing his fog lights. Wipers on high. The men let the truck warm up. They smoke. John will be the first corpse to spend the winter in the Death Man's shed. The Death Man will be waiting for the men by his sliding glass door. The men will be announced by the mania of his gulls, their shrill cries. The Death Man will invite the men into his trailer. Have a bit of liquor, listen to some speed metal, sit on his plastic furniture. Take a load off. Sorry, man. Can't. Another night, for sure. The men will make excuses. The wife, the kids. Then they will place John in the Death Man's shed, between stacks of empty, body-size shelves.

Fur Thumb asks, "What do you think got him? Like, what *did that* to John the Leader? Do you think there are animals in there?"

"In the reservoir?"

Pony and I watch the men climb into the front seat of the DEALR truck and belt themselves in alongside my father.

"And, I hate to say it, but also *out* there?"

The men look through my father's custom windshield, tinted and made of bulletproof glass.

"Animals we don't have names for," says Hot Dollar, feeling a creep over his skin.

"Animals we don't know how to kill," says Fur Thumb, and he looks over to my father, who, for the first time in his life, is quiet, quiet as a nuclear winter.

Pony opens the back door of her bungalow and lays me out on the living room carpet. Panic darts through her eyes, which she tries to subdue. She knows there's something wrong with me—hypothermia? Shock? Grief detonating in my body? Billie's portrait above the mantel. 4:42 P.M. Confirmation my watch is waterproof. "You are obsessed with time," Billie said to me. No, I am obsessed with the *passing* of time. All I have not said and done. The life *not* lived. The bungalow feels vacated. Where is The Heavy? It was John in the reservoir, I want to tell him. Not Billie. John the Leader. Where is he? "You're totally thrashing," Pony says. "Easy, Supes." She unlaces my boots and pulls them off. She tugs at the frozen cuffs of my jeans. She wraps a black bedcover around my shaking body and then takes the stairs two at a time to get dry clothes for me.

When I ran alongside Pony, and we came to a stop in front of her bungalow, Friday, sun up, she took my hand and held my palm. Traced the lines. "Something about your father," she said, and she looked away from my hand and toward the lightless house where my father slept, and one floor above him, The Heavy.

Pony returns and dresses me. Gets me to my feet. What is this feeling? I put my head in my hands. My heart jolts. Love does hurt. The Heavy pulls back the hood of his black recliner and looks at me without my ball cap, without my hood, my thick, shoulder-length brown hair, in his clothes, his clothes that fit me. "Time you go home, Son."

The moon is bright as I run home full of questions for my mother. Am I who I think I am? Am I who I think I am? Am I who I think I am? Saturday night, when I know I will have her to myself. My mother's words. My mother's words on Saturday nights only.

WHEN I WORRIED about how my mother got home with the baby, I remembered she was the only woman in the territory with her own truck. My father had a tract of land he had cleared of trees and filled with various-size trucks. Above it, he hung a sign, FULLY LOADED, that flashed on at night. Some of the trucks had been there for the five years he had been in business. When my father saw rust on a truck, he painted it matte black. The men buying trucks caught on, so even the newest models were painted matte black. Now, all of the trucks in the territory were matte black. When my father wouldn't mark down the price of the older trucks, he made the scales of justice with his hands and cited inflation. One hand went up and one hand went down. If you thought through the value of the dollar then, the value of the dollar now, the price was a bargain.

The night after my mother told my father they were going to have a baby, at last, a second child, my father gave my mother her own truck. "I can't believe it, I just can't believe it," my father said, and he held his palms to his eyes. Then my father shook my hand, cried openly, and was unembarrassed. He shook my hand for a long time. The truck he gave my mother was the oldest truck off the lot, and half-eaten by rust. Six months later, my mother would use it to bring home the child she had fooled him into believing was his.

The Mother Trick.

WHEN IT WAS too cold to meet in the clearing, Billie and I would lie on the floor of the trailer at the back of the truck lot. The Golden Falcon trailer that served as the Fully Loaded office from 8:30 A.M. to 4:30 P.M., Monday to Saturday. Sundays, by appointment, and closed for all final restings. Billie and I put our heads down on the gray slush that had built up that day and listened to the ice dent the roof. There was a small stove we lit for heat. The metal desk coated in frost. And on the walls, my father's collages. Some nights, he would disappear into our toolshed with his scissors and slice up magazines, coupons, pamphlets, then glue them onto rectangles of paper. To me, they looked like ransom notes. To him, they looked like a new world order.

Billie's dog stood watch by the trailer door. I never once read to Billie without her dog only feet away. Billie would say, "Oh, she's keeping guard. She knows things," but I always felt the dog would, if given the chance, close her teeth around my throat and read to Billie herself. Billie talked about how the dog left dead animals under her pillow, never under The Heavy's—though he was always the one to carry the bodies from the house—and the dog would leap for the body until The Heavy unhanded it, and the dog would devour it in the yard.

There was a forty-channel CB radio in the trailer, and Billie and I listened to the territory girls' plotting voices. Pushing the talk bar and whispering, "Do you read me?" a girl would ask nervously. "I read you," another girl would reassure. One night, Billie looked at me, and not knowing what else to say, what could be left to say (so much), quoted the girls, "We just have to commit to the motions. Make a list of the motions. We can't get lost."

We can't get lost.

BILLIE SAW OUR DAUGHTER one time. Once. Briefly, they were in the same room. It was the first Delivery Day after she was born. I heard about it from the territory men who, every afternoon, their windburned faces, bottom lips bulging with chewing tobacco, filed into the trailer. Above the small stove, my father had a black-and-white television mounted in the corner—never turned it off—and the men, while they looked up at the television, told us,

"The Fontaine mother just . . . It was her turn at the cash—"

"And she just left her basket right there and walked out."

"I heard Debra Marie checked out her basket."

"Yeah."

"Your mother checked out her basket." The men looked to me.

"Pony Darlene had to run to catch up to her."

"And Pamela Jo told me she didn't even have her door closed behind her let alone her safety belt on when the Fontaine mother pulled away."

"She didn't pull away."

"It was Pony who pulled away."

"The girl pulled away."

"A good driver though. A real capable driver."

THE LAST TIME I read to Billie in the clearing before the baby came, she said after, "Women only warn you about the tiredness. You won't sleep for two years, the mothers love to warn you when you're going to have a baby. And they brag about how little they slept when they had their babies. They gloat about their sleepless years. Falling asleep on the floor. At the table. In the shower. But no one warns you about the love. No one even speaks about it. The love for your baby comes with something dark. It comes with death. When you look at your child for the first time, you feel the presence of death. How death is looking at your child too. That is why you don't sleep. Not because of the child, but because you are watching over her. Keeping death away. It is death that keeps you up. Not the child." Billie, who kept Pony's milk teeth in a box in a drawer beside her bed, spoke about her own mother to me only once. "My mother completely missed this feeling."

I WOULD SEE Billie Jean Fontaine three more times. The third last time, we met in the clearing soon after our daughter's birth. When I arrived early, feeling triumphant, Billie was already standing there in her faded workdress (she had worn the wrong color that day to the Banquet Hall; the women of the territory were dressed in yellow; she was at her station, the only one in pink) and handed me an envelope. It contained a handful of her hair.

"Forensic." I tried to make a joke.

"It's falling out," she said tonelessly. "That's what happens after a woman has a baby." On the envelope she had written:

Mrs. Supernatural

"I was going to put a question mark after the name." Billie held her hands out to stop me from touching her. She had the shrink wrap around her breasts now. They were hard with milk and made her wince. I couldn't go anywhere near her body. She didn't cry. Even when she asked me: "How is she sleeping? What is she eating? What is she like? Tell me about her face."

The second last time I saw Billie was two months later at the final resting for our little girl. I saw Billie's effort, standing in her large dark dress in front of the black square, how she held her spine straight. Then, how the will left her body. I couldn't move to help her. My mother's hand on one wrist, and my father's hand on the other. I was only feet away. The Heavy carried her out, and she fought him. I heard a woman call Billie vicious. The woman had mascara all over her face. Billie did not. Watching Billie's struggling body, throwing fists, the woman muttered, "Like a dog with a catch in its teeth trying to snap the neck." The IV poles, the cots, the refrigerators filled with blood pushed to the walls. "Trying to snap her own neck," said Rita Star. The Heavy kicked open the metal doors of the Banquet Hall, and Pony Darlene followed. She turned back and yelled at everyone. Everyone looked away from Pony Darlene. The Heavy said, "Enough." He walked out with Billie into the sun.

That night, I stood in the woods across from the Fontaine bungalow. The Heavy had started pulling down the east wall of the house and was under a blue tarp beside a work light, sawing through lumber. Pony had her back to the wide rectangular window. She was watching television. *Teen Psychic.* I went around to the back of the house. The Heavy's outerwear hung damp on the laundry line. I threw rocks up at Billie's window. Where's your stupidity? Where's my stupidity? Come on, Billie. She came to the glass. I ran through the woods to the reservoir and, knowing she had a clear view, swam the strokes she had taught me. It was late July and the air was thick. It was going to rain. I arched my back and dropped beneath the surface and held my breath for as long as I could, and when I came back up, it was The Heavy who stood in Billie's place. He watched me through a squint. Billie had given him a black eye that day, and as The Heavy and I stared at each other, we heard the sky open and rain fell on rain.

"When she cries, she sounds like she is trying to swallow her cries. Like already she is trying to be brave. She has black hair and it's falling out. New hair is coming in and it's white. Her eyes are blue. Not sure where that came from, the blue. She's the most mysterious person. I can almost watch her eyelashes grow. She has your cheekbones, your mouth. But really, she just looks like herself. She is so *complete*. Sometimes she gets so angry. It's as if she's in a fight with the world. Can't believe this place. She is long. Her grip is firm. She sleeps on her back and kicks off her blankets. Hates to be wrapped in blankets. Doesn't like to sleep alone. Makes these whale sounds when she is dreaming. Screams when she's hungry. She wakes up once, sometimes twice in the night and I give her a bottle. She just started to look up at me. To study me. Before that, it was like I was a stranger. Like she was in a separate life, one that ran alongside this one, but one I couldn't reach. I can hardly take it. Her stare. It's like, I don't know, it's like she knows every secret. Every cure. And she's just about to tell me."

As I stood there in the clearing holding an envelope of her hair, unsure of how to be, Billie said, "Babies' eyes change color. Her eyes won't be blue for long." And even though she knew I did not like questions, she had asked me the questions, wanted answers to her questions; she said, "Now, I want you to stop talking to me. I don't want to hear the sound of your voice anymore."

It happened to babies. The women crowded around my mother and stroked her back through her final resting dress. "It's not your fault," they consoled her. "Babies die in their sleep and no one knows why. It's hideous. It's cruel. It's not your fault. Debra Marie, oh, Debra Marie. Poor Debra Marie." But my mother could see a strange joy inside the women. She had lost something, and, for the women, this was directly their gain. They thought she should have been a grandmother, not a mother. That her age had made the baby die. That her good fortune in everything else had made the baby die.

"The thing is, Will Jr.," my mother said to me later that night, forgetting my nickname, "my pain is real. My grief is real. The strain on my heart is real."

I had memorized her face. Billie was right. Her eyes were no longer blue. They were dark. My daughter's eyes were Billie's. Do you read me? they said. I read you.

HOURS AFTER I stood in front of the black square, my father opened the door to my bedroom, flicked on the overhead light, and sat on the end of my bed. As he spoke, he filled my room with the smell of alcohol. He told me about a place that was famous for its mountains. The mountains were snow-capped, and people visited the place to see the snowcapped mountains. But the snow had stopped falling, and now the place was no longer beautiful. People had stopped visiting, and the place was in decline. In an attempt to save his people, one man climbed the mountains with cans of white paint. He painted the mountaintops. Tried to return beauty to the place. Prosperity. "I am the guy with the cans of paint," my father said, laughing a little to himself, playing with his pinkie ring, then zeroing in on me. "I'm just trying to do good, Son. To do right."

I was still wet from swimming in the reservoir, and my father, just in from the rain, was wet too. Water spilled down his face. He soaked my bed. His black mood, the mean hurt of his body. He told me he felt ill. He said it was his fault the baby died.

Did you do something to her?

My darkest question.

I had to move my feet out of the way when my father sat down. I could hear the squelch of his jeans when he did. My bed was too short for me, and my feet hung off the end of my mattress and touched the wall. My mother had given me a mirror from her purse that was the size of a playing card. I had it propped up on two old nails. Under my bed, I had books and parts of books from the Lending Library. I made the reading to Billie seem random, but it wasn't. I had thought it through. Like everything I did, I had thought it through.

I knew in the morning, my father would wake angry with his eyes red and his boots on, unable to move his body properly. I knew I would have to wait for him to pass out. His long and uncontrollable sentences. "I have never felt so tired. I have never felt so cold. I've never wanted so much to talk. I have things to say. I have no one to talk to," my father said to me. "Why won't you talk to me?"

"You don't have to hold it in," I said to Billie the last time I saw her. We were in the clearing the day after the final resting for our daughter.

"Hold what in? I mean what would you even call it? What would you call this? Do you have a name for it? With all your reading, you must have a name for it. Tell me! Tell me what you would call this because I don't have a name for it." And Billie pounded at her body, fell to the ground. Eventually, she grew quiet, and, when she looked up, the owl hung there, many feet wide and not flying. "Did you make that happen?"

She looked from the owl to me like it was the owl she knew, but I was unfamiliar.

Billie – Will

My father propped my desk chair under the handle of my bedroom door with my mother on the other side of it asking if everything is okay in there. And then we could hear as her body slid down, and she hit her head against the door until my father and I told her everything is okay, we will be out in a moment. The sun burned through the curtains of my bedroom window, and, looking like he was on fire, my father, still at the end of my bed, sat on my feet now. Sober, he would not let me go. His wasted days. How little he has felt. He has been disloyal to his wife, jealous of his son. He is the only man who slows to a stop on Saturday night. No other man can bring himself to cheat with the daughter of The Heavy. The Heavy, who has lost so much. He is the only one. He keeps men low and broken. He sewed up his best friend's gaping wrists with bright blue thread. He nearly let him die. One woman had told him she loved him, and for twenty years she was lying. It was his fault the baby died. He had wished it. Just the night before he had wished it. And his wish had come true. He could not love. He could only trap. And The Silentest Man had seen that in him at a young age. "Traps," my father spoke his own name. *"Traps."*

Then he said, "Remember when The Heavy and the Fontaine mother had that party? People talked about the party for a long time. It was her idea. Remember when we showed up, the first thing we noticed was that badminton net strung across their yard. Remember it came out that the Fontaine mother had made the net. Woven the net. You know it became so after the party, whenever one of the men saw something in town— a truck, a coat, an apple—he'd say, 'The Heavy's wife made that.' We'd joke, 'Oh that? That ATV? The Heavy's wife made that. The fucking sun? The Heavy's wife.' That baby? Yeah, The Heavy's wife made that baby too. The Heavy's wife made that baby. The Heavy's wife made that baby. With *you*. The scene at Delivery Day. Your mother walking in, and the Fontaine mother walking out. I couldn't get it out of my head. And something had gotten into you; that much was clear. I followed you. One night, a few weeks later. Took my binoculars and watched you as you hid yourself there in the woods opposite the Fontaine bungalow. The look on you. That's when I knew I was right. That's when I made the wish. Only wish I ever made that came true—"

"Did you do something to her?"

"I didn't touch the baby. I swear I didn't touch her. I would never have touched her. Never have harmed her. I'm not sick. I'm not a bad man. Can you see that, Son? Can't you see that? Just trying to do good. To do right. I'm not a bad man. But I did wish her gone. I did. I could not look at one more thing that was not mine. One more thing *I* didn't make." And when my father went to punch my face, I let him. His pinkie ring caught on then sliced through my top lip. Same room, same bed, same sun. I needed something to look different.

It was the one night I didn't bring her into my room. When she didn't cry, I must have slept.

When my father and I finally opened the door to my bedroom, my mother was in her nightdress and directionless in our hallway. "Look at you," my father spat at my mother, "just look at you. I believed you. Do you have any idea how much I needed to believe you?" And when he pushed past my mother, she tried to hold him back by the shoulders then by the waistband of his jeans and eventually by the ankles. Her tendons lifting, she had him by the boots. Then, my mother's noble face, she held her hands to it, and she let my father go.

I watched my mother in her awkward shoes lift her body into the driver's seat of her small truck. How she made herself keep going. Forever bent over the kitchen table. Doing nothing. Then raking the yard. Then folding the black sheets. Having the baby gave her the chance to move with effect. Now, she moved with no effect, and one morning, on a day that was not garbage day, she put all of the small clothes she had made for the baby, everything she had knit, into a box, and left the box where our yard meets the north highway; then she turned back toward the bungalow, toward me, an empty woman.

"I LOVED HIM," my mother tells me now when I come through our side door and into the kitchen. Her coat is on, and her face is glossed and certain. Behind her, a cast-iron pan is bare and smoking. I turn the stove off. Outside, the snow has stopped falling. "I still love him." She looks away from me standing before her in The Heavy's clothes. With his hair. His body. The kitchen ceiling has always been too low. "It started before I was married to your father and it lasted until the night of our engagement. I had dreams and I lost track of them,

Will Jr. A person is more than one thing; a person is many things. Why can't a woman be more than one person in a lifetime? Why can't she be two or three? I know I was unfaithful, in so many different ways, unfaithful, but I don't know how to explain the need I had for my freedom. My dutiful mother, my dutiful grandmother. That was what I saw lying in wait for me. He was Jay Jr. then. We would jump from the windows of our bedrooms and see each other whenever we could. We kept the relationship a secret. It is good to take risks, Son. It is important to take risks. When I finally gathered my nerve and raised the question of marriage, Jay Jr. could not explain why he wouldn't marry me. I was desperate for an explanation, and he broke down. He was sorry. He was so sorry, but he never could tell me why. I thought I might die with the pain. I had never felt so much pain. To hurt him, I turned to his best friend, Traps. We were young. You have such a sense of justice and vengefulness when you are young. It is so enlivening! And by these two things, I was moved—not by love—to seduce your father, and your father, easily flattered, proposed. I married him only so The Heavy would have to see me in a wedding dress standing next to another man, in the arms of another man. My thinking became sectional. I put people into sections, and I had to work to keep up with the sections. When Jay's house caught on fire, and he lost his family, your father, upon seeing my grief, how the sections of my mind caved in, wondered if something had happened between me and Jay. He looked at me differently, our life together differently. He looked at you differently. When I told him we would be parents again, all of his doubt went away. Doubt is desperate.

Doubt is lonely. Traps was awash with belief, and it made him soft for a time. I never told him. Never told him that when we married, I was already pregnant with you, Jay's son. The Heavy's son. Heav."

My father = The Heavy.
My daughter = The Heavy's granddaughter.

THE FLOOR IS COLD. "Please forgive me." My mother crouches. She is the lone, dim light above me. "I don't know why I have told you so little over the years when inside there was always so much to tell."

BILLIE SAID TO ME, "Is love all you need? Is all you need love? Have I loved well enough? Does Pony know how she is loved, that the love I feel for her is an injury? My worst permanent injury. And still I try to walk around."

AND STILL I TRY to walk around.
6:42 P.M. October 26, 1985. Saturday. The porch light is on at the Fontaine bungalow. The only question I had for my mother—"Does he know?"—she could not answer. Pony opens the front door before I can knock. Her face is expectant. Behind her, The Heavy stands in the middle of the living room floor. Where I lay just two hours ago. Seeing him, my chest cracks open. I do not say remarkable things to him. Son-like things. I have two strengths, and this is not one of them. Okay. I think of myself as having two strengths. Neither has made itself apparent to me yet.

The Heavy is unwrapping a wooden frame. He drops the black bedcover. The rope that bound it. Square in his hands, he holds the last portrait taken of him, when he was still Jay Jr. The Heavy has never seen the portrait. Never showed it to Pony. Never showed it to Billie. He studies himself now, who he was before the fire that killed his family.

Nearly twenty years ago, after his suicide attempt, The Heavy's portrait was briefly propped up in the Banquet Hall. The nickname he had been given after his bungalow was destroyed (the Fontaine bungalow was bungalow 2, next door to his best friend, Traps; it was Traps's father who was having the affair with The Heavy's mother, and it was The Heavy's father who started the fire out of heartbreak; when Lana Barbara Sr. and her husband, Visible Thinker, decided to build their bungalow on the site of the Fontaine family tragedy, they were cautioned against it; the newly married couple made it known they did not believe in ghosts) THE HEAVY, was burned into plywood and, as is the territory way, placed beneath the portrait of the young man. The lights and flowers were set up. It was August, and his grave, beside his sister's, was swiftly and easily dug by Traps. A day later, it was filled with clay and rock. The portrait was taken down. Looked like The Heavy would make it after all.

The Heavy would tell me later—we would talk, oh, how we would talk—that his younger sister had taken the picture. It was late summer, the end of the day. Their father said, "It's time, Jay Jr." His sister had to tilt the camera up to get his face. Really get his face. She stacked wood pallets and chipboard, and stood on them in her combat boots. She was particular about the slant of the sun, about Jay Jr. being in the center of it. She got Jay Jr. to look this way and that. "You're so serious," she said. "Lighten up!" The other young men in the territory took off their shirts and held cinder blocks over their heads, thick chains. The Heavy was not like the other young men. His sister had the same green eyes as him. They were honest, bracing. She had her headphones around her neck, and on her bicep, FOCUS THINE ANARCHY written in permanent marker. She begged him not to go hunting that night. To stay home with her. To hang out. She had a funny feeling, she said. She couldn't name it. Wanted him near. But The Heavy had had an affair with Debra Marie, and felt Traps was catching on. He needed to defuse Traps's suspicions, and keep the peace. He felt guilty. The Heavy wasn't a cheat. "Sorry, Pony," Jay Jr. said to his younger sister, conflict in his heart. Outside the frame is The Heavy's dog. Her perfect posture, her grave face. She sat at his feet. Behind him is his house. That night, it would burn to the ground.

Everything The Heavy loved was inside that moment. He was nineteen. My age. The Heavy looks at his former face, the defiant face, the one he could not stand to look at until now, and in it, he sees me. The Heavy confirms I am his.

The Heavy and I do not hug each other. It is Pony and I who hug each other. And there it is, my first strength: brother to Pony Darlene Fontaine.

My sister.

A TRUCK PULLS INTO the Fontaine driveway. With his fog lights, Traps is the only man in the territory who can light up so much of it. He cuts the engine. We are standing in the picture window. Pony, The Heavy, and I. We watch Traps jump down. A slick of black ice, and Traps steadies himself against the body of the truck, the FULLY LOADED slogan at his back. And then Traps punches the air. I put my hand to my mouth, where his ring tore through my lip. Traps had tried so many times to teach me how to throw a good punch. "When you make contact with your target, don't stop," Traps said. "You gotta *go through it*. The motion is about completeness." He spoke the words his father had to him. "Come on, kid. Try it." I wouldn't.

7:16 P.M. Traps gave me this watch. He would have had to organize the gift months in advance. Found a picture of the watch in one of his magazines and slipped the cut-out image and an envelope of money to the Delivery Man. On the face of the watch it says WATER RESISTANT. I always took it off before going in the reservoir. Never forgot. Fastened it to my belt loop, jeans neatly folded and at least ten strides from the water. Traps handed the gift to me the night I turned eighteen. It was wrapped in deerskin and duct tape. It was the one night I felt Traps got me. I put the watch on and shook his hand. "Thank you." Then from across the kitchen table, candles blown out between us, he passed me a card he had made. The card was a collage of letters: Dear Son, Live a little.

"You need my truck. You need my fog lights. You need to find Billie Jean." On the Fontaine front porch, Pony and I watch as Traps hands his truck keys to The Heavy. His breath spirals white in the cold. About Traps, The Heavy would tell me, "He was a good man, a good friend, and then he became a vain man and, after my family died, a deceitful one." The Heavy spent time with him only so he could spend time with me. His boy.

Traps takes my hand in his and looks into my eyes. This is his goodbye. The gold incisor; he flashes it at The Heavy. "Nothing to tell me, eh, friend?" He smiles, cocking his head and running a palm over his forearm, the one with the mouth-shaped scar. He turns his body away from us. We watch him walk down the driveway. Under the glare of the moon. In his trapper hat and his cowboy boots. The shined black leather, the red stitching. He makes his way toward home, toward my mother.

"SHE's NOT HERE," The Heavy says. "We've had it all wrong. She's not in the woods. She's not in the territory. She's not even close." Pony and I leave the cement porch for her stash of jerry cans in the north woods. When we pull back the black tarp to load them into the DEALR truck, we see it has already been stocked. In the space where John the Leader had been laid out only hours before, Traps has put water, canned food, ammunition, and plenty of fuel.

The Heavy switches off the light in the front hall. When he reaches for the knob to close the door behind him to the Last House, the mostly empty house, he pauses and his dog comes bounding down the stairs. She winds herself between The Heavy's boots. "Don't think we would have forgotten you," he says to the dog, and he kneels down. Face-to-face, he runs his hand along the ridge of her spine. While search teams combed the woods for Billie, the dog allowed The Heavy to lift her ragged body off the master bed and wash her in the bathtub. She let The Heavy pull the remnants of the muskrat she had killed, the frozen blood, from her snout. She let him wash her clean. Bring her back to life.

Once The Heavy gets into the truck, sliding the driver's seat back as far as it will go, the dog leaps over him and arranges herself in the passenger seat. Pony and I are together in the back. The last Fontaines. This is a new feeling for me. I am ready. I have always been ready for this feeling. Pony holds a book in her hands, *Brutal Errors of the Human Body.* She opens the cover to show me a thick stack of money. "Drug money," she mouths. "Le Pony," I mouth back. And then, as The Heavy reverses onto the highway, he reaches for the CB. "Do you read me, Billie Jean? Do you read me?"

8:19 P.M. We are driving along the north highway toward the perimeter of the territory. The closest I have been to the perimeter (it lies a mile past the truck lot) was at dawn, yesterday, when I watched Pony pull off her first and last armed robbery. I knew what she had done with Traps to get fuel. Traps had left her card in the top drawer of his metal desk. I tucked it into my jean pocket.

THE COMPLAINT DEPARTMENT
1-800-OH-MY-GOD

I knew the lengths she was willing to go to get Billie back. I wanted to keep Pony safe.

Tonight, there are no teenage girls walking the ditch. No

boys pedaling fast on their dirt bikes. No white barking dogs. No bonfires. No men salting their driveways. Staring into their high beams, mugs in hand. I can make out the chandelier in Drink-Mart that is only partly working, the mottled mirror behind the bar. The place is empty. The lights are out at Home of the Beef Candy, Furniture City, Gold Lady Gold, Value Smoke and Grocer. Though it says CLOSED in the window, the mirror ball spins at Hot Dollar's Hi-Fi Discount Karaoke and Sporting Lounge. When we pass the truck lot, the FULLY LOADED sign blinks on. I can see the black-and-white flicker of the television from the trailer. I look back at the territory, the only place I have ever known, expecting the ground to gape open and swallow it whole.

The Heavy picks up his speed. We blow by the perimeter. 8:31 P.M. October 26. Saturday. A wall does not suddenly form behind us. We had believed this as children; we had been told that if we ever left the territory, even stepped a toe over the line, a steel wall would rise and it would be unclimbable. No doors to open, no grips to use. No way to reenter. To see your people again. Even though we knew there was no logic to it—the Delivery Man came and went every month—we pictured ourselves stranded in oblivion, at the mercy of larger animals.

So far, only static from the CB.

2:09 A.M. Pony is asleep. The Heavy is driving fast, and outside the truck windows are trees, miles and miles of trees. The Heavy looks out at the trees, and then back to me, in the rearview mirror—his eyes are my eyes—and there it is, a quiet at last, my second strength: son of The Heavy.

My father.

——

I THOUGHT GREAT PARTS of the land would be on fire. The people of the territory talked about the world beyond the perimeter this way. Or submerged by water. Or pavement. Sometimes, I pictured a grid of beige bungalows identical to our own. Snowmobiles corroding in the yards. The Delivery Man had told Pony it was two days before you hit the end of navigable road and arrived at a small airstrip to get you over the water. "Airstrip won't be there long," he said. "Already, trees are coming down around it." We were still a while away from knowing whether the Delivery Man had ever told the truth.

6:45 A.M. My watch alarm goes off. I wake up to see Pony is driving. I look behind me. Nothing but open road. The highway is smooth and unbuckled. Not the gravel roads we are used to. Pony drives even faster than The Heavy. She has her hunting glasses on. She has rolled down all of the windows. Her hair snaps in the wind like flags pointing in every direction. Their dog is in the passenger seat on The Heavy's lap with her eyes closed and her head leaning out.

The air has the same sharpness as the territory air. The light is the same, and this morning, it is gold. 7:59 A.M. October 27. Sunday. We are almost twelve hours past the perimeter. We have refilled the tank three times. Seventeen jerry cans left. Ample water, bullets, canned food.

Where will this road end? In a crater, an inferno, a rush of water? I have spent my entire life inside a ten-mile radius. There is something to be said about a place you can memorize. As the road goes on and on, uninterrupted, I see that the world is bigger than a lifetime and just as unknown to me. It has been sixty hours since Billie left. She could be anywhere by now.

As if reading my mind, Pony turns on the radio. She cranks it. A guy with a slight drawl talks about sports. He comes in loud and clear. He talks about a team, their winning streak. "And that caps a stellar season for 2018." I can tell Pony wants to slow down to absorb this information, but she wouldn't dare. We've lost enough ground as it is. It's not 1985. We're thirty-three years into the future. The Heavy would tell me that, in a fire, you can actually hear the flames suck the air from a room. This is how it feels now in the truck. Pony shuts off the radio. She doesn't even throw me a look. She doesn't have to. We stare through the windshield, and the bubble we have been living in breaks apart.

I squint into the sun. The sky is cloudless. Satellite view: a narrow highway that winds through dense forest, and two trucks on a crash course. Driving toward each other at very high speeds.

We nearly collide with the matte black truck. The road is just wide enough for both of us. A slight swerve and then the high pitch of the brakes as we each come to a stop and gear into reverse. It's Billie. In the driver's seat. FONTN. It's Billie.

She is in The Heavy's arms. The moment she gets out of the truck, this is where she goes. She wears The Heavy's spare outerwear, his socks, his workboots. She broke into the aluminum supply box with her bare hands, she tells us. She holds Pony for a long time. She holds me. She has to glide between

us. The size thirteen boots. She looks down, laughs at herself—
the laugh is brief, barely leaving her throat—and then she
stands with The Heavy, who can only look at Billie, their dog
settling herself at their feet. One of Billie's hands goes straight
to the dog's fur, up and behind her ears. The dog's eyes shut.
Steam comes from her mouth. Everything falls still. Not even
a single bird. The driver's side door to The Heavy's truck
swings open. The truck is on an angle. Partly in the ditch.
Motor hums. Billie left it running. From the stereo, a song
plays. I don't know the song. Something about love. Trading
everything for love. "I figured it out," Billie says, looking from
The Heavy to me. "When I was driving, I put it all together."

Billie tells us she had tried to empty her mind as she had so
many years before, but found she couldn't. Her life was what
she wanted. We were what she wanted. She had turned
around, she says. She was coming back for us. We would leave
the territory together. We would find a new place together.
"Forgive me," she says to The Heavy. "Forgive me," she says
to Pony and then to me. She had nearly hit a bison. Last night.
It stepped into her high beams and stayed motionless in the
middle of the highway. "You cannot believe how dark it was,"
she says, "and then suddenly." She extends her arms to indicate the beautiful animal and then takes in a breath. She came
to a stop about a foot from its body. Its massive, peaceful body.
"You know the truth when you look into the eyes of something
wild," Billie says. The four of us stand in the space between
the two trucks. There is no end in sight to the road. The sun
rises higher and higher. It is white now, and, with it, comes
decision. We wonder how far we can go.

Acknowledgments

Thank you to Jennifer Lambert and Martha Webb for their expertise and heart. Thank you also to Anne McDermid, Suzanne Brandreth, Charlotte Cray, the teams at HarperCollins, The Borough Press, and Random House—especially the brilliant Anna Pitoniak.

For close reading and radical thinking: Ishan Davé, Martha Sharpe, Jason Logan, and my sister-in-arms, Heidi Sopinka.

For tracking down Jimmy Page and other forms of *genio:* Jill Connell.

On how not to get killed by a wild dog and countless other life-giving directions: Michael Ondaatje.

Grateful acknowledgment to the short films of Emily Vey Duke and Cooper Battersby, the parlor games of One Yellow Rabbit Performance Theatre, Annie Baker's *John,* the Talmud on mercy, Brian May on asteroids, Pico Iyer on ant colonies, and, dearest to me, Alisha Piercy on hair—also the many journalists who have written about free divers—notably, Alec Wilkinson.

For solidarity: Caia Hagel, Jason Collett, Chala Hunter, Damian Rogers, Allie Yonick, Michelle Giroux, Alysha Haugen, Daniela Gesundheit, Tom Daniels, Gabrielle MacLellan, and Kerri MacLellan. For talk and wisdom of all kinds: Marie-Josée Lefebvre, Christie Smythe, Christine Pountney, Michael Winter, and, rarest bird, Gillian Frise.

Thank you always to Marion Bowers, the Kerr family, my beloved parents, Peter and Janet Dey, and my sister, Sarah.

For the above and all that is beautiful and true: Thank you to Don Kerr and our boys, Dove and Austin, my company in this wilderness.

For Morwyn.

And in memory of Chas Bowers, librarian, caretaker, and a lion of a man.

About the Author

CLAUDIA DEY is the author of *Stunt*, a *Globe and Mail* and *Quill & Quire* Book of the Year. Her plays have been produced internationally and nominated for the Governor General's Award and Trillium Book Award. Dey's writing has appeared in many publications, including *The Paris Review* and *The Believer*. She has also worked as a horror film actress and as a cook in lumber camps across northern Canada, and is co-designer of Horses Atelier. Claudia Dey lives in Toronto. *Heartbreaker* is her American debut.

claudiadey.com
Twitter: @claudiadey
Instagram: @claudiadeytona